Savannah Sweethearts

THREE SWEET NOVELLAS

ALLISON WELLS

WELL VERSED PUBLICATIONS

SAVANNAH SWEETHEARTS

Contents

Ashley & Tyrell

Second Chance Romance

Ashley

THE PARTY WAS AWFUL, and my date was a huge bore. My parents demanded that my brother and I come to present a united Gloss family for all their swanky business events and charities. My dress—gorgeous though it may be—could have purchased a month's worth of food for one of the families this charity event is supposed to be supporting. My mother bought the dress and had it delivered to my studio apartment.

Evan Browning, my date, was about as exciting and appealing as a flea. He also kind of looked like one. He was a nice man, sure, but he was the same age as my father and spoke slower than a sloth. He kept putting his arm around me, and I had to keep shrugging him off.

I looked around, noting my brother and his wife laughing in the corner with people I didn't know. My mother's watchful gaze landed on me, and she nodded. I smiled back as expected. Evan excused himself to get a fresh drink without asking me if I needed one. I did. But I took a deep breath, glad he had stepped away. How I wished I was in sweats instead of sequins.

Laughter caught my attention a few tables down. At least someone was having a good time tonight at this charity event. I picked up my empty glass and meandered toward the group laughing. As I got a little closer, I could hear individual voices. One in particular jumped out to me, and my entire body broke into goosebumps.

It was a voice that called to me like a siren song. My heartbeat quickened; my palms began to sweat. It had been ten years since I had last heard Tyrell Harris's voice. Ten years and we had not run into each other—until now. I had worked hard to move on, and I was sure he had as well. My body's and mind's reactions, however, did not care. They urged me to find him. Demanded it.

The drink in my hand suddenly weighed a ton, and I set it on the table in front of me. A quick glance showed my date chatting with someone I didn't know, so I moved toward the voice that begged me to find it.

And then, there he was. He wore a navy blue suit that was perfectly tailored to fit over his shoulders. He stood with one hand in his pocket; the other held a glass as he laughed at someone else's words.

The group around him was all men, and I wondered if he was here with a date or if he was married. For years, I had imagined what his life would be like without me—and if I talked to him now, I would find out.

For a moment, I could only stare at him. Tyrell was really here, twenty feet in front of me. My heart implored me to run to him, even all these years later, but my feet stayed planted where they were.

Then he looked up and saw me. The smile fell, and his eyes widened. My breath hitched as I watched recognition hit him. Without excusing himself from his friends, he walked toward me like a man on a mission.

"Ashley?" He asked as if he didn't know who I was, as if we hadn't been together every day for years as teenagers. His eyes searched me up and down as if looking for the teenager I once had been.

I swallowed hard, but my voice came out hoarse. "Tyrell. How are you?" I didn't want to notice, but when I inhaled, he still smelled the same—like bergamot and pepper. It brought a smile to my lips. It was from an aftershave I had bought him as a high school graduation gift.

"It's been a long time. I'm good. How are you? You look fabulous." He stepped back and looked me over.

I wore a long, blue sheath dress that shimmered in the light. I had thought it was demure when I put it on, but now I felt wanton. Nothing was on display, but neither was my body hidden away; and with his eyes on me, I felt naked.

Nodding, I stepped closer to him. "I'm good. I'm surprised to see you here." He hadn't been one to mix with this crowd of people. In fact, that had been why we had broken up. We came from two extremely different worlds.

The left side of his mouth went up in a half-smile, and he gazed into my eyes. "I'm a producer now, so I've met a lot of people at places like this. I have wondered if I would ever run into you."

At that moment, my date reappeared and stood at my elbow. Being the dutiful Savannah daughter I was, I made introductions. "Tyrell Harris, this is Evan Browning. Evan, Tyrell Harris."

The look Evan gave Tyrell was pure disgust. Tyrell didn't even register with him, since he clearly wasn't old money. He put his arm around me as if to claim me as his, and I gently stepped out of his embrace.

Rolling his shoulders back, Evan stayed close to my side. "Ashley, are you about ready to go?"

In all honesty, I was ready to leave the party, but I did not want to leave with him. I looked to Tyrell and raised an eyebrow. Then I turned to Evan. "You know, why don't you say goodbye to the Lambeths, and I'll get my jacket."

I had not brought a jacket, but Evan didn't argue. He nodded and stepped away.

"Boyfriend?" Tyrell tried not to laugh. He hid his glorious smile behind his hand.

I stepped closer to him and tried to hide my own giggles. "Hardly. He was my mother's pick. I'm sure you remember her preferred type." I rolled my eyes and folded my arms. "I would love to leave, but not with him."

Then he said three simple words that would stay with me forever. "Leave with me." There was excitement in his eyes, like we were eighteen again and sneaking off before going to college.

My first instinct was to grab his hand and run. My second instinct was that Tyrell was here with other people, and I had my own date and family in the room as well. I needed to keep up appearances. Didn't I? I had spent my whole life being the socialite my parents wanted me to be.

A raised eyebrow from Tyrell and a peek at his very bare left hand gave me my answer. I agreed, and without a backward glance, I took his hand, and we disappeared from the room. It was April in Savannah, so it was already warm and humid as we went through the door. We hid out away from the lamplight for a moment. The thrill I felt at not just running away but running away with Tyrell was euphoric.

"Now what?" I licked my lips, unsure what we would do now that we had escaped. I guessed he didn't have a date, since he had suggested leaving together.

There was a sparkle in his eye. "Coffee? I'd love to catch up." It was a grown-up answer from a now grown-up Tyrell.

I nodded, and he took my hand, leading me down the sidewalk. There was a coffee shop two blocks from where we were, and we headed toward it. His hand in mine felt warm and familiar, like a favorite sweater that's both comfortable and sexy. The corners of my lips turned up, and I could feel the blush warm my cheeks.

My thoughts momentarily turned back to Evan. I wondered if he was now turning in circles looking for me, and I giggled. My parents would have a beratement for me in the morning, but for now, I didn't care. Maybe I wouldn't care at all anymore.

We slipped into the shop and picked a couch in the back. I sat—or, rather, fell—into the worn couch with a laugh. Tyrell perched on the edge.

"You want the usual? My treat." His smile was warm and his eyes inviting. While he had certainly matured, he was still the same Tyrell I had known years ago.

"You remember?" We had started drinking coffee together, wanting to seem more grown-up. When he nodded, I agreed, and he went to the counter to order.

He returned with two mugs in hand and a cheese Danish to split. He knew my weakness for Danish. I picked it up and tore it in half, biting into a piece. It wasn't until I was chewing that I realized he was just staring at me.

"So, Ashley Gloss, what are you up to these days?" He leaned away from me and folded his arms in front of him.

Sitting on the low couch was not the most flattering position, especially in a clingy dress. And especially when I was stuffing my face with pastry. "I'm a preschool teacher, and I live right near Baldwin Park. How about you?"

He laughed. "That's it? No epic love story? No kids? No scientific breakthroughs?"

"Unfortunately, no. You know I was never much for science. I got my degree in early childhood education and started working. I love my school. It pays the bills." I took a sip of coffee, realizing I hadn't done a whole lot with my life thus far. "I have a cat. I try to do some philanthropy. But tell me about you."

His smile fell, and I wondered if he had run into unfortunate circumstances since we had last seen each other. "Well, I'm a producer for Action News now, living here in the city, just a few blocks from Mom." He hesitated and winced a little. "I have twin daughters, who are four. They are the light of my life."

Oh. He had kids. The cozy atmosphere suddenly became suffocating—not that it had a reason. Tyrell was not mine to claim. At all. I had always thought he and I would end up together and have children one day. I wondered why he had left the party with me if he had a wife and children at home waiting for him.

I plastered a smile onto my face. "Oh my goodness, twins! That must be so much fun. I'm sure you and their mother are always on the go." I stuffed another bite of Danish into my mouth to keep myself from breaking down.

He quickly stepped in to correct me. "No, no. We're not together. We've never been together. She was a mistake. A complete, one-time mistake. But that gave me the biggest blessing of my life with the girls, so we share custody."

He showed me a picture of two identical little girls with braided ponytails. They were precious and looked very much like Tyrell. I was relieved that he wasn't with their mother, though I had no reason to be.

We chatted about his children and his mother. Then we talked about my parents and my brother with his new baby. Before we knew it, two hours had passed, and my sides hurt from laughing so much.

"I really should go. My classroom will be very lively in the morning." I stifled a yawn.

"Where do you teach?"

"Lighthouse Preschool. It's a great place." I picked up my small purse and put it in my lap.

A knowing grin crossed his face. "I knew it. It had to be fate. The girls start there tomorrow. I'm transferring them to be closer to Mom."

"That's wild. I can't wait to meet them. I guess I'll see you around, then." I stood, and he followed suit.

After a slightly awkward hug, we parted ways. I went home to my cat, and we curled up on the bed where I lay awake wondering what might have been. I fell asleep to dreams of the family that might have been mine if I had only ignored my father.

Tyrell

BACK HOME, I GENTLY woke my mom to relieve her of her babysitting duties. I decided not to mention Ashley to her, even though they had been close when we dated. If nothing came of it, there was no point in giving my mother hope. She left, and I changed into sweats and a t-shirt.

I still couldn't believe it. My Ashley. No, not *my* Ashley. Never again *my* Ashley. Her father saw to that. And all the better. Because of him, I fought for what I wanted. Because of him, I had made something of myself. Nobody would call me a good-for-nothing ever again. And because my relationship with Ashley had ended, I now had my girls, sleeping side by side in the next room.

A text came through on my phone, and I knew it would be Sabra, the girls' mother.

SABRA: HOW MY BABIES?

Me: They're fine. Fast asleep. Goodnight.

Sabra: You know we could be a whole family if you'd take me back to your bed.

I ignored the message. She always wanted me to take her back when she was between other boyfriends. We had never dated in the first place. If it hadn't been for a DNA test, I wouldn't have known the girls were mine. Sabra had been a mistake, one I would be saddled with for the rest of my life. But the girls—they were my greatest miracle.

There was too much nervous energy after seeing Ashley, so I called my work buddy AO. In truth, he was probably my closest friend. When he didn't answer, I gave up, flipping my phone onto the couch. He was probably at P's and Cues, our usual after-work hangout.

I stood and went to the doorway of the girls' room. They shared a double bed that looked like a swimming pool compared to their tiny frames. Saffi was curled up against Sami, her arm draped over her sister's face. Even though they were identical, I could tell them apart easily. Saffi was just a hair taller, and Sami had a freckle just in front of her right ear. Saffi's face was ever so slightly fuller, and Sami's facial expressions were much more dramatic.

Leaving their door cracked in case they needed me, I wandered to my own room and stretched out on my bed. I wondered if I would see Ashley in the morning when I took the girls to school. Would she be their teacher? I didn't really want her and Sabra to meet.

But I did want to see her again. I pulled her up on social media after years of avoiding looking up her name and scrolled through what little I found. Her accounts were private, but she was frequently tagged in posts and articles. As the daughter of one of Savannah's most prominent businessmen, she was a Southern socialite if ever there was one. Her father never thought I was good enough for his little girl.

Once I became a father myself, I understood. No man would ever be good enough for my girls. But for Jonathan Gloss, it was more about what neighborhood I came from and how much was in my family's bank accounts that mattered. I was from the wrong side of the tracks, and he made sure I knew it.

The next morning, the girls—with their boundless energy—woke me at the crack of dawn. I scrambled some eggs and fried some bacon for them. My mom always made the best breakfasts for me, and I wanted to make sure I did that for the girls. Even though my mom lived only a few blocks away, it was important that I make that memory with Sami and Saffi.

Having a mother and not a father hadn't been easy for me—not that it had been the plan. My father had been killed in a work accident when I was three. I barely remembered him, but from what I did remember, he was a fun and loving guy. I wanted to make sure my girls knew the same kind of dad from an early age.

We loaded up in my car, and I took the girls to school before I went to work. We were early and had to wait for the doors to open before being allowed into the building. The cool Savannah morning helped calm my nerves as I thought about what I might say to Ashley that wouldn't sound like I was trying too hard.

Before I knew it, the door unlocked, and Ashley stood there, holding it open. Another family came in before us, and then my girls went tearing into the building toward their class. Since I was holding their backpacks, I followed them.

God help me, but she still smelled like honeysuckle. My steps slowed as she allowed the door to close behind us. "Good morning." The smell was just as intoxicating as it always had been.

"Morning." Her gaze stayed fixed on the floor, and she didn't move.

Without thinking, I fell into step beside her. "How are you this morning?" I felt awkward, but I wanted to be friendly.

No, what I wanted to do was grab her by the hand, pull her into an empty room, and kiss her. But I couldn't do that at a preschool with my children only a few steps away, so I made uncomfortable conversation instead.

"I'm good." Ashley hoisted up a little boy and took his backpack from his mother before turning around and heading for their classroom. Before she stepped over the gate, however, she turned back toward me, nodded once, and smiled. "Have a good one, Tyrell."

She disappeared behind the door, and I was left standing in her wake. Last night, she had been stunning in the blue dress she wore. Now in leggings and a flowy top with her hair pulled back, she looked just as beautiful. Perhaps even more so. After a moment, I turned and left for work.

I went through the day as if I were in a daze. My buddy AO laughed at me and told me I looked like a lovesick schoolgirl. I shook my head at his comment. His life goal was perpetual bachelorhood, so I knew he didn't get it. But when he invited me to P's and Cues that night, I agreed. I needed to get my mind clear.

"No kids tonight?" AO Ortiz clapped me on the back as we left the building.

Shaking my head, I pulled my keys out. "No. Sabra has them for the next week."

He raised his hand for a high-five. "Nice."

Even though it was against the 'bro code,' I left him hanging. "Man, those girls are my life. I hate being away from them." I opened my car door. "I'll meet you there."

At the bar, we racked up a pool table and both grabbed a beer. I wasn't much of a drinker, and neither was AO, but we would nurse a beer throughout the night.

"So, what had you in la-la land all day?" He broke the rack, and the sound of pool balls cracking filled the air.

I surveyed the table for a moment before answering. "I ran into my old girlfriend last night. We wound up talking for hours."

He wagged his eyebrows. "Talking?"

As much as I wanted to whack him with the pool cue, I didn't. "Just talking. But it got me thinking about what might have been. Even though we were kids, I thought she was the one. And seeing her last night…" I could still see us together, growing old.

"So, why did you break up before?"

I shook my head. "We were young and easily swayed. Her dad was a grade-A elitist. Still is, I'd wager. But we let him break us up."

"Love is for the birds." AO sunk a ball, then scratched.

I sunk three balls in a row. "That's why they're called love birds."

<h1 style="text-align:center">Ashley</h1>

I DIDN'T SEE TYRELL pick the girls up that afternoon, and the next morning, a woman dropped them off. Three-inch heels, full-face make-up, and nails that reminded me of Edward Scissorhands sashayed through with them. She must be their mother. I said a warm hello to her when she walked by my classroom, but she gave me the side eye and ignored me.

In the late afternoon, I had hoped to see Tyrell again, but no such luck. The same woman came for them. She asked one of the twins about the whereabouts of something, and when the girl responded that it was still at her father's house, the mom rolled her eyes. I did my best not to look like I was watching.

I hadn't thought to ask Tyrell for his number, and he didn't have mine either. I knew it might look over-eager to text him, but I didn't care. Too much time had already been wasted. If we were both unattached, I felt like we owed it to our younger selves to see if there was still something between us.

Tyrell's contact information was probably in the director's office, as well as in their classroom. Did I want to be sneaky and find it? What if I got caught? The last thing I wanted was to be fired. Working not only gave me something to do but also extra money because most of my trust went right back into investments.

I grabbed a hairbow from the lost and found and went to the twins' classroom. Now if I could only remember the teacher's name. Even though we had worked together for a year I struggled. I sucked at names. Bailey? Bree? Oh, thank goodness it was on the door.

"Hey, Britt, one of those twins dropped a hairbow on her way out. Do you want me to call and tell them?"

Britt scowled and cocked her head to the side. "I don't recall either of them wearing a bow, but you can just leave it, and they'll get it Monday."

Shoot. I should have thought of that. "Of course." I put the bow on the counter, defeated.

"I saw you talking to their dad." Britt gave me a sly smile. "And he was definitely looking at you."

I could feel the heat rise on my cheeks. "Oh, no, it's not—"

She hip-checked me. We were definitely not close enough for that; I barely knew her name. "Girl, I don't know how you knew the parents weren't together, but you're right. And that mom? Sabra? Oh, she's a piece of work. Mr. Harris is definitely the better parent."

Before I could stop myself, I blurted out our story to her. "Tyrell and I were high school sweethearts, but we broke up in college because my father is an idiot and I was an idiot for listening to him. We haven't talked in ten years, but after running into him, all those feelings came rushing back." My chest heaved from my rapid speech.

Britt's jaw did not hang open as I thought it might. But she nodded as if she approved. She grabbed a notebook and flipped it open, winking at me before she turned around. The ball was in my court. She was letting me take Tyrell's number.

Before I could think any further, I pulled out my phone and created a new contact. Tyrell Harris. I double-checked I was getting his number and not his ex's and flipped the notebook closed.

"I guess that wasn't their hairbow, after all." I winked at Britt as I exited the room, a certain bounce in my step.

"I got you, Ashley."

Suddenly, I felt like we were hip-check close. Maybe I would have to give Britt a call and see if she wanted to hang out sometime. I bet we had some similar interests.

At home, I stared at my phone. Should I text him? Texting was more innocuous than calling. But then, he might think someone was pranking him. Calling was probably the way to go. Oh, but he might be busy. He might be out on a date, or out with friends. It was a Friday night. And I was at home with

Trainer, my cat, wondering what my ex-boyfriend from many years ago was doing.

My phone buzzed in my hand and I jumped, screamed, and threw the phone all at the same time. My heart hammered in my chest. I was not expecting that. Retrieving the phone, I saw a text from my sister-in-law, Morgan. She thought we were best of friends. We were not.

MORGAN: WANT TO COME OVER FOR DINNER? TANNER WANTS TO MAKE CLAMS.

I detested clams. And Morgan. And Tanner. Okay, maybe I didn't detest my brother, but we weren't close.

ASHLEY: SORRY, MORGAN! I HAVE PLANS TONIGHT. KISS LITTLE JONNY FOR ME.

MORGAN: I KNOW IT'S LAST MINUTE. HAVE FUN GOING OUT. I CERTAINLY MISS MY DAYS OF FREEDOM.

My nephew Jonny—Jonathan Tanner Gloss IV—was the most adorable thing in my life, and I would give my left kidney for him. But not if it meant a clam dinner with his parents. I should have offered to babysit. Maybe next weekend.

I loved kids. I loved their easy smiles and their dimples and how even when they were upset, they were easy to make happy. That's why I had majored in early education. I didn't even mind the diapers too much. I just adored being around kids.

That brought my mind back around to Tyrell's twins. Sapphire and Sam-something. It was not Samantha. Samita? He called them Saffi and Sami—that, I remembered. Worked for me.

Before I could stop myself, I texted him.

ASHLEY: TYRELL, THIS IS ASHLEY.

ASHLEY: ASHLEY GLOSS.

I held my breath and waited until the count of ten. No instant reply. I closed my eyes, said a little prayer, and fired off again.

ASHLEY: I GOT YOUR NUMBER FROM LIGHTHOUSE. I HOPE THAT'S OKAY. IT WAS GOOD TO RUN INTO YOU.

ASHLEY: SAVE MY NUMBER.

With that, I flung my phone down again. I wasn't going to watch it all night. I wasn't going to open myself up for that disappointment, even though it seemed I just had.

"Why am I doing this, Trainer?" My cat, in all her infinite wisdom, did not reply. How smart of her. "I know. All those old feelings came right back, didn't they? You never met Tyrell, but he was such a gentleman and a hard worker."

Trainer blinked and stretched out a paw so it was touching my arm.

"Thanks for the understanding. You see, I was sure Tyrell was my forever. Apparently, Daddy did not. Tyrell was 'from the wrong side of the tracks,' according to Daddy. He didn't come from money. But that meant he didn't have everything handed to him, and he worked hard." I thought about Tyrell in high school, how he wore old shoes and never had the latest fashions. I never minded riding in his fifteen-year-old compact car because he had earned the money and bought it himself.

Unlike me. When I turned sixteen, I was handed the keys to a brand-new Lexus. It was even the shade of teal I had requested. Life for me had been easy. It still was. I had chosen my father and the life he had given me. And Tyrell had chosen to move on.

Maybe now, though, we could be friends. I missed him. We would tell each other everything. He hadn't just been my boyfriend, but my best friend as well.

My phone vibrated on the couch. "I'm not checking, Trainer. It's probably just Morgan again." I stood and walked around my bed. "Don't let me pick it up, Trainer."

Bad cat. She did nothing but flick her ears, which I took as a signal to check my phone. So I did.

TYRELL: WELL, WELL! GLAD YOU FOUND MY NUMBER. WE'LL HAVE TO CATCH UP SOMETIME.

The giggle that came from within me exploded out into the air, scaring Trainer. I flopped onto my bed, feet in the air, as I squealed like a teenager. Whatever happened, Tyrell would be back in my life, and I would not mess it up this time.

Tyrell

I WOULD NOT MESS it up this time. She had found my number, which meant she wanted to talk to me on some level. Even if it wasn't romantic, we could at least be friendly. It would be hard, but I could do it. I read over the texts again, a stupid grin plastered to my face.

She didn't respond, which was fine. I could take it slow. But I did miss her. When I had graduated from college, I wished she had been there. When Sabra told me the twins *might* be mine—then they *were* mine—I wished I had her to talk to. Even though if she had been around, I probably wouldn't have ever looked at Sabra. The girls were worth the hassle of Sabra Thomas, but I'd be lying if I didn't wish at least once a year they were Ashley's and my kids.

The next day I was off work and I didn't have the girls, so I did what any bachelor would do. I slept in. When I woke up around 10:30, I decided I wasn't going to waste time. I had already wasted ten years. I wasn't the same kid who could only afford college on a scholarship. I had a good job; I took care of my kids; I had even coached their peewee soccer team. My hat was officially going into the ring. I texted Ashley.

Me: I know this is last minute, but want to have lunch in about an hour?

I hopped in the shower while I waited. I didn't want to seem over-eager. Never mind that the phone came with me into the bathroom—or that I made a sudsy grab for it when it dinged a few minutes later.

Ashley: I'm tied up. But I could do dinner. Want to meet at Luck's? 5:30?

Me: See you there.

I lingered through my shower, neatened up my beard, and put on my favorite cologne. She had been the first to give it to me after we graduated from high school. There was no way I would part with it. Especially not today. The mirror showed a man in his prime, young but wise, intelligent but fun. Not to be arrogant, but I thought I looked good.

Luck's was where Ashley and I had gone all through high school. I hadn't been back since, but I passed it all the time. Teenagers still hung out there before their curfews. It was a step above a diner and a step below a steakhouse, hovering in a strange niche we had loved as kids. I tried not to read into what meeting there meant. Perhaps it was just comfortable, familiar.

Just before 5:30, I parked in the lot and realized I didn't know what Ashley drove. Deciding it would look better if I was waiting at the door, I went to the bench just outside. Ashley pulled up in a small Lexus SUV, newer than the one she had gotten in high school. There was no way to afford it on a preschool teacher's salary, and I scowled at the thought of her still living off her father's money.

Mr. Gloss was an investor and business owner. In and of what I'm not entirely sure, but he puts in money and comes out with more money. Because of that, Ashley never wanted for anything. They made her work hard, but in the end, they provided everything for her and her brother. Unlike me, raised by a single mother after my dad died, struggling to make ends meet. I went to school, played soccer, and worked to help Momma with the bills. I was never good enough for Ashley in her father's eyes.

Ashley approached me slowly. "Hi, Tyrell. You okay?" Her hair rolled in soft waves around her shoulders while sunglasses perched on top of her head. She wore a short-sleeved sweater with jeans, and her eyes were bright as they searched me over. Even casual, she looked like a million bucks.

It took a second to focus on her face. "Yes, hi. Sorry, I got lost in thought." I stood and wiped my hands on my pants. Did I hug her? Shake her hand?

"I haven't been back here in years." Dark eyes looked around the building as she took in the once-familiar scenery.

It had definitely been a long time since it was updated. The same red paint on the door was faded and peeling, but the awning had been replaced since we had last ventured inside. The booths had been updated at some point, but they were still worn. The carpet looked just as ragged as it had a decade before.

When the waitress approached and asked for our drink order, I spoke for us both. "I'll have a sweet tea, and she'll have lemonade and tea mixed together." It was pretty smooth that I remembered her go-to drinks.

Ashley's cheeks turned pink as she smiled. "You remembered my coffee order and my tea-ade? You'll make me wonder if you've been thinking of me all this time." While the rest of the world called the mix an Arnold Palmer, she had dubbed it tea-ade, and the name had always stuck in my mind.

"How could I forget?" The urge to reach my hand out to cover hers was strong, so I hid my hands under the table. I licked my lips and felt self-conscious. Was I being ridiculous? Probably. "How have you been?"

A stray lock of hair fell over her shoulder, and she gently tucked it back. "I've been good. How long have you been back in Savannah?"

Aside from college, I hadn't really left the area, so I know I made a face at her question. "Since after school. I mean, I moved back in with my mom after I graduated; then I got my own place after the girls were born."

Our drinks were slid onto the table, breaking up the conversation. Ashley thanked the server, then cleared her throat. "And the girls are four?"

I could talk about Sami and Saffi all day long. A soft smile broke out on my face, and I pulled out my phone to show Ashley more pictures of them. "Yeah, they're four. They'll be five in July; then they'll start kindergarten this year. I can't believe they're getting so big."

Ashley only nodded at the picture of the girls before grabbing her drink and downing it in a few gulps. Her face flushed, and she shifted in her seat. It may have been ten years, but I still knew when Ashley was uncomfortable.

"You okay, Ash?"

She nodded, but the swipe under her eye told me she was not.

"Are you—are you upset that I have kids?" My whole body got hot. No matter how much I had missed Ashley over the years, my girls came first and foremost in my life. No flame would ever compete.

Her hand shot out in protest. "No! No, not at all. It's been ten years, Ty; I figured you'd be married and have a family at this point."

The eye roll couldn't be stopped. "Well, I'm definitely not married to Sabra or anyone else. Sami and Saffi are all I have time for outside of work." I realized she had gotten the topic away from herself. Her hand was on the table, so I covered it with my own. "Now, why are you so upset?"

She shook her head. "It's nothing. I'm just being sentimental, that's all." Classic Ashley, she straightened her back and put a smile on her face.

"Do you like teaching kids?"

Her eyes lit up, and I knew I had hit a sweet spot. She had always loved kids. "Oh my gosh, you have no idea. I adore it. Even if I'm in a class that still has diapers. Can you believe it? I'm hoping I can work my way up to being a school director one day. I just need to remember the kids' names. And their parents."

Remembering names was not Ashley's strong suit. It had taken her weeks to remember that I was Tyrell and not Tyler. She constantly mixed up her friends' names. She knew them and knew details about them, but she somehow lost it when it came to names, especially similar names.

"So, my girls being Samirya and Sapphire?" I chuckled.

She pretended to wipe her brow. "Yeah, I'm glad they're not in my class. I'd never get them right."

Ashley

Thankful Tyrell had distracted me from the tears that threatened, I was determined that I would not cry. I would not be telling Tyrell that I couldn't have children when we weren't even dating. Technically, we weren't anything at this point. It wasn't information I offered easily. That conversation could wait until later—much later.

The jealousy that someone else had given him children mixed with the joy that he was a father at all made my mind a jumbled mess. "It's been so long."

Tyrell's expression softened. "It's been too long."

Our server returned and took our orders. We never looked at the menus but ordered our usual favorites. They must still be available because she didn't question us.

"Tell me about your twins."

That was all it took for him to spend the next ten minutes telling me all about school, their soccer team, what each one loved and hated to eat, and that they both adored K-pop music.

I raised an eyebrow. "K-pop? Really?"

The laughter was so familiar and so magical. "Really. I think they learned about it from friends. They love to watch these Korean boy bands on YouTube. They know all the words."

When the food was set before us, we fell into a comfortable silence. I stole little glances of Tyrell as we ate. He looked much the same, but a little more filled out, more mature. He had changed from being a boy to a man. I wondered what changes he saw in me.

"What's been going on with you over the years? No one has been able to catch you?" He made a show of looking at my bare left hand.

"Nope. No man has ever caught my eye and held it for more than a few months. My last boyfriend was probably two years ago; but after four or five months, I realized he was just like Tanner, and I gave him the axe." I took a bite from a still-steaming, crispy fry.

The face Tyrell made told me what he still thought of my over-the-top brother. "Oh, Tanner. I haven't thought about him in forever."

With a giggle, I told him about Tanner's marriage to Morgan and how the world now revolved around Jonny. "I just try to stay in my own lane and live my best life. Maybe one day, I'll find the right person to settle down with."

I didn't try to hide the look I gave him. I couldn't. My eyes caught his, and I stared him down. He had been the one. The beat of my heart told me he still was—or at least, I wanted him to be.

His hand enveloped mine from across the table. "Oh, Ash. I'm so sorry I didn't fight for you. I should have."

"No, no, you were right in going to college. We were kids. We weren't ready for a lifetime commitment back then." The warmth of his hand on mine sent a shiver through my body.

He licked his lips and leaned forward. "Are we ready now?"

I leaned back in my seat away from him. "What do you mean?" I wanted to get to know him again, yes, but was he...

His eyes grew wide, and he snatched his hand back. "I'm sorry. That was too much. I told myself I wasn't going to give up this time if you gave me a chance. Will you? Give me a chance again?"

A coy shrug was my only reply, and I bit into a greasy french fry that tasted like heaven. Would I give him a chance again? Oh yeah. How could I not? It's not like we had wanted to break up when we did. I had never stopped loving Tyrell, even after all this time. He was the standard every other guy was held to, and none measured up.

"Is that a yes?"

Instinct told me to look away from him before answering, but I held his gaze. "Of course. That's why I'm here."

"You wanna take a walk like we used to do?" He put cash on the table and reached his hand out to me. The smile on his face told me exactly what he was thinking.

Butterflies erupted in my stomach. How many times would I feel like this with Tyrell back in my life? I felt like a schoolgirl again, staying out past my curfew and spending all my spare time with the man across from me now. Except it was broad daylight and instead of micro skirts and stilettos, I was in jeans and wedges.

Nonetheless, I took his hand and stood next to him, my eyes never leaving his. "Are you going to take me under the bridge, Mr. Harris?" That had been our favorite make out spot as kids, hiding under an old bridge near Tyrell's neighborhood.

He wrapped his arm around me, and I could have melted right there. He leaned in and spoke low. "No, that wouldn't be safe these days. Besides, I think we need a fresh start, don't you?"

There was no way I was going to argue with that. I nodded, and he led the way out of Luck's and down East Gwinnett until we got to Forsyth Park. It was a stunning park with the famous fountain, gorgeous trees, and a lovely lawn. As a local, I never thought much about going there; I was too busy going past it to stop.

As we passed through the gates, a bride walked by in her pristine white dress. Someone held her train up off the ground as a photographer rushed past to find the next perfect spot in the fading light. I stopped and watched for a moment as the photographer directed how the dress was to be fanned out and how the bride was to pose. She looked so calm and collected. I think I would have been a bundle of nerves.

"Ash?"

My head turned to Tyrell, and I shrugged. "I can't pass up a pretty dress."

"Then that hasn't changed one bit." He took me by the hand. "You should see some of the things Mom has gotten for Sami and Saffi—the biggest, puffiest dresses you've ever seen."

One of my dreams had always been to have a daughter to put in frilly dresses. I would imagine it when I was in high school. Working with preschoolers, I always fawned over the girls who came to school in fancy dresses. The rainbow ones were my favorites.

Mrs. Harris still held a soft spot in my heart. She had accepted me from the get-go without question. She sobered me if I had drunk too much at a party; she gave me a talking to when I needed it; and she loved me without condition. While I knew my parents loved me, it wasn't the same as the way Mrs. Harris had loved me.

"Oh, I bet your mom is over the moon having granddaughters. I always thought she'd be a perfect grandma." My mother, on the other hand, wasn't very hands-on with Jonny. She was more of a 'seen and not heard' type of grandmother.

Tyrell began walking in the direction of an ice cream cart. He had always had a weakness for mint chocolate chip. "You have no idea. She is so smitten, and she loves to spoil those girls.

Sabra doesn't buy them cute, little girl things. She gets them tiny versions of what she would wear." A scowl crossed his face as he talked about the girls' mother. Clearly, he didn't have a good relationship with her.

I wasn't sure what to say to that, so I just laid my hand on his arm. His large hand covered mine, and the feeling of safety and security enveloped me.

After getting our ice cream, we found a bench to sit on. We watched people walk past with strollers, dogs, and even a pot-bellied pig on a leash. Savannah was a city like no other.

"I'm sorry if I talk about the girls too much. They're my life outside of work." Tyrell bit into his cone, and mint green ice cream dribbled down his fingers.

Oh, how I wanted to be the napkin to clean him up. Melted ice cream dripped off his thumb. Even in the shade, I felt the temperature rise a few degrees. "It's fine. I love hearing about them."

The cone crunched again. "You always did love kids. I figured you'd have some by now."

Truth be told, I had thought that as well. I was thirty with no prospects; and even if I did have any, once I told them I couldn't have kids, I was sure they would walk away. That's what my mom told me would happen. "Nobody wanted a defective wife" were her exact words.

"If I had found someone to settle down with, I might have. I, um, have thought a lot about adoption, actually. If I don't find a guy—or even if I do." Let's see what he did with that information.

He leaned his elbows on his knees. "Ah, you'll find someone. Maybe you already have." He raised an eyebrow as he looked at me.

Oh, this was going to be harder than I thought.

Tyrell

IT WAS LIKE NO time had passed. But then the realization that a decade had gone by would rear its ugly head. I knew one thing for sure, though. I was not going to let Ashley Gloss go without a fight. And this time, I was prepared. I had a home, a career, and the wisdom to not back down from her father.

When I went to pick Sami and Saffi up at school on Monday, I took a very simple, small bouquet of those colorful daisies she always liked. I also got two single carnations for the girls. Because I'm that dad. When I walked up to the girls' class, Miss Britt called for the girls and eyed the flowers.

"Those for someone special?"

Crud. Did she think they were for her? Then she winked, and I realized she was the one who had given Ashley my number. I smiled as the girls came running to me. I presented each of them with a beautiful pink carnation, and they squealed with delight.

Saffi eyed the other flowers. "Who are those for, Daddy?"

I had prepared for this question. "Do you know Miss Ashley across the hall? She's an old friend of mine; and I'm so excited she's my friend again, I got her flowers."

Her sister looked from their single flowers to the bouquet with nine flowers. "Why does she get more than us?" There was a reason I called her Sassy Sami.

"Because she's older." Miss Britt came to the rescue.

Twin sets of doe eyes stared up at me. Saffi beat her sister to the question I knew was coming. "Is Miss Ashley your girlfriend?"

I squatted to be eye to eye with them. "No, she's not. Maybe she will be one day. I don't know. But right now, she's just an old friend of mine—and one I've missed for a long time. Okay?"

They led me over to the door across the hall. Ashley had to have heard the entire exchange, but she waved to a child who was leaving instead of watching us approach. When she looked our direction, her eyes lit up.

"Miss Ashley, these are for you." Sami made a show of her hands to present the flowers.

Color rose to her cheeks, and she pulled her dark hair over her shoulder as if to cover herself. "Oh my goodness. Really?" Her eyes met mine as I held them out for her. "You really didn't have to."

Now it was my turn to blush. I had felt like a knight in shining armor bringing them in, and now I felt like a crazy man giving them to her. "I know, but I wanted to."

The tender moment was interrupted by Saffi announcing that her mother was there. The fluttering in my stomach turned into lead as Sabra approached us.

"What are you doing here today, Tyrell?" She crossed her arms in front of her and narrowed her eyes at us. "And why are you giving flowers to that teacher?"

My sweet Sami never knew when to keep her mouth shut. "She's Daddy's old friend, and he likes her."

Drawn-on eyebrows shot up, and Sabra's posture stiffened. "Excuse me? You're hitting on this teacher in front of our children?"

Sabra and I had only been a one-time thing. We never dated. I know that made me look like a grade-A player, but she was a mistake. The girls were not, but Sabra was. I have never called her my ex, just the girls' mom. She has brought boyfriend after boyfriend into and out of the girls' lives, and I've tried really hard not to speak ill of her. Since the girls were born, I have had one semi-serious girlfriend who didn't last long enough to introduce to the girls.

I ignored the comment and turned to Ashley. "Give me a minute, if you don't mind." I didn't wait for an answer before approaching Sabra. Needing to control the level of my voice, I took a steadying breath.

"Ashley and I go way back; we knew each other in high school. I'm not hitting on her. I am bringing her flowers because she deserves them. If you notice, I also brought Sami and Saffi each a flower." Another breath came through clenched teeth. "Now, it's my day to get them, is it not?"

Sabra pouted. A thirty-year-old woman pouting was not attractive. "I know, Tyrell, but I thought we could do something as a family." She pulled my arm around her waist and looked over my shoulder, I presume at Ashley and the girls.

Stepping back, I knew I needed to maintain my distance. "We spend Christmas and the girls' birthday together and anything else that might be really important. And that's it. No more than that. We may share Sapphire and Samirya, but we,"—I gestured between her and me—"are not a family."

Anger rose up in her, and I wasn't sure I could shield anyone from it. "Fine. Fine, Tyrell. Girls! Want to come home with Momma today?"

I could feel the girls crowd into the back of my legs, shaking their heads. "I have them today and tomorrow," I reminded her.

"But I want them." She stepped toward us and reached out for Sami. "Sami. Come with me."

My Sassy Sami wasn't afraid to speak up. "No. We want to be with Daddy. He's nice, and Gigi makes us cookies."

A scowl that could scare a lion came across Sabra's face. "Unreal. Saffi? Want to come with Momma?"

Sami put her arms around her sister as Saffi hid her face. "I'm staying with Sami. And Daddy." Her voice was muffled, but I could hear it just fine.

"Argh!" Sabra threw up her hands and turned on her spiked heel. She sashayed out of the building, leaving a crowd of onlookers in her wake.

The school director, Miss Smith, came from her office and raised an eyebrow at me.

"I'm so sorry." I didn't know what else to say. I was relieved when she simply nodded, her face drawn but her eyes kind.

I turned back to Ashley and furrowed my brow. "I—"

She shook her head. "No, it's fine. Thank you for the flowers. I think you better take your girls home and give them some reassurance."

Saffi and Sami were still huddled close to me. I mouthed my thanks to Ashley and ushered them out to my car.

After a silent ride home, we went inside and all sagged onto the couch. I wasn't sure what to say, but as I gathered my thoughts, Saffi was the first to speak.

Fat tears rolled down her cheek. "Why is Momma so mean sometimes?"

How do I answer that? I drew her into my lap. "Oh, Saf, I'm sorry if Momma was mean. I don't think she tries to be mean. I think maybe she's just confused."

"What about?"

What, indeed. I certainly had no idea. Confused about the four of us as a family unit? Confused as to why the girls preferred to be with me than her sometimes? "Baby, life is always confusing. Even for grown-ups. We don't know everything; we just do what we think is right."

Sami stood up and stomped her foot. "Maybe Miss Ashley can be our new mom." She folded her arms and scrunched up her nose.

It was my job as their father to treat their mother with respect. I knew that. Hard as it was, I would have to keep doing it. "No. You have a mom; and she loves you, and you love her. Even if Miss Ashley and I were to date, Momma would always be your mom. Even when you and Momma fight, you love each other. Got me?"

She fell back on the couch. "Okay, fine." It only took about three seconds for her to change the topic. "Can we pick up burgers on the way to Gigi's?"

I smiled. We all loved our nights with Gigi, and my mom loved her nights with us. "Let's call her and see."

After collecting her order, I sent a quick text to Ashley, hoping she wouldn't go running for the hills after the performance by Sabra.

TYRELL: I PROMISE IT'S NOT ALWAYS LIKE THAT WITH SABRA. SOMETIMES WHEN SHE'S BETWEEN GUYS SHE WANTS TO ACT LIKE WE'RE A HAPPY FAMILY. WE HAVE NEVER BEEN THAT.

ASHLEY: IT'S OKAY. SHE'S SOMEONE YOU WILL HAVE IN YOUR LIFE FOREVER, SO I KNOW YOU NEED TO BE DIPLO-MATIC.

Ashley: Thank you for the flowers. They're gorgeous.

Tyrell: Like you.

I pocketed the phone with a smile on my face. The girls and I loaded up and went to pick up dinner before heading to my childhood home.

Ashley

D ID SABRA THOMAS SCARE me? Yes, she did. Did I
think Tyrell and his girls would be worth the hassle of
dealing with Sabra? I wondered. I knew Tyrell was worth it,
and he had explained the situation to me already. Still, she was
a force to be reckoned with, and I didn't want to get trampled
by her.

The flowers from Tyrell looked cheerful on my table. I
couldn't see the television with them there, but that was okay.
I'd move them to the counter when I was done admiring them.
The texts from him were reassuring, and of course, I blushed
like mad at his comment that the flowers were gorgeous "like
me."

When my phone rang, I thought it might be Tyrell, but
I grimaced upon seeing Morgan's name once again on my

phone. I readied my saccharine voice. "Morgan, to what do I owe the pleasure?"

Her perky voice grated on my nerves. "Ashley, honey, what are you doing tonight? Tanner was asked to a business dinner, and I was hoping you could watch Jonny for us."

An evening with my cuddly nephew might be just what I needed, so I agreed. It would likely be a late night, but I grabbed my laptop so I could watch something while Jonny slept. I didn't use their streaming services because I didn't need Morgan and Tanner knowing what I watched. It wasn't bad, but I was sure there would be comments about it.

On my way to their house, my mother called. I couldn't handle all this Gloss family communication. "Mom, I'm on my way over to watch Jonny."

I could picture her recoil. "Oh, well. That's lovely Ashley. It's too bad you like children so much." Unlike her, who thought they were tiny leeches.

It felt like a stab to the heart when she made comments like that. "I do love children, Mom. My inability to bear them doesn't mean I would begin to hate them."

Her Savannah drawl sounded bored, even though she was the one who had called me. "I know, sugar, but it's just torturing yourself since you'll never be a mother."

Do not engage, Ashley. Do not comment back; it will only encourage her. "What did you call for, Mother?"

"There's a charity ball this weekend, and I thought you'd like to go. I have two tickets for you if you can find a date.

You're on your own for this one, since you left Mr. Browning searching high and low for you. Do you know how embarrassing it was that you had just up and left?"

I did my best to ignore the fact that I was an embarrassment to her. There had to be a catch to her generosity. I waited for her to announce it, but she remained silent.

"What's the charity?"

"Oh, something your father is involved in. Raising money for underprivileged people of some kind. Apparently that actress who used to live on Tybee will be there. Tanner and Morgan can't go." Ah-ha. There was the reason for the last-minute offer.

My brother and his wife couldn't attend, so the tickets were being discarded in my direction. That was fine. I would be happy to take them, and I told her as much. After hanging up and pulling into my brother's driveway, I texted Tyrell.

Ashley: Any chance you're interested in attending a black-tie charity ball with me Friday night? I have two tickets.

It didn't take long for a reply to pop up.

Tyrell: What's the charity? Some of my reporters are going to one this weekend for Savvy Kids.

Ashley: That might be it. My mother didn't say specifically.

Tyrell: Oh, your parents will be there?

Ashley: Does that change your mind?

Tyrell: Absolutely not. In fact, I would love to see them again and show them how well I'm doing despite their predictions to the contrary.

I couldn't help the smile that spread across my face. I would also love for my parents to see how well he was doing. Tyrell was pretty much at the top of his game and still only thirty years old. It would be a pleasure to wipe their smug smiles from their faces.

It was a thin line I walked with my family and I knew it. I was the black sheep that had somehow turned into a bitter disappointment to them, but I still reaped the benefits of being a Gloss. I got a monthly allowance from my parents, plus the payouts from my stock in the family business and my trust. Having a job wasn't a necessity for me; it was a choice.

Still smiling, I got out of the car and headed toward the house for babysitting duty.

Once Tanner and Morgan had left me with a list of instructions for Jonny, I stripped him from his prim pajamas and left him in just a diaper. He seemed so much more relaxed that way without itchy knits on his skin and no tags rubbing him.

"What do you want to do before bed, Jonny?" I held him close, running my fingers along his soft skin.

He was just a year old, so he didn't have much to say, but he pointed to a few toys and crawled over to them. They were all soft, organic, and as bland as you could get. I scooped him up and took him into the kitchen, where I pulled out Morgan's expensive pots and pans and her designer mixing spoons.

It took a minute of my showing Jonny what to do before a wicked grin crossed his face and he laughed. Spoon in hand, he began banging the pots and pans as if his life depended on it. I knew he led a quiet, calm life, and little boys weren't meant to be quiet and calm.

He relished the noise he was creating, and while it gave me a slight headache, it wasn't anything I couldn't handle. Anyway, the poor boy needed an occasional outlet away from Morgan's smothering. Plus, it wore the kid out. After ten minutes, he was slowing down and rubbing his eyes.

Aunt Ashley for the win. I redressed him, read him a book, sang him a song, and laid him down. As his eyes drooped closed, I felt the squeeze on my heart.

I would be a mother one day. Even if I didn't birth a child myself, it didn't matter. I had saved so much of my money and invested it wisely, I could adopt ten children if I wanted. It didn't matter how it happened. A deep breath caught in my throat, and I left the room before I woke the baby from his slumber.

My phone was ringing from the living room, and I raced to pick it up before it woke Jonny. Looking at the screen, I groaned before answering, "Hello again, Mother."

She didn't greet me before launching into why she called. "Ashley, I found someone you can take with you to this gala. You remember Ben Baxter?"

Pinching the bridge of my nose, I shook my head as if she could see it. I did remember Mr. Baxter, emphasis on the *Mis-*

ter. He had been my tennis coach and was even older than my father. "Mom, I don't need you to find me a date. I've already asked someone."

There was no attempt at hiding her shock. "You have? Who? Someone I know?"

I wanted Tyrell's presence to be a total surprise, so naturally, I couldn't tell her who it was. "Yes, someone you have known for a long time, so tell Mr. Baxter sorry."

I hung up with my mom still puzzled over who I might have invited to her special charity event.

At about ten o'clock, as I scrolled through social media pictures, Tyrell texted and asked if he could call me. Of course, I said yes. The phone lit up with his number instantly.

"Hey, there."

"How are you doing?" His smooth, baritone voice still gave me goosebumps.

"I'm not too bad. I'm babysitting at my brother's house." I sighed as I looked around Tanner's massive living room.

"I can't believe Tanner has a kid. I never thought I would see the day he'd settled down." Tyrell laughed quietly. The girls must be asleep nearby. "Anyway, I wanted to apologize for earlier."

"You don't need to apologize at all. That woman was a little scary, though. Is she always like that?" I shivered as I recalled the look she shot me while she was trying to latch onto Tyrell.

He groaned a little, and I heard him move. "Yeah, that's how I ended up the father of her twins. I took it as flattery at first, but then, she got very possessive. When I told her no, she moved on to someone else. Five guys did DNA tests for the girls. Five. I was the lucky one."

"They're sweet girls." I wasn't sure what else to say.

"They are. I was the only one of the five ready and willing to be a father. One of the guys was only sixteen, Ash. I'm so glad they're mine. I wish Sabra wasn't attached, but I love those girls."

I put my hand to my mouth; his words about his girls were so beautiful. He wanted them, which was such a change from many people these days. Sami and Saffi were definitely blessed with a father who was present and doted on them.

"Don't even think about it. And thank you again for the flowers. That was such a treat." I couldn't wait to get back home to look at them again.

We chatted about everything and nothing for the next thirty minutes until he yawned and said he had to be at work at five the next morning. We hung up, and I closed my eyes until Tanner and Morgan came home.

Tyrell

T HE CHARITY BALL WAS in a few hours, and I was getting ready at my mom's house. The girls would be staying the night with her, which was a special treat for all of them. Judy Harris was meant to be a grandmother, and she relished in her role.

"Daddy you look so handsome." Sami batted her eyelashes at me. "I want to go to the ball and be a princess." She twirled around in her pink princess dress.

"When you're big, you can attend all the balls you want. There will be plenty of time for that." I picked her up and twirled her around until I got dizzy. I tossed her tiny frame onto the couch, where she fell into a fit of giggles.

"You want a turn?" I looked at Saffi.

Always the more cautious child, Saffi's big, dark eyes looked up at me. "Can you go slow?"

I nodded as I lifted her up. Her blue princess dress draped over my arm as I carefully danced a basic box step with her instead of spinning her into oblivion. When she rested her head on my shoulder, I pulled her closer to me. They were both Daddy's girls, but Saffi was definitely my cuddler.

My mother appeared in the doorway and snapped a picture on her phone. "Don't you need to get going to pick her up?" She was over the moon that Ashley had reappeared in my life but nervous about what might happen with Mr. and Mrs. Gloss.

"That's the best part, Mom. She's coming here. Ashley has asked about you every time I talk to her, so I asked if she wanted to leave from here." I beamed, knowing this would please my mother to no end.

"I'm not prepared for guests, Tyrell." She turned in a circle, her hand to her chest. "It's a good thing I made tea earlier. I think I have cookies somewhere."

"Momma, we won't have time for tea and cookies. She can hug your neck and officially meet the girls, and then, we have to go."

As if on cue, the doorbell rang. Sami jumped up and opened the door, swinging it wide open for Ashley to enter. She wore a dress the color of peaches with ruffles all along the edges. It hugged all the right places and showed some skin without being vulgar. My heartbeat quickened, and my mouth actually began to salivate.

Before I could say a word, dumbstruck as I was, my mother pushed past me. "Ashley Gloss, my sweet girl. Come give me some sugar!"

Nobody turned down one of my mom's hugs, and Ashley was no different. She nearly glowed as she embraced my mother. Her eyes closed tightly, and Ashley held on to my mom like she was a life raft. After ten seconds, I cleared my throat, but Momma waved me off and let Ashley hold her.

When they finally separated, I saw the wetness on Ashley's cheeks. She took a shaky breath. "I'm so sorry, Mrs. Harris. I don't know what came over me, but I have missed that hug for a long time."

Taking Ashley's hand, Mom led her inside and sat her down. "Sweet girl, don't you worry about it. Sometimes, we need those kinds of hugs. And I have missed you, too." A tissue appeared from her pocket. "Here you go, sweet girl. Now, you're a grown-up, and you need to call me Judy."

Ashley laughed. "I don't know that I can do that, Mrs. Harris." She dabbed her eyes and took a deep breath.

Sami took a step toward them. "We call her Gigi."

Realizing they had an audience, Ashley's face transformed from lost child to teacher. "Gigi? That's the best grandma name ever. You have a very special one."

Saff took up position next to her sister. "You can call her Gigi."

"No, she can't. Gigi isn't her grandma."

Saffi scrunched her nose. "She can if Gigi says she can." They both turned to their grandmother.

Unphased, my mom shook her head. "Ashley, you can call me whatever pleases you. Judy, Gigi, Your Highness. It's all fine." Everyone giggled at the last one.

Sitting down behind the girls, I pulled them close to me. "Girls, I know you have seen Miss Ashley at school, but I would like to actually introduce you. Samirya, Sapphire, this is Ashley Gloss. We've known each other for a very long time, and she used to be my very best friend."

I put my hands on Sami's shoulders. "This is Samirya—or Sami, as we call her." Then I switched to the other girl. "And this is Sapphire. Saffi."

One of Ashley's admitted flaws was her inability to remember names, which is probably why she always called my mother Mrs. Harris. How she would tell the twins apart and remember their names would be a challenge, I knew. But she would rise to the occasion.

With her hands in her lap, she looked from one to the other. "Sami. Saffi. It's so nice to meet you outside of school. I love your dresses. Are you coming with us to the ball?"

Squeals erupted, and the girls began bouncing around. "Can we? Can we go?"

It took a minute to settle them before I had to break the news that this was a grown-ups-only event. Thankfully, Gigi knew just how to rein them in with promises of watching Princess Tiana and eating cookies and ice cream.

As we stood to leave, Ashley stopped and sat on the coffee table in front of the girls. "Thank you for letting me take your daddy out when it's your time with him. I really appreciate it." She spoke to the girls like they were adults, and they stared at her, a little awed by the respect she was showing them.

Saffi's little voice whispered back, "You're welcome."

Mom shooed us off, and we climbed into Ashley's car. I had offered to drive, but she said she knew the way. She navigated the streets of Savannah with ease as she worked her way to The Promenade, where the ball was being held.

She bit her lip as she drummed her fingernails on the steering wheel. "Did that go okay? Did I mess up by asking if they were coming with us?"

I chuckled. "No, it was fine. I'm impressed with how respectful you were to them."

"Good."

"Mom sure missed you."

She sighed. "I had no idea just how much I missed your mom. I don't get hugs like that from my parents. It's been a long time since someone just held me because they loved me. And Mrs. Harris has always loved me simply for being me."

A truer statement had never been uttered. My mother loved everyone for exactly who they were, no questions asked. And she had loved Ashley from the start, realizing she was an affection-starved teenager who needed that unconditional love from somewhere.

As The Promenade came into view, Ashley gulped. "Are you ready to face the totally conditional-love crew who will not be happy to see either of us?"

I steeled myself. This was as prepared as I would ever get. I knew I would never win the approval of Mr. and Mrs. Gloss, and that was okay. Their approval did not factor into my self-worth or anything else. Facing them was something I had dreamed of for years—showing them that I was not the delinquent they thought I was. Doing it with Ashley at my side was icing on the cake.

"I'm ready. My good friend from work, AO, will be there, along with Jennifer Marcingill and Karry Draper. We can always spend our evening with them." AO Ortiz was a producer at Action News, where I worked, while Jennifer and Karry were reporters.

"That's exciting you know them and work with them. I watch Karry Draper on the news every day." Ashley's eyes shone in the low light as she spoke. "Let's get this party started."

After a deep breath for fortification, I exited the car, circling around to get Ashley's door. We walked into the open-air lobby and right into the sights of her parents.

Ashley

WHY DID MY PARENTS have to be the very first people we saw when we came in? My father wore his navy blue suit, even though this was a black-tie event. It showed he didn't care as much about this charity as he could. Mother was dressed to the nines in a flowing, burgundy organza gown that had a train. A train. On a sixty-year-old woman.

When Mom spotted me, she looked me up and down and nodded in approval. Then she looked beside me to the man in the black suit. Her eyes grew wide, and the glass of chardonnay in her hand wobbled slightly. With her other hand, she took my father's arm, drawing his attention to us.

I clenched my teeth and put my hand through Tyrell's arm. "Prepare for battle." My game-face smile spread across my lips as we approached them.

"Ashley, I—" My mother stammered.

We stopped in front of them, and I puffed my chest a little. "Mom, Dad, you remember Tyrell Harris, don't you?"

While my mother was at a loss for words, my father absolutely was not. "Hello, Ashley. Mr. Harris. It's certainly been a long time. I didn't realize you were still in our fair city." He spoke through clenched teeth, and his voice was not warm in any way.

My father did not offer his hand, and neither did Tyrell. Instead, my date wrapped his right hand around my own as it rested on his arm. "Mr. Gloss. Mrs. Gloss, it's a pleasure. I am, indeed, still here in Savannah. I'm actually a producer at Action News."

Voice finally found, my mother scoffed. "A producer?"

"Managing producer, actually. I run the show." He looked at me as he said that and tightened his grip on my hand.

I could have swooned right then and there with how sexy Tyrell was in that moment. He had overcome whatever obstacles my parents projected him to have. Growing up, his family had been lower-middle class. He never went without food and necessities, but he did have to do without most of life's niceties. Whereas, I grew up with nothing but niceties and excess. Mrs. Harris had worked exceptionally hard to make ends meet, and I had nothing but the utmost respect for her and Tyrell for their successes.

"So, you made something of yourself after all. How did you find him again, Ashley?" My father appraised Tyrell, looking him up and down.

If I knew my father, he was assessing the cost of Tyrell's suit and trying to figure out what income bracket to now place him. Ire rose in my throat.

I stepped even closer to Tyrell, and I could feel the heat coming off his body. "We ran into each other a few weeks ago, Dad, at your event. And when Mom said I needed to find a date for this lovely function, I immediately knew who to ask." I looked at my date with complete adoration. I had started off doing it for effect, but I realized I truly did adore him. I always had.

My mother stepped toward us. "Ashley, darling, might I speak with you in private for a moment?" She held out her hand for me to take and walk away with her.

Instead, I drew back even more into Tyrell. I knew the game she was playing. "I'm sorry, Mom. It will have to wait a bit. I know Tyrell is eager to introduce me to his co-workers, and I see Karry just ahead." My head was swimming as I blatantly defied my mother. Usually, it was more subvert. "Shall we?"

Knowing his cue, Tyrell nodded to my parents. "Mr. and Mrs. Gloss, excuse us. We'll have to catch up more later." He held me tightly as he turned me away from my parents and led me over to the table of Action News crew carefully munching on hors d'oeuvres and sipping wine.

Exhaling, I flexed my fingers so the feeling would return after having been dug into Tyrell's arm. "I'm so sorry. I didn't realize I was gripping so tight." I rubbed his arm. "But that was amazing."

He stopped and lifted my hand to his lips, kissing it lightly. "I am so proud of you, Ashley."

I beamed. "Thank you. I'm proud of you, too. Look at us growing up."

As we approached his coworkers, a man with a mass of wild curls on top of his head called out, "Tyrell! Hey, man!" I recognized him from the last event.

After a round of introductions, I noticed the room becoming more crowded. I couldn't see my parents any longer, and I was grateful. My entire body began to relax, and I rolled my shoulders back.

A voice behind me caused me to spin on my heel. "Ashley Gloss, I thought that was you."

Evan Browning—the thorn in my side my parents had set me up with. Apparently, my giving him the slip at the last function didn't get the message across that I wasn't interested in him. There was no doubt in my mind that my parents had found him and sent him after me to try to get me away from Tyrell.

Evan's hand extended toward me. "Might I steal you from your party for a dance?" I backed away on instinct.

Before I could speak, Tyrell pushed between us. "I'm sorry, but this next song is spoken for."

The smug smile on Evan's face fell as he eyed Tyrell. "Oh, well, perhaps a little later then." He fiddled with his diamond-encrusted Rolex.

Without expensive jewelry to show off, Tyrell rolled his shoulders back and cracked his neck as if he was a prize fighter. "I'm afraid her whole night is booked."

I could feel someone step up behind me. I heard knuckles crack, and Evan looked over my shoulder. He put his hands up and nodded, backing away slowly.

A gush of air rushed from my lungs. "Oh my gosh, thank you so much." I put my arms are Tyrell.

Reaching behind me, Tyrell shook hands with the man who had shown up to back him. "That's why you're the man, AO. Thanks."

Turning toward AO, I smiled. "Thank you, too."

"What a creep." AO went back to the table and picked up his plate as if nothing had happened.

Tyrell put his finger on my chin and tilted my gaze up to him. "How about that dance?"

"Anytime."

As we began a basic box step, I enjoyed his hands around my waist. I could feel the muscles in his back flex as we moved, and I wondered if he looked the same without a shirt. He had worked out as a kid, but he had been thin and wiry. His shoulders were more filled out now, and I wondered if his abs were as well.

"You wanna tell me who that a-hole was?"

I shook my head. "Exactly that. He's a country club friend of my father's and someone my mom has tried to set me up with countless times. My parents would love to marry me into his money." A shiver ran through my body.

"You don't want all the riches in the world?" Tyrell's voice was low and soft.

I knew what he was asking. He was asking why I would want a man who works hard and basically lives paycheck to paycheck when I could have a man with all the money in the world and want for nothing. He was asking why I would want him.

"Money is not where all the riches in the world are, and you know it." I snuggled in closer to him, running my finger up and down his lapel. "Financial security is great, and I admit I enjoy it. But I would rather have a loving family, a cozy home, and lots of laughter than a steel vault full of cold money."

His chin rested on the top of my head. He spoke, but I couldn't understand him. I didn't want to move, though, so I said nothing. When he ran his hand up my bare back, it tickled, and I disengaged from his arms.

"Did you hear me?"

"No."

He pulled me close. "I said, 'That's what I always loved about you—that you were humble and honest.' I wish I hadn't let things come between us, Ash."

Tears swam in my eyes. We were still box-stepping, even though the music had become more up-tempo. "We both let things come between us. But it wasn't our time then."

"Is it our time now?"

Was he going to kiss me? I wanted to lick my lips, but I also didn't want to seem overeager. Instead, I nodded. "I think it might be."

We stopped moving, and his head lowered. Gently, he pressed his lips to mine, and his hands came up behind my neck, pulling me closer. I wrapped my arms around him in an attempt to get as close as possible to him. It was the same as it had been, but it was also better than it ever was. My Tyrell.

Tyrell

M Y ASHLEY. FROM THE time we were fifteen, I knew I would love her and protect her forever. And now at thirty, it was no different. How could I have wasted the past ten years? Why had I not fought for her? Why had I not searched for her?

It didn't matter now. She was in my arms, and I was never going to let her go. When I lifted my lips off hers, what I really wanted to do was take her home. Instead, I put my forehead to hers and closed my eyes.

I brought my lips close to her ear and kissed it lightly. "Yes, it's definitely our time now, Ash."

The shiver that ran through her at my words made me want to devour her on the spot.

Someone cleared their throat behind me, and Ashley's eyes grew large before she pulled her head away from mine. "Daddy."

I turned and came face to face with Mr. Gloss. He nodded slightly, and I returned the gesture. He looked no different than he had a decade before—the same salt-and-pepper hair, the same sharp, blue eyes.

As he stepped forward, he reached out his hand. "I thought I might have a dance with my daughter."

Knowing I needed to play his game and play it well, I stepped aside and put Ashley's hand into his. "Of course, Mr. Gloss."

Ashley looked at me, and I nodded. I would be waiting for her when they finished, and no amount of intimidation would scare me off. Her father twirled her out onto the dance floor and started a beautiful routine with her. Ashley had grown up with formal dance lessons. I learned the box step purely so I could dance with her in high school.

I backed up to AO and Jennifer. Jennifer leaned in close to me. "She's a cutie-patootie, Tyrell. How does she know Jonathan Gloss?"

My coworkers knew just about every name in Savannah. I hadn't thought of that. "She's his daughter."

The shock in her voice was not at all masked. "How do you know her, then?" She wasn't being rude, just being Jennifer. It was how she was.

Looking out to the dance floor, Mr. Gloss was talking to Ashley in earnest. I didn't take my eyes off of them. "She was my high school sweetheart."

From the corner of my eye, I could see Jennifer and Karry lean together and giggle. Even in their fifties, they giggled like my twins. Karry patted my arm. "Was? Or still is?"

"If her parents have anything to do about it, it will stay past-tense. But as far as I see it, we're picking up where we left off."

Ashley's mouth was in a tight line, and I could see the anger in her eyes from across the room. I started to move toward her, but AO stopped me and told me to wait. He was right; causing a scene would help nothing. We were mature adults now.

When the music stopped, Ashley kissed her father's cheek and turned my direction, but he caught her by the wrist. Ever so gently, she removed her hand from his, shook her head, and walked away from him.

And once again, I wondered if I was worth losing everything for. I knew I wasn't. All the love in the world couldn't replace income and lifestyle. That's why I had walked away before. There was no way I would ever be good enough.

No. No more would I think that way. Those words had been planted in my brain by the Gloss family, and I had believed them as a kid. Now, I was a man, and I knew I was good enough—for Ashley, for my daughters, for them. I was better. Money didn't buy the things that mattered most. Besides, I wasn't poor; I just wasn't as rich as they were.

Ashley kissed my cheek. "Are you okay, *mon ange?*"

Fire lit through my body. I hadn't heard that nickname in so long, I had completely forgotten about it. It meant my angel in French, and she had taken to calling me that when we took French together in school.

I took her hands in mine and searched her face. "*Mon ange?*"

Pink lit up her cheeks as she bit her lip and nodded. "*Oui.* You've always been *mon ange.* Do you not like it anymore?"

I looked her in the eyes; my throat felt raw, and I could almost feel moisture prick at my own eyes. "Am I still *ton ange?*"

She brought my hands up to her cheeks and kissed one, then the other. Her voice was a soft whisper. "If you want to be, Tyrell."

Licking my lips, I tried to wrap my head around the fact that she had more or less said she loves me without actually saying it. And she had just come from what looked like a heated discussion with her father. "Your dad? What did he say?"

She shook her head and took my hand. Leading me outside, she sat me down on a bench and paced in front of me. "No, you first. Are you *mon ange?* Regardless of what my parents or anyone else might say? Because I can't go through that heartbreak again."

I knew if I hesitated, she would think I didn't love her, and I did—with everything in my being. Was it enough? I would never know.

Throwing caution to the wind, I took her hands and recalled the pet name I had given her. "As long as you're mine, Dream Girl."

Tears rolled down her cheeks as she fell into my lap. Her arms wrapped around me, and she buried her head in my shoulder. Naturally, my arms went around her as I held her, my hand smoothing her hair. This I would protect with every fiber of my being. Along with my girls, Ashley had returned to her place as the center of my world.

When she lifted her head and swiped her tears, I brushed her hair back from her damp cheek. "See? Everything is okay. We can take this as quickly as you want. For the girls' sake, though, I ask that it not be lightning speed."

A deep, wavering breath expelled from her chest. "Well, for my parents, as well. Daddy was not happy when I told him he no longer got to say who I spent time with. And he was not happy I had turned down his greasy friend. He said he could cut me off."

"Ashley, I—"

Her hand went up to stop me. "Please, let me finish." I shut my mouth. "Thank you. He said he could cut me off, and I told him he could do no such thing. I'm well into my majority, so my trust is no longer in his hands. And as I'm over twenty-five, my shares of the company are mine, and I reap the benefits. I haven't lived off his money in years, which I doubt he realized because Tanner still lives off Daddy's money whenever he can."

She took a deep breath and stood up from my lap. "I live in a studio apartment to keep costs down. I scrimp and save. I don't have all the streaming services or the top internet plan, and I don't eat at fancy restaurants. Now, I know I can spend money with the best of them—and certainly, I have when it's called for—but day to day, I'm just an average girl trying to survive and put money into savings."

When she finished her rant, I stared at her for a few moments to see if she would pick back up. Her hands were balled into fists, and her shoulders were tense. After a few seconds, her hands released, and her shoulders dropped back down. I just watched as she relaxed.

My raised eyebrow made her giggle. She knew I was looking for permission to speak, and she nodded. I stood and faced her. "Ashley, I have never doubted your ability to survive and thrive on your own. But I can take care of you. I make enough for you, me, and the girls to do all right."

Big, doe eyes widened and reflected the moonlight. "Are you…"

"Oh, no! No! Not at this point." That definitely had not been a proposal. "You'll know when I'm asking you to become Mrs. Harris. But not yet."

Taking her hand in mine, I pulled her close. "Can I have this dance, *Miss* Gloss?"

"I thought you'd never ask, *Mr.* Harris."

Ashley

T HE PHONE RANG BRIGHT and early, and I wondered who would be calling me before sunrise. When I saw Tyrell's name, I perked up, but the panic in his voice when I answered popped the bubble.

"Ash, my mom fell, and I need to take her to the hospital. I can't get ahold of Sabra. Can I bring the girls to you?" He spoke with such speed, it took a moment for my brain to catch up with what he had said.

"Of course, of course. Is Mrs. Harris okay?" I sat upright, prompting Trainer to start meowing for her breakfast. "Shush, Trainer."

There was a commotion on the other end of the phone, and Tyrell was barking orders. "She can't walk. I think she broke her leg; I'm not sure. It's a miracle the girls thought to call me and tell me Gigi was hurt."

That must have frightened the girls terribly. How could I take their mind off what had happened? "She'll be okay, *mon ange*. Bring the girls here and don't give it a second thought. Get your mom better."

"We'll be there in five."

I threw on a dress—who had time for pants?—and pulled my hair up in a bun. After a quick stop in the bathroom, I tidied up just in time for the doorbell to ring.

The girls bound into my apartment, talking a mile a minute. "Miss Ashley, Daddy said you have a cat!"

"I'm hungry. Can we have McDonald's?"

"Oh, that's so pretty."

"Gigi got hurt."

Tyrell looked frazzled. "Mom's in the car. I had to carry her." He thrust a bag toward me with a few toys, tablets, and blankets in it.

I put my hands on his cheeks to make him hold still. "Ty. Stop. Take a deep breath." I looked into his eyes as he breathed in and out. "I know you're worried, but she will be okay. And the girls will be fine. Take care of your mom, but stop panicking. It helps no one."

He closed his eyes and pulled me in for a hug. "Thank you, Dream Girl." He kissed my forehead before saying goodbye to the girls and disappearing.

Two little girls sat on my hastily made bed and stared at me. I stared back. Trainer jumped up on the coffee table between us, and the girls squealed in delight. Sensing a need to flee,

Trainer took off, and the girls followed her around the kitchen island and back to my bed where Trainer slid underneath to safety.

"I want to play with the kitty." One of the girls tried to fit under the bed but couldn't, while the other climbed on the bed and dangled her head off the side.

That's when I realized I had no idea which girl was which. I was doing good to remember that their names were Sami and Saffi, but I couldn't tell them apart. Looking from one to the other, I breathed a sigh of relief that they were not in matching outfits. One wore a green shirt, while the other was in pink.

"That's Trainer. Let's give her a few minutes, and maybe she'll come out to play. How about I make pancakes?" I clapped my hands like I would in my classroom. Both girls' heads popped up to attention. "Come sit up here and tell me what you did with Gigi last night while I cook."

I whipped up pancake batter and heated the skillet while they rattled off everything they had done with their grand-mother. By the time they were done, the pancakes were ready, and Trainer had finally peaked her head out from under the bed.

"Why don't we go to the park?" I suggested. "The bath-room is right over there." I pointed to the first door down the hallway. "How about you both go potty, and we'll go play."

I cleaned up a little bit while they tore off for the bathroom. Those girls did everything in a hurry. I threw some water bottles in my bag, along with a few apples and a frisbee. The benefit of living in Savannah is there are plenty of green spaces to play, and I was grateful to have Baldwin Park right outside my front door. After a quick text to Tyrell checking in, we headed out.

Still not sure which girl was which, I stretched my hand out toward them. "Saffi, take my hand." The girl in green took my hand. Saffi was in green. I repeated that in my head a few times. "Sami, take Saffi's hand." The one in pink latched onto her sister.

As we marched across the street, I recited in my head Saffi green, Sami pink. Saffi green, Sami pink. The girls were thrilled to run wild for a few minutes on their own while I watched. They attempted cartwheels and danced arm in arm. It was like being at work with my class. Keep them occupied and in sight, and everything would be all right.

We played and ran outside for almost an hour, the girls happily shrieking as they chased birds, squirrels, and me.

When we sat down for some water and a snack, a police officer approached us. "Ma'am? Are these your children?"

The girls clearly did not resemble me in any way, but seeing sitters or nannies were commonplace in the city, so I thought the question a little odd. "No, sir. I'm watching them for their father, who had an emergency."

"Where is their mother?"

I scooted forward on the bench so the girls were a little more behind me. "Their father, Tyrell Harris, could not get ahold of her. His mother needed to go to the hospital right away, and he asked me to keep them."

Sabra came up a sidewalk in that moment dressed in a skin-tight catsuit. "She's a liar. She kidnapped my children. She also stole my man. Arrest her."

Kidnapped? What? I stood and stepped forward, thinking that putting space between the adults and the girls would spare them from hearing this. "Ms. Thomas, I assure you I did not kidnap the girls. Tyrell asked me to watch them while he took his mother to the hospital." But my words fell on deaf ears.

She waved her arms wildly. "I want her arrested." The girls had seen her and gone running to her. "Don't worry, girls, Momma is here."

The one in green—Saffi?—pulled on her mom's shirt. "Momma, Miss Ashley is from school. She's Daddy's friend."

The officer turned and spoke in hushed tones to Sabra. While he did, I pulled out my phone and texted Tyrell that he needed to come as soon as he could because Sabra was accusing me of kidnapping the girls. I slipped my phone back in my pocket without waiting for a reply.

My entire body shook as people pulled out phones and began recording Sabra's rant. There was nothing I could do, and I would not walk away from Sami and Saffi. The girls had taken up residence between us and were silent as they made dandelion chains. Their mother's screaming didn't seem to faze them, but I knew that wasn't healthy for kids to overhear the kind of words she was spewing.

After talking with Sabra, one officer came over to me. He already looked exasperated. "Miss, tell me again what's going on."

"Gladly." I sighed and stood up as I explained everything again. Sabra kept repeating that I was a kidnapper, and I had to tune her out.

The officer nodded. "And what hospital did your friend take his mother to?"

"I'm honestly not sure. I was more concerned about taking care of the girls than where they were headed, but I'm sure if you could get ahold of him, he will clear this up." I crossed my arms, then uncrossed them and stuffed my hands into my pockets. "If Ms. Thomas had just approached me and said she would take the girls from there, it would have been fine. I'm a teacher at their school, so we have seen each other frequently."

In that moment, Tyrell came into sight and was running toward us. "Stop!"

The twins jumped up and ran to their father, wrapping their arms around his legs. "Daddy! Daddy!"

Sabra approached him as well, her hips swaying as she went. "Oh, babe, I was so worried. I thought this lady had stolen the girls from you." She put her hand on his chest, but he flicked it off as if it were a bug.

"I will deal with you in a minute." Tyrell shot her a menacing glance. He went to the officer near me. "I'm Tyrell Harris, the father of the girls. I can prove it. I have pictures of them all the way back to their birth." He began to pull out his phone, but the officer waved it off.

"You know both these women?" The officer looked from Sabra to me.

With a nod to Sabra, he said she was the mother of his girls. Then he looked to me. "Ashley Gloss is my girlfriend."

I would have jumped for joy in any other situation. In this one, however, I merely gave him a weak smile.

After talking with Tyrell for a minute, the officers went back to Sabra, and Tyrell approached me. "Are you okay?"

I wanted to tell him no, but I nodded instead. "I'm fine. But, Tyrell, the way she came at me yelling and the things she was yelling that didn't even faze the girls... That concerns me."

Sabra came up to us before he could respond. "I'm taking the girls home with me."

One of the officers stopped her in her tracks. "Do you have a custody agreement?"

Tyrell ran his hands over his head. "We have a verbal agreement only. Though I think that might be changing soon. But I have the girls until this coming Wednesday."

The officer looked from Tyrell to Sabra. When she nodded, the officers shrugged and backed off. After a final warning for us all to behave like civilized people, they began walking away.

Tyrell

THERE WAS TOO MUCH happening at once, and my head was spinning. Mom was safe at the hospital, but I needed to get back to her. Ashley would probably be done with me after this fiasco, and things with Sabra were coming to a head.

The twins gathered behind me and cowered from their mother. I had never seen them cower before, and I realized I was done with her charades. I stood and blocked the girls from her view. "You will not be taking them anywhere. This stunt was the last straw, Sabra. I'll be hiring an attorney to get custody of the girls."

Up until this point, we had done everything civilly without the courts involved. We had worked out a good deal with the girls spending equal time between us, but I had long suspected that Sabra wasn't giving the girls a stable home life. Foolishly, I had opted to ignore it because I could see that she loved them.

Crossing her arms, Sabra looked up at me. She was a tiny woman, but she was fierce. "You will not. I'm their mother."

"And I'm their father. And I don't go around cussing and raising Cain around them." I looked over to where the girls were now playing frisbee, Ashley having snuck them away from us so Sabra and I could argue in private. The police officers were walking away slowly, checking back every few steps. "I have them until Wednesday. You can pick them up from school then. But be prepared. I'm going to fight for full custody. Everything will be documented from here on out."

Her eyes grew wide as she backed away from me. She called to the girls for a hug before exiting the park alone.

I approached Ashley as she held the disc, waiting for the girls to resume playing. "I'm so sorry."

"No, I'm sorry. I wouldn't have pulled you away from your mother if Sabra had come up to us and been pleasant." Ashley rolled her shoulders back. "If she had been polite and asked to take the girls back home, I wouldn't have argued. She is their mother."

I rubbed her back as Saffi ran after the frisbee. "I know. She's been a pain for a while now, and I've been biding my time. I'm ready for full custody of the girls. I don't think it's good for them to be with her so much."

The frisbee came flying to us, and I caught it mid-air. "Go long, Sam!" I flung it far and high; both girls ran after it. "I do need to get back to Mom in a few minutes. She's okay for now, but I don't want to leave her alone too long."

Ashley bit her lip. "I can take them back inside. My apartment isn't very big, though, and Trainer wasn't too happy for the invasion."

The girls came back and bowled into us. We all sat on the grass for a minute, and the girls said what animals the clouds looked like.

I took Ashley's hand in mine. "You're doing fine. She won't bother you again, since I told her I was getting a lawyer."

"Daddy, is Miss Ashley your girlfriend?" Saffi blushed as she asked.

That caught Sami's attention. "Will she be our stepmom?"

I coughed. "How do you know what a stepmom is?" She was only four. How did she know that term? Both girls shrugged. With a glance to Ashley, I smiled. "Yes, Ashley is my girlfriend. Beyond that, we will see. But I need to get back to Gigi at the hospital. I'll be back for you soon."

The girls jumped on me and knocked me over with their hugs. Ashley laughed. This was the family I had always envisioned with her. Getting full custody of the girls could make it a reality.

I left them as they headed back toward her apartment and I went back to the hospital. Once Mom was feeling better, I would have to ask her about it. She was the wisest person I knew and wouldn't steer me wrong.

By the time I had mom ready to go home, I realized she wouldn't be able to do much on her own. She would need constant help. My house was half the size of hers, so the girls and I would need to stay at her place for a while.

When she was settled in her own bed and resting, I went to pack some things and retrieve the girls from Ashley. I wondered how the rest of the day had gone. Lunchtime had passed hours ago; she had to have been exhausted caring for two girls on the fly like that.

I knocked on her door, and she opened it, looking refreshed. How had she done that? My jaw dropped at how gorgeous she was. "Wow, here I thought you'd be completely worn out."

She winked at me. "Guess again." Allowing me inside, her apartment was cleaner than it had been that morning, and the girls were both passed out on her bed.

"Did you poison them?"

"Tyrell, really. They wanted to find Trainer, so I got them to help me clean up while we looked for her. Lunch, a movie, cuddles, and they were out." She looked proud of herself. "I can even tell you who is who."

Now I was impressed. Ashley knew which girl was which? I raised an eyebrow. "Do you now?"

"Saffi is in the green, Sami in the pink." She beamed. And she was right. "How's Gigi? The girls were worried, so we made cards."

I filled her in on Mom's break and her cast. "I think we'll need to stay with her for a while. She won't be able to move around easily with her leg in that cast. But she'll be okay.

Doctor said it was a clean break. And she's young, so it will heal."

The offer of coffee was made, and I accepted it. I sat at her bar while she popped a pod into her single cup coffeemaker. We were silent as I watched her prepare the coffee for me with a heaping spoonful of sugar and a splash of half-and-half. She popped another pod into the coffeemaker before handing me the steaming mug.

She leaned in close to me. "How about Sabra?"

I had been thinking about it all day while waiting for doctors. "I'm going to call some lawyers on Monday and see what my options are. I've been working toward this for a while, and I think it's time. I don't want to take them from her, but I've seen the string of men she's brought around, and after hearing her today..." I shook my head, afraid to say more.

Ashley's hand patted mine. "Say no more. It's none of my business, but that outburst worried me."

"Me, too. And I'm so sorry, again, for this mess. You didn't sign up for this. You've barely signed up for me." I stared down into my coffee. Once again, I felt as though I wasn't good enough for her. I had too much baggage.

She turned and got her coffee, then looked back at me while she leaned on the counter. "Stop that right now. Stop feeling like you're not enough. While I'm learning what I'm getting into, I'm not scared off."

One of the girls sighed, but when I turned to look, they were still sound asleep. Turning back to Ashley, I saw she had tears in her eyes. Maybe she was scared. "Ash, I'm sorry. This is too much, too fast. I'll wake the girls and take them home."

She choked back a sob. "No, wait. That's not why I'm like this. I need to tell you something. In case it's a deal-breaker for you."

A deal-breaker for me? I was the one with the crazy baby momma and two children. A thousand thoughts went through my mind, and my body flushed. I swallowed the lump that had formed in my throat and nodded for her to continue.

With a deep breath, she whispered, "I can't have children, Tyrell. I had some extensive issues during and after college, and it ended up being the best choice for me to have a hysterectomy. That's why I've never had a long-term relationship. I'm defective."

Shock did not cover what I thought in that moment—not that she couldn't have children, though that did surprise me, but that she would think she was defective. I went around the counter to her and wrapped my arms around her as silent tears slid down her cheeks. I had the feeling she had already cried plenty over this.

"Hey, Dream Girl, you are not defective. Not at all. It's okay if you can't carry children. If some guy can't see that, then he's the one who's defective." I soothed her as best I could, rubbing her back and kissing her hair.

She pulled back and looked up at me, her mouth turned down. "Not according to my mother."

If Rebecca Gloss had one talent, it would be filling her children with self-doubt. My mother had worked hard to keep us afloat and happy, always building me up. Rebecca Gloss didn't care if Ashley or Tanner were happy or drowning, as long as they looked the part of dutiful daughter and son.

"Your mother is a piece of work. You know she's wrong. You are not defective. You are not unworthy." There were several more thoughts in my head that I didn't dare say out loud because I was attempting to be respectful, even though the miserable cow didn't deserve it.

There wasn't time for her to respond beyond a nod because the girls did wake up then. Sami jumped up, startling the cat from her spot on a chair. Saffi blinked several times, trying to figure out where she was.

"Daddy! We had so much fun with Ashley. How's Gigi?" Sami scrambled across the bed. Then she stopped cold.

I knew the look. Bathroom.

Ashley knew it, too. "Hurry, hurry!"

Without even closing the door behind her, Sami made it to the toilet, and we heard a huge sigh of relief. Sami, in all her decorum, hollered to us. "That was close!" We couldn't help laughing at her declaration.

Saffi stumbled out of the bed and trudged after her sister, pushing past her as Sami came out.

"Wash your hands." Ashley pointed back to the bathroom, and Sami turned on her heel to comply.

"How did you do that? I have to beg, plead, and chase the girls with soap to get them to remember to wash after using the bathroom."

Her giggle made me relax. "I'm a teacher, remember?"

I hoisted Saffi up when she came from the bathroom, hands dutifully washed. "We need to go. Gigi is waiting for us. We're going to stay with her for a few days."

Sami went over to Ashley and stared up at her. Ashley picked her up effortlessly, and Sami rested her head on Ashley's shoulder. The pang in my heart was immediate. That was where my daughter's head belonged, snuggled up with Ashley.

"You be good for Gigi, okay? Help her out." Ashley rubbed Sami's back, and Sami nodded.

Sami looked at me. "Can we come back again tomorrow?"

I looked over her to Ashley, who blinked rapidly. I could tell it meant a lot to her that Sami liked and accepted her. Saffi would be a little harder, but she would follow her sister. Ashley hugged her tight.

"We'll see Ashley soon, don't worry." I led the way downstairs to my car, Ashley following behind.

When the girls were buckled into their seats, I rubbed her shoulders. "Thanks again for keeping them."

She shook her head. "Don't mention it. Let me know if your mom needs anything." She raised up on her toes and whispered. "And let me know if you need anything, too."

The only thing I needed right then was a kiss, and I took that with joy. I would happily drown in this woman's kisses. When we finally broke apart for air, I remembered the girls and pulled away from Ashley.

"I'll call you later."

She nodded. "You better."

In the car, Sami was giggling. "Daddy, you were kissing Ashley."

I couldn't help the grin that spread across my face. "Yes, yes, I was."

Ashley

T HE NEXT DAY, I called my brother. On purpose. "Tan, I need a good family lawyer."

He chuckled. "You're not suing Dad and Mom are you?"

I slid my shoes on before rushing out the door. "No. I have a, uh, friend who needs an excellent lawyer for a custody battle." I jumped into my car, pressed the start button, and waited for the Bluetooth to pick up the call.

The shuffling that I had heard behind him stopped. "Would this happen to be an old friend of yours from high school?"

I squeezed my eyes shut, not that he could see me. Tanner had never been unfriendly to Tyrell, but they had never been friends. "Possibly. I guess you heard who I took to the ball."

My brother's tone turned serious. "He has kids?"

I have never prayed so hard for my brother to be on my side for a change. I needed him to be okay with this. "Yes. Twin girls, four years old. Never married to the mother—and they've worked everything out without the courts so far—but this woman is legit nuts."

Instead of a harsh reaction, Tanner's voice softened. "Are you prepared for this? Not just what will come from Mom and Dad but having a boyfriend with kids? Especially with what you've been through in the last few years."

Tears pricked my eyes, and I took a deep breath. "I think so. I hope so. You know how heartbroken I was. What if he's my forever? And he already has children, so it's a built-in family."

Then he asked a question that was like a punch to the gut. "Do you want Tyrell, or do you want a ready-made family, Ash?"

All my breath left me, and I blinked rapidly as I grasped for words—not because I was upset with his question but because I wondered if he was right. I had always loved Tyrell, but did the fact that he now came with children make me want him more?

"I'm sorry, Ashley. I'm sorry. I shouldn't have said that. Listen, I will text you a few people's numbers." A door closed, and I heard Morgan's shrill voice behind him.

Choking back tears and a harsh retort, I cleared my throat. "It's okay. I can't say you're wrong. I'm not sure you're right, but I can't say you're wrong." I sighed. "Thank you, big brother. Kiss Jonny for me." We hung up, and I put the car in reverse.

At church, I sat beside Carly Rivers as I usually did. And she sat beside Alyssa and Riley Norman. We were the unmarried spinsters of the church. Not that they called us that, of course. We were the single women over the age of twenty-five. I always felt like there was a blinking light over our area that announced us as unmarried women ripe for the choosing. Maybe overripe. We had a singles' group for a while; but then the two single men married the other two single women, and that left the four of us.

While the pastor preached the sermon, I found myself contemplating Tanner's question. Was I feeling so heady about Tyrell because he was now a package deal with kids? It would take the pressure off my feeling like I needed to give him children. And he said anyone who thought I was defective was defective themselves. I wanted children, even if they were only parttime and not biologically my own. I had looked into all the options for adopting over the past few years, and it didn't bother me to raise children I had not birthed.

By the end of the service, I concluded that while I felt that Tyrell was the man of my dreams, and the girls definitely did up the ante, they were not my sole reason for wanting to move a little more quickly with him. I felt it was time. I was thirty, and I was ready to move off this row of perpetual availability.

Getting my mother to stop setting me up with men fifteen years older was another reason for me to consider moving a little quicker. Just dating Tyrell wouldn't satisfy her; she wouldn't consider me off the market until I had spoken vows. I wondered if even that would work.

I headed toward home for my usual Sunday afternoon chores of laundry and grocery shopping. What I was not expecting at my door was my mother, her stilettos tapping as she waited impatiently for me.

Approaching with caution, I put on a fake smile. "Mom, what a pleasant surprise. I just got out of church." I went past her and into my building, knowing she would follow closely behind without an invitation. She did.

Her silence was deafening as we went up the stairs to my apartment. As soon as I swung my door open, however, she launched into me. "That man has children?"

I cringed. Had my brother already ratted me out? I could shoot him. "Yes, Mother."

"So, you found a deadbeat dad with a crazed ex?" She then flung a newspaper onto my counter. "Ashley, what is the meaning of this?"

The paper was opened and folded to a photo of me, sitting on the bench, being yelled at by Sabra Thomas. The two officers were standing there, and the girls were watching their mother, wide-eyed. There was no time to contemplate who had taken the photo or what the article said. My mother cared about neither, only that I was photographed and displayed in a negative light.

"I was watching those girls, and their mother went off the deep end saying I had kidnapped them." I put my purse down and turned toward her.

"And these are Tyrell Harris's children?"

I braced myself. "Yes."

She pinched the bridge of her nose and looked like the world was ending. I leaned back on the counter and folded my arms, preparing for the onslaught.

My mother blew out a long breath and readied her rant. It happened often enough. "It's bad enough you found him and brought him out of whatever pit he had been in and brought him to the charity event. But to find out, like this, that he has children with someone else—someone who is clearly unstable. He had too much baggage back then, and it's only gotten worse."

Only my mother would think this way. I scoffed. "How can you call two beautiful, little girls baggage? They are sweet, kind children, thanks to Tyrell and Mrs. Harris." I looked at the picture again, the girls staring wide-eyed at their mother. I should have shielded them, but it wasn't exactly my place.

"Are you dating him again?"

I turned my gaze to my mother and smiled sweetly. "I am."

"Your father said he would cut you off." She used it as a threat. She had used it for years to get me to do what she wanted.

But this time, I was prepared. I knew my financial situation. The money my father passed out to keep me under his thumb would no longer be useful.

"He can't cut me off from my trust or my share in the business. If I mean that little to him, if my happiness and well-being mean nothing, then that's fine." I went to the door and opened it. "Thank you for stopping by."

Heels clicked on the laminate flooring. Her hand lightly touched my arm. "Think about what you're doing, Ashley. Is he worth it? Is someone else's children worth it?"

I looked her straight in the eyes; the dark brown color matched my own. "Absolutely. Goodbye, Mother."

The door closed behind her and I flung myself onto my bed, curled up, and cried myself to sleep.

Tyrell

THE WORLD WAS IMPLODING around me. First, my mother broke her leg, then, Sabra and her nonsense, and now Ashley's mom. Why was the world against us? I wasn't usually one to believe in such things, but what else was I supposed to think?

I had called several attorneys and found one that was willing to work with me. She had said it would be better if I were married, but I certainly wasn't going to rush into that for the sake of a custody battle. I'd seen enough movies with that premise to know it never worked out. Living close to my mom was a bonus, though.

And Mom was getting better every day. The pain was finally subsiding, and she was figuring out how to move on crutches. The girls were being especially helpful and attentive.

On the attorney's advice, we stuck to our current custody agreement, but I was not happy to drop the girls off at school Wednesday knowing Sabra would be the one picking them up. What if she ran off with them? What if she went after Ashley again?

I hated to admit it, but I didn't have much time to worry about Ashley's predicament with her parents. I had known they were toxic before the term "toxic people" was a thing. But they were her family, and she loved them. Still, putting space between her and them was needed. When she told me about her mother calling the girls "baggage," I just shook my head. That woman would end up alone in life.

"Tyrell, man, what are you doing?"

I snapped out of my trance and realized I was standing in the middle of the newsroom, papers in hand, just staring out into space.

My co-worker, Rex, clapped me on the back. "You okay, man? You look like me after pulling staying up all night with the baby."

Shaking out my arms and legs, I nodded. "Yeah, sorry. Just a lot going on. I guess I'm not getting much sleep, either."

He laughed. "Well, the boss wants to see you. Greenhorn interviews are happening soon." He shook his head and walked off toward his edit bay.

As if my home life wasn't screwy enough, one of our on-air reporters was leaving, meaning we had to hire someone new.

And as one of the news directors, I had to sit in on interviews. I wondered if I could just take a vacation for the next six months.

At 5:30, I got a text from Ashley.

ASHLEY: THE GIRLS ARE STILL HERE. BRITT CAN'T GET AHOLD OF SABRA.

TYRELL: I'M HEADING INTO A MEETING. CAN YOU CALL MY MOM?

TYRELL: NEVER MIND, SHE CAN'T DRIVE.

ASHLEY: I CAN TAKE THEM TO HER. THEIR CAR SEATS ARE HERE.

What should I do? We had an interview, so I couldn't leave. My mom was out of commission. Where was Sabra? The last thing I needed was her showing up for the girls after Ashley left with them.

TYRELL: GIVE SABRA TEN MORE MINUTES. I'LL TEXT HER. IF SHE'S A NO-SHOW, TAKE THE GIRLS TO MOM'S.

ASHLEY: WILL DO.

I fired a text to Sabra telling her my mom would be getting the girls in ten minutes if she didn't show up. Slipping into the conference room, I put my phone on silent and prayed when I left, everything would be okay.

Thirty minutes later, I pulled out my phone to find that Ashley had taken the girls to my mom's house. Sabra had not come. While I was happy to keep the girls, it would have been nice to have a heads up. Rage welled up inside me.

I stopped by my office to grab a few things and lock up when AO came by and slapped my door. "Tyrell! P's and Cues tonight?"

"I can't, bro; the girls' mom didn't show up to get them." That's when the worry set in.

Sabra was always on time when it came to Saffi and Sami. She was good about taking them to doctor's appointments and getting them everything they needed. It wasn't like her to be a no-show. What if something had happened to her? I didn't know if I should be furious or scared, so I rushed out, dialing Sabra as I went.

When her voicemail picked up, I tried to be calm. "Sabra, you didn't pick the girls up from school. My mom had to get them." No need to tell her Ashley had taken them to my mom. "Let me know if you're going to get them tonight or what."

Ashley was still there when I got to Mom's house. "I didn't want to stay in case she showed up, but your mom asked me to help her with them." She looked to the girls, who were snuggled up on either side of Mom watching television. "They asked why their mommy hadn't come to get them. And Sami is worried about her pet snail?"

"That would be Saffi. And it's a stuffed snail, so it will be okay." I opened the fridge and rummaged around, deciding to make a quick ham and cheese sandwich. "I just don't know why Sabra wouldn't show up."

"You don't think something happened to her, do you?"

I tried not to let my mind go there. I was prepared to fight for custody, but I didn't want anything bad to happen to Sabra. She was the girls' mother. I shook my head. "I hope not. I guess we'll wait and see. If I don't hear from her by tomorrow, I'll call her mom."

The next morning, I still had no word from Sabra, so I called Anita Thomas after I dropped the girls off at school. She was just as good a grandmother as my own mom, but she and Sabra had a volatile relationship. I was pretty sure it was all Sabra's doing.

She said Sabra had called her and told her she was going to Atlanta to audition for a television show and that I was keeping the girls longer. This was news to me.

Her concern for the girls was evident as her voice shook. "They can come stay here if you need them to."

She didn't get to see the girls as often as she would like, so I was happy to make her an offer. "How about they come over tonight and stay the weekend with you? Maybe Sabra will be back by then."

"God bless you, Tyrell. You are a good man, a good daddy." She sniffled as she hung up.

It was hard to believe Sabra had been so reckless to leave like that. She wasn't usually that irresponsible to just run off when it was her time with the girls. I knew when I had them she liked to go off with her girlfriends for long weekends, but I usually knew ahead of time.

All I could figure was that at this point, she had abandoned her daughters, and my custody case had just become a whole lot easier. It was documented in the school schedule that she was supposed to get the girls, and she hadn't shown up. It broke my heart for Saffi and Sami, but it gave me hope.

When I picked up the girls, I told them they were going to Granny Anita's house for the weekend because Momma was out of town. They were thrilled to have fun with Anita and their cousins.

As we were leaving, Ashley stopped me. "Since they're going to their grandmother's, how about I take you out on a date tonight?"

"You're going to take me out?" Despite my stress levels, the idea of Ashley taking me out was fascinating.

She crinkled up her nose at my smile. "Yes. My treat. You need some time to relax after this week."

We set up a time for her to pick me up, and I took the girls to their grandmother's house. The day was already looking brighter.

Ashley

I PICKED TYRELL UP at his mother's house, just like I used to do in high school. He could never pick me up when we were teenagers because my parents did not approve. It had been easier for me to go to his house. Plus, I loved his mother.

I knocked on the door wearing the same jeans and blouse I had worn to work. Thankfully, nobody had peed on me or spilled juice all over me. It was a banner day.

Mrs. Harris hollered through the window. "Come on in, Ashley. It's open."

I let myself in and went straight for a hug from Mrs. Harris, who sat in her favorite chair. She was positioned in front of the television with her leg propped up, a sandwich on a stool next to her.

"Do you want us to bring something back for you? Or we could order in and stay here." I mentally began thinking of who delivered nearby.

She waved me off. "No, no, darlin'. You two go and have fun. I'm just gonna sit here and catch up on my shows that I can't watch with little eyes nearby." She looked me up and down. "I don't need big eyes, either."

I giggled at the thought of her watching something racy. "Mrs. H., what are you watching these days?"

She wrinkled her nose at me. "Never you mind. How about you refill my tea real quick? I don't know what's keeping that boy."

Her glass of tea sat nearly empty, so I took it to the kitchen and refilled it. When I set it down next to her, Tyrell came out from a back room.

"You didn't tell me you were here." He kissed my temple.

Glancing at the clock, I chuckled. "It's just now 5:30. I was here to see your mom first."

Again, Mrs. Harris waved me off. "Both of you, go on. I have a date with Netflix. I'm fine."

We bade her goodbye and exited the house. In the car, I laughed. "I never thought your mother would force us on a date."

"She tried so hard to convince me to try to get you back. She has always known." He shook his head. "Well, I've always known, but she was willing to say it." With that, he leaned over and kissed me.

Since we were both casually dressed, I took us downtown to the more touristy area of the city. I loved playing tourist from time to time. There were cheesy gift stores and chocolate shops and restaurants galore, all with the water nearby. It made for a relaxing date night.

As we strolled along, I took Tyrell's hand. "I'm glad you figured out where Sabra went. That had to worry you."

He nodded, his face grim. "It did. Not for my sake, but for the girls. They knew she was going to get them, and she didn't show up. So, she let them down. Again. I don't want to call it child abandonment, especially if she comes back in a few days, but what else could it be?"

I shrugged. "We were taught, as teachers, to look for signs of abuse. But we're taught to look for physical signs. Things like this just aren't covered. At least, they have you for stability."

A shop filled with children's toys seemed to beckon to me, and I pulled Tyrell inside. We spent fifteen minutes playing with toys and laughing. I picked out two little princess wands and bought them. Green for Saffi and pink for Sami. At least I could color-code them to know who was who.

Taking my hands in his, Tyrell looked at me with a serious expression. "You don't have to buy them gifts. They like you just fine."

I nodded, knowing what he was trying to really say. "I'm not trying to buy their affection. Or yours. I just want to do something nice for them. Gifts are my love language."

A grim smile crossed his face as he looked away from me. "I can't give you all those gifts, Ash."

We exited the store, and I stopped him on the sidewalk. "It's not about money, and you know it. You could grab my favorite candy bar at the store. Or I can get the girls cheap, plastic wands or give you something small. It's just something that shows the giver was thinking about the receiver. That's all. It's not about diamonds or expensive perfumes or anything else. It's a simple thing."

He jammed his hands in his pockets. "Are you sure?"

I tilted my head. "Have I ever lied to you?"

"No."

"Okay, then. And since I don't lie, I'm starving, and I want shrimp."

One of my favorite places was a block down, so we went there and sat on the same side of the booth, cuddled up and eating bottomless plates of shrimp and fries.

As we left, I asked Tyrell one of my favorite questions. "What's your five-year plan?"

"You still ask people that?" The laughter made his words nearly indecipherable.

It was true—I had loved to ask that question my whole life. I had learned it from my father. "Of course, I do. How else will I know what their five-year plan is?"

We linked arms and moved away from the crowd that always inhabited the area. A comfortable silence came over us, and I allowed him time to think.

It took a moment before he finally began to speak. "Before you showed back up, I had just hoped to keep the pace—watch the girls grow, take care of Mom, do good at work. I wondered about moving up the ladder at the station, but there's not much else for me without moving. And you know I can't leave my family."

"What about finding love?"

He shrugged. "If it had suddenly happened, maybe. But I wasn't looking. At least, not looking hard. Between Mom, Sami, and Saffi, I had enough women around me."

He was not wrong there. There were plenty of women in his life. I stopped walking and faced him. "How about now that we have reconnected?"

The grin on his face told me enough, but I wanted to hear it. "Now? In the next five years, I want to get married to a gorgeous brunette, maybe find a bigger house for everyone. I would love to add to the family, if that's in the cards, but if not, I'm content."

Of course, he wanted more children. Why wouldn't he? I shook my head. "Tyrell, you know..."

He put a finger to my lips. "We can adopt. We can look into whatever you would like. But I know you, and I know you would love to raise a child from day one. As long as we're together, Ashley." He closed the gap between us and hugged me tight.

The scent of bergamot and cinnamon filled the air as I breathed him in. "Are you sure?"

"You listen to me, Dream Girl. I will never be rich enough or come from old money. Does that matter?" He pulled back and looked me in the eyes.

"Of course not."

Then he grabbed me by the shoulders. "You will never give birth to a child, and that does not matter to me. You are still perfect."

I cried. The big, ugly cry that you see in movies. Ten years' worth of tears.

"I love you."

He cradled my head in his hands. "I love you, too."

Tyrell

THE PHONE IN MY office rang a lot. I wasn't usually in there to answer it because I generally ran around like a chicken without a head. While I could have attached the number to a cell, I preferred the office line to stay in my office. The people who knew me had my cell number. Those office voicemails would be dealt with later.

So when the phone rang and I was there to pick it up, I was not expecting to hear Jonathan Gloss on the other end of the phone.

"Tyrell Harris. You managed to find my daughter again." It sounded like he had me on speaker phone, and I wondered who else was listening in on the call.

I did not have the time or the patience to deal with him. We had a new reporter coming in, and her producer, AO, was already up in arms about it. "Mr. Gloss, I'm afraid I don't have the time to play your power games right now. I'm trying to run a news floor."

He snorted in response. "Well, then allow me to cut to the chase. Do you intend to keep seeing Ashley?"

"Yes, I do." I stood up straight and planted my free hand on my hip as if he could see me in a power stance.

"And my wife is correct in telling me that you have two children running around the city?"

My girls were not any of his concern, and as a fellow parent, I would think he'd understand that. "My daughters are four. They do not run around the city. What are you getting at?"

"I'm a father, so I understand how much you must love your children." He took a deep breath. "I would like to set up a college fund for your two daughters. Fifty thousand each."

He was offering me one hundred thousand dollars for the girls to go to college? There had to be a catch. "And what do you get out of it, Mr. Gloss?"

"You always were a bright boy." I could hear the shuffling of papers. "Fifty thousand for each of your daughters will go into an interest-bearing college account if you will stop this nonsense with Ashley right now and never see her again."

The new hire would have to wait.

I sank into my chair. "You hate me that much that you would pay me off, using my children, to keep me away from Ashley?"

He laughed. "You're a father. I hoped you would see that I love her that much."

The rage that rose in my throat caused a metallic taste. No, I had bit into my lip so hard, it was bleeding. I could not believe what he was saying. "That's not love, Mr. Gloss. That's control."

"Just wait until your daughters are teenagers, Mr. Harris. You'll understand." He hummed for a few seconds. "I tell you what. I'll throw in an extra fifty grand to help your mother fix up her house. The three women in your life will be taken care of. You don't need another one."

Thinking I could get the better of him, I tried a different approach. "I assume there would be a contract of sorts if I entertained this idea?"

"Of course, there would be. But don't think you could show it to Ashley to make her turn on me. It would be cleverly worded. I have people for that."

"I figured you would. How about we meet in person to discuss this?" That would give me time to figure out something.

"Come by in the morning. I think you'll find you suddenly have a few hours off work." He laughed softly. Sure enough, when I checked my calendar, it said I was off in the morning.

He was beyond belief. My entire body shook with fury. "Do you own the station?"

"No, I don't. But Mr. Andrews owes me a favor, so I called in this one. Be glad you still have a job, Mr. Harris. I will see you in the morning." With that, he hung up, and I was left dumbfounded, staring at my phone.

My first thought was to call Ashley; but she was working, and I was late. Before I left my office, though, I slammed my fist into my desk. It's a good thing it's made of solid wood. Then I took a cleansing breath, cracked my neck, and walked out the door. There was a reason I didn't stay in my office where the phone was.

As I showed our new hire around, I thought about what I could do. How could I beat Mr. Gloss at his own game? Then it hit me. I knew exactly what to do, and I was in just the right place to do it.

The next morning, I walked up to Gloss Enterprises ready to battle. I didn't want to turn Ashley on her father, but I also wanted to reveal just how low he was willing to stoop to get his way. Before going through the large double doors, I looked around the parking lot. A mix of SUVs, luxury cars, and compact cars filled the spots. It was perfect.

Once inside, I was led right to Mr. Gloss's office, where I stuffed my hands in my pockets out of nerves. I could only hope this turned out all right, and Ashley wouldn't hate me forever for not telling her ahead of time.

An older secretary told me to go on into the office, and I swung the door open to see Mr. Gloss sitting confidently behind his massive desk.

"Mr. Harris, so nice of you to come see me this morning." Mr. Gloss was tall and trim, but the air of authority around him made him a force to be reckoned with.

In my younger days, I had been intimidated by him. Now, he was just a man, no better or worse than me. I went to his desk; but he did not offer to shake my hand, so I did not offer mine either. When he motioned for me to sit, I remained standing.

"Let's get down to business." He pulled a few papers from his desk. "If you'll just sign these, I can get everything started, and your children and mother will be taken care of."

I shook my head. "I'm not blindly signing anything." I needed him to talk more. "How do I know you'll be true to your word, Mr. Gloss?"

He licked his lips. "Don't you know by now, Mr. Harris, that I'm a man of my word? Once this is signed, I can hand you cash."

Playing dumb, I tilted my head and scratched my chin. "Cash? I thought you were going to set up accounts for everything."

Now, he stood, his hands splayed on the desk between us. "Don't be stupid, Harris. You didn't think I'd be as easy as that, did you? You sign that document saying you will never see Ashley again, and I will hand you one hundred and fifty grand right here and now. Put it away for your offspring's college, blow it all on drugs—I don't care."

I adjusted my stance and folded my arms. "You think so little of me, Mr. Gloss? You want me to give up on a lifetime of love with Ashley for cash? Don't you want her to find a good man to settle down with?"

A devious smile came across his face. "Of course, I do, Tyrell. That's why I'm getting rid of you." He opened a drawer and pulled out a stack of bills. Pushing it toward me, he winked. "Here. All the money I promised you. Just sign on the dotted line."

Now I did sit in the chair across from him. I picked up the paper and began reading it out loud to myself. He was right; it was cleverly worded, but I still read it in its entirety. If I were to break the agreement, he could break me—that much was clear.

I drew in a deep breath and blew it out slowly as I brought my gaze up to his. "Mr. Gloss, I love my children."

"And I love mine."

"I also love your daughter."

He scoffed. "It will never be enough."

I stood again. "Is that enough?"

A quizzical look came across Mr. Gloss's face, but he didn't realize I wasn't talking to him. I was talking to Rex, who sat outside in the parking lot with recording equipment. Georgia was a single-party-recording state, which meant I could record him without his knowledge. Everything in our exchange had been recorded via a hidden mic I wore under my shirt.

My phone buzzed twice, the signal that we were good to go.

Mr. Gloss was still in the dark. "I just said it would never be enough."

I smiled. "Maybe not for you. But it's enough for Action News to air tonight. Have a good day, Mr. Gloss." With a wink,

I turned and walked out of his office, leaving him sputtering behind me.

The contract that he had already signed was still in my hand.

Ashley

I WAS CALLED OUT of work by two frantic people – Tyrell and my father. The director stepped into the classroom for me while I went outside to call them back. I opted to call Tyrell first.

"Have you spoken to your father?"

I put my hand on my hip. "No, but he just called me as well. I called you back first."

He sighed. "Good. I just came from his office. He tried to pay me one hundred and fifty grand to never see you again."

My knees buckled, and I sat on the curb. "I'm sorry, what? Surely you're mistaken."

"I wish I was, Ash. But I went to his office, and I have the entire thing recorded. Rex set me up with a mic and recorded it from a car in the parking lot." He spoke rapidly, and I could hear someone else in the car with him. That must be Rex.

"Okay, back up and explain this to me." I put my head in my hands as he explained everything that had transpired with my father.

The very thought that my father called this love was beyond me. It was not love. It was control. This was why I didn't use the monthly "allowance" he gave me. It was either donated or invested. I lived off my own money, and I had never been so glad of that until this.

"So, what will you do with that recording?" I chewed on my bottom lip. On one hand, my father could use a big helping of humble pie. On the other hand, I owned a good chunk of the business, and if my father went down, the business would as well.

Tyrell spoke to Rex before coming back to me. "That's why I'm calling. I can have this on air all day today. It would certainly be breaking news. Your father is one of the most prominent names in Savannah."

It would ruin him, I knew. My head began to pound, which wasn't helped when the director opened the door and glared at me before slamming it shut again. "What's the other idea?"

Tyrell's voice softened. "You talk to him and hope he's learned his lesson. We can get rid of the evidence, and he accepts that we're together."

Would my father ever learn his lesson? Even without hearing the recording, I believed Tyrell. He would have no reason to make up everything. I told Tyrell I needed to think about it for a little while and speak with my father. After hanging up with Tyrell, I called my dad.

"Ashley, that hoodlum you've been seeing…"

I interrupted him. "Stop it right now, Dad. I know everything. How could you?"

"He's no good for you, Ashley." His voice wasn't harsh, and he spoke plainly.

I shook my head. "How would you know? You don't know him. He's an amazing father."

"He has children out of wedlock, Ashley."

Standing to stretch my legs, I paced back and forth. "I know that. So does half of America at this point, Dad. That's neither here nor there. I won't ever have children; these girls might one day be your grandchildren."

"They'll never be my grandchildren."

Bitterness rose in me. How could he be so callous? "I'm sorry to hear that, Dad. I'm done. I hope you're happy with the results of your actions today because you'll be reaping them for years to come."

The backtracking began in earnest. "Wait, Ashley, sweetie. You're not going to let him…"

Laughter bubbled in my throat. "You'll just have to watch Action News tonight and see what happens. Maybe you'll be exposed. Maybe you won't. Tyrell is smarter than you give him credit for. I'm just sorry you're too small-minded to realize it."

I hung up and kicked the curb as hard as I could. The tennis shoes on my feet weren't exactly great protection, and I yelped in pain. As tears swam in my eyes, I realized just how toxic my parents actually were. There was no reason for me to continue playing into their plan.

Opening my text messages, I fired one off to Tyrell.

ASHLEY: Hold off. Let's make him sweat.

TYRELL: I love that idea.

ASHLEY: I'm so sorry. About everything.

TYRELL: You did nothing wrong, Dream Girl. I'm sorry it came to this.

ASHLEY: I guess I'm without a family now.

The tears were now in a free flow down my cheeks. I knew my boss was watching me, but I didn't care. For all intents and purposes, I had just lost my father. Perhaps my mother and brother as well. The tears turned to sobs at the thought of never seeing Jonny again.

TYRELL: We're your family now, Ash. We all love you.

A touch on my shoulder had me spinning around. Britt stood there, her arms outstretched. I fell into them and cried until I was all out of tears. Through hiccupping breaths, I told her my father was gone. She told me to go home, and she would explain it to the director.

Not wanting to argue, I simply nodded and went inside to get my things. My class was outside on the play equipment, and I slipped in and out without fuss. I went home, curled up with Trainer, and closed my eyes.

It was dusk when the sound of my phone ringing woke me. Tanner's name came across my screen, and I debated ignoring him. Knowing Daddy had surely made his side known, I answered so I could give my own. Whether he wanted to hear it or not would remain to be seen.

"Let's hear it, Tanner." I stayed on my bed, staring up at the ceiling.

He chuckled. "I was more thinking I needed to say that to you. What on earth happened? Dad is preparing for the apocalypse."

I blew out a heavy breath. "Good. After what he tried to pull, I'm done. And if he's sweating in his Brooks Brothers, all the better."

"Tyrell threatened him?"

Of course, that was Dad's side of the story. "No. Tyrell has the entire thing recorded. Dad tried to pay Tyrell off to never see me again." I told him what Tyrell had told me.

"Dad is just looking out for you. He doesn't want to see you end up with the wrong person." Tanner's defense of our father wasn't a surprise.

The snort that came through my nose, however, was a surprise. "The wrong person? You mean, the only guy I've ever loved? The only one who doesn't care that I can't have children? The man who has done nothing but protect me? Dad is only trying to keep me away from Tyrell because he comes from the wrong family."

"Dad loves you. This is his way of showing it."

Now I did sit up. "That's not love. He's using money to control us, Tanner. You and me both. That monthly allowance you get? It controls you. You do what Dad says to do, and he gives you ten grand a month. See what happens if you stop following his orders."

The voice on the other end became hardened. "Doesn't he give you that money every month as well?"

"I donate it or invest it. I don't use it."

"You still accept it."

"No more. I'll close out that account tomorrow. I'm done being Dad's pawn." I huffed. "I'm sorry, Tanner. I can't do it. I cannot be around someone who would control me like this. I'm just mad at myself for not seeing it until now." More tears came. "I love you. And you know I adore Jonny. But I have to choose myself."

A deep sigh came through the phone. "I know. You're braver than I am. I have a lot to think about, but we'll talk again soon, okay?"

"Okay." I threw the phone down and fell back onto my pillow.

Tyrell

AFTER TWO DAYS, THE recording still sat in my desk at work. It was also backed up at my mom's house, just in case. I could air it anytime. Our new reporter would probably love to do an exposé on Jonathan Gloss, especially since she had just been sent out to get a story on invasive vines.

As the weekend began, my thoughts turned back to my own family issues. Living with my mother again was not as much fun without the girls to be a buffer. I adored my mom, but I was a grown man, not a teenager who needed to be tended—especially by a woman who could barely move around her house.

Not only was I working full time, but I was also trying to maintain two households, get reacquainted with Ashley, get my mom to appointments, and still trying to get in touch with the mother of my children. It was Friday, and she still hadn't shown back up in Savannah.

Going for a run seemed like a good way to get out of the house and think through everything going on. I popped earbuds in and took off from Mom's house, thinking I could run the two miles to my own house, then back again.

I needed to solve the easiest problem first—dating Ashley. Well, there was no problem there. She was perfection. Okay, maybe not perfection, but she was close. We saw each other a few times a week, not counting when I took the girls to school, and the girls were getting to know her, too. Nope, no problems there.

Next, my mom. She was adjusting to the crutches and was hobbling okay. She had five more weeks with the cast, and I didn't think I could live with her for that long. Maybe I could just stop by after work and help her make dinner and pop in a load of laundry if she needed it. The girls and I could stay on weekends and clean the house. Maybe I could sweet-talk Ashley into going by as well to check on her.

That left Sabra and Ashley's father. There wasn't much I could do about either one of them with a quick turnout. But what could I do? I could support Ashley however she needed it. I could keep or destroy the recording of my confrontation with Mr. Gloss – keeping it hidden away seemed the best course of inaction. As far as Sabra went, I had spoken to an attorney who said I had a great case against her, but then we were at the mercy of the courts and their timeline, which could drag on for months. I needed to actually talk to her before anything else happened.

I stopped on a corner, winded. Sweat dripped down my neck and my back, and I was beginning to get a stitch in my side. Running used to be one of my favorite things. Soccer had been my life in high school and college. But since then? Not so much. I didn't have the time to devote to my physique, nor did I care that much. I had a dad bod, and I was a dad; it hadn't bothered me in the last several years. The run that would have been easy as pie five years before was now a struggle. By the time I got to my own house, I was drenched in sweat, and I feared my legs were permanently damaged.

I struggled to open the lock and went straight for the kitchen, where I downed the entire pitcher of water. Then I collapsed on the couch and laid there, panting. My phone dinged, and I struggled to hold it up.

Ashley: Whatcha doing?

I had to use voice-to-text to answer. I couldn't lift my other hand to type.

Tyrell: Trying not to die. I ran from Momma's house to my house.

The phone rang then. I answered with a weak grunt.

"Why did you run from Gigi's house to your house?" Ashley couldn't decide if she was concerned or amused because her tone changed halfway through the question.

The fact that she had taken to calling my mom Gigi always made my heart jump. I didn't know why. But the last thing I needed right then was for my heart to start acting up again. I was still trying to get it to beat normally.

"I needed to clear my head, and I thought a run might help."

"Did it?" She giggled this time.

"Absolutely not." I gasped for effect. "I can see the light. You better say your goodbyes."

This time, she burst into laughter. "Oh, no. You cannot die on me, Mr. Harris. I just found you again. I will not give you up this easily. How are you getting home?"

Crawling back army-style had crossed my mind, and I told her as much. She made the generous offer to pick me up. I agreed.

After we hung up, I managed to stand on my noodle legs and get myself to the bathroom for a quick shower to both cool me down and make me smell better. Even though I was growing out my beard, I splashed my aftershave on my neck. I knew how much she loved the scent.

I was dressed and once again sprawled out on the couch when a knock came at the door. "If that's Ashley, come in. If it's not Ashley, nobody's home."

The door opened, and I looked up to see my petite brunette enter. She leaned over the couch and kissed my cheek. "Oh, you smell so good." She kissed it again.

Bolstered by her affection, I reached up and grabbed her, pulling her over the couch and onto my lap. She squealed and laughed; the sound was like music to my ears. Kissing her more thoroughly, I groaned with hunger for her.

"I thought you were too weak to move, and yet here you are grabbing me and kissing me." She ran her fingers lightly over my face, giving me goosebumps.

I leaned in and nibbled on her neck, making her shriek again. "Ha! That was all a ploy to get you here."

We were interrupted from anything further when my phone gave off a special ring. Sabra's ring. Yes, she had her own ring—mainly because she only called when it had to do with the girls, and I wanted to make sure I took those calls. I cursed under my breath and grabbed for the phone. Ashley sat up but stayed close.

"Sabra, where have you been?"

"Some greeting, Tyrell. I'm trying to provide for my babies." She already sounded exasperated, but then I guess I did, too. I put her on speakerphone.

"You left without telling me, without telling the girls good-bye. Where are you?" I ran my hand over my head, my blood heating back up.

It sounded like she was in her car. "I'm on my way home from Atlanta. I landed an audition for this reality show called Circle Up, and I made it. I'm going to be on it. I have a week to pack up some stuff and get back."

"What about the girls?" I pushed off from the couch, causing Ashley to fall over a little; but in that moment, I was more concerned with the vitriol Sabra was feeding me.

"You're a great dad, Tyrell. You can handle them. And I'll still see them. The taping is only three months. And we have a family day halfway through when they can come visit."

I closed my eyes and paced the room. "You know you're just making my court case stronger. Not that I mind, but I thought you'd at least fight for your children."

Ashley pulled her phone out and began typing. While I waited for Sabra's reply, Ashley showed me a website for Circle Up. It was a reality dating show. I would not subject the girls to that kind of environment.

Finally, Sabra spoke. "I'm doing my best. I get paid good money to be on this show, and if it goes well, they think I could do a spin-off one as well. This could be my big break, which means I can provide more for Samirya and Sapphire. Speaking of, I want to talk to them."

Through gritted teeth, I replied, "They're at your mother's house."

"Oh. I'll call there, then. But I do need to sit down and talk with you before I come back to Atlanta." I heard her turn signal come on, and she yelled at another car.

"Yes, we sure do." We hung up, and I again fell to the couch. Ashley only wrapped her arms around me silently as my mind reeled.

I didn't know what to do, but I guess I had time to figure it out. Three months at least.

"Tyrell?"

Looking up at Ashley's big, doe eyes, I raised an eyebrow.

"I love you."

Relief flooded over me. She was in this with me. "I love you, too, Dream Girl."

Ashley

LIFE WAS HARD. I knew that. And as I laid in my bed, my pillow hugged close, I wondered if life with Tyrell was too much. The girls were easy to love, and Mrs. Harris—Gigi—was a dream. But the drama with Sabra gave me pause. Did I want to deal with her for the foreseeable future?

The minute I had heard Tyrell's voice, I knew he was my future. I knew I couldn't walk away again. Regardless of him having kids. He was my soulmate, my best friend, and my rock. We could weather any storm together. And if he could weather my parents, I could weather Sabra Thomas.

My thoughts then turned to the girls. Didn't they deserve a woman in their corner? Both their grandmothers were, of course, but they had raised their children and couldn't easily keep up with Sami and Saffi. Their mother certainly loved them—I could see that—but she had a convoluted way of showing it at times. They were completely worth the hassle.

I fell asleep weighing the pros and cons of everything and woke up knowing that regardless of how many things were on the cons side, the weight of the pros would win. I had told Tyrell I was in this with him, and I meant it.

My phone rang as I finished getting ready for work. My mother's name appeared on the screen. With a roll of my eyes, I answered. "Good morning, Mother."

"Did you just wake up? You don't sound very enthusiastic." Neither did she, but that was beside the point. "We haven't spoken since that boy came and tried to blackmail your father. Let's clear the air, Ashley."

Tying my sneakers, I put the phone on the coffee table and put my mother on speaker. "You're right. Let's clear a few things. First, Tyrell is no longer a boy. He's thirty. He's a man and deserves to be treated as one." I took a fortifying breath. "Second, Daddy tried to pay him off to stop seeing me. That is a horrid, horrid thing to do. There is no blackmail. Tyrell did not ask for anything, nor did he air the very clear evidence he has against Daddy."

Before my mother could come up with a retort, I continued, "And another thing—I will no longer be accepting the allowance you and Daddy dole out every month. I have a job; I have good investments; and I own a decent share of Gloss Enterprises. I don't need your money or your control. Unless you are willing to accept me for me—and that includes Tyrell and his girls—you can hang up now."

Silence. For a brief moment, I thought my mother had actually hung up, but then I could hear her breathing. With a shaky voice, she finally spoke. "You're right. You are a grown woman, and you can make your own decisions. I think...I need some time to think. I'll call you soon."

With that, she hung up. I laid back on my bed and took a deep breath, letting the tiny tear that formed escape into my hair. If nothing else, I had stood up for myself, and that was something. Hopefully, my parents would see the error of their ways.

If for some reason they didn't, I had a family. I had Mrs. Harris and Tyrell. I had the girls. And I was fairly certain Tanner wouldn't give up on me. Even though we struggled, he seemed accepting of Tyrell. In fact... I pulled out my phone again and texted.

ASHLEY: TANNER, WHY DON'T YOU AND MORGAN BRING JONNY AND MEET US FOR DINNER TONIGHT?

A reply only took a few moments.

TANNER: US?

ASHLEY: ME, TYRELL, AND THE GIRLS.

TANNER: WHERE?

ASHLEY: LUCK'S?

TANNER: THAT GREASY SPOON IS STILL STANDING? LET ME CHECK WITH MORGAN.

ASHLEY: PLEASE, TANNER. IT WOULD MEAN A LOT.

My phone went silent, and I hoped my brother was actually checking with Morgan. I got in the car and made my way to the preschool. As I got out of the car, my phone alerted me to a text.

Tanner: We're in. Six o'clock?

Ashley: See you there.

A huge smile broke out on my face, and I quickly fired off a text to Tyrell telling him about the plans. He responded when he dropped the girls off, cautiously saying it sounded good.

Wary was a good word to use as we all convened that night at Luck's. It was fairly busy, and we just blended into the crowd. Morgan looked a little grossed out by the well-worn décor and tables, but she would get over it. Tyrell and Tanner shook hands as we met, and I gave them both a cautious smile.

My sweet Jonny launched himself from his father's arms to mine upon seeing me, and he blew a raspberry on my cheek.

"Ashley, who is he?" Sami's giant eyes took in Jonny. He was in the place she liked to occupy herself.

"This is my nephew, Jonny. I babysit him a lot, and we have a lot of fun." I knelt down so they could be eye to eye. "Can you say hi to him?"

There was a small amount of stink eye going from Sami to Jonny, but she greeted him cautiously. Saffi, on the other hand, immediately began to coo at him and play peek-a-boo.

At the table, we put the girls and Jonny on one side and the adults on the other. Tanner and I sat side by side, buffering our partners. Morgan wasn't too happy to be in a dive, and Tyrell wasn't too sure about Tanner's sincerity. While we eyed each other with suspicion, the kids were happily playing peek-a-boo and giggling uncontrollably.

"What prompted this night out, Ash?" Tanner never was one to beat around the bush.

The rhythm of my heart picked up, and I licked my lips. "You haven't seen Tyrell since we were kids, and I wanted you two to meet again. On my terms. And since I think he and the girls will be a big part of my life from here on out, I wanted your family to meet my new family."

Under the table, Tyrell gripped my hand and squeezed it tightly. I squeezed back.

Morgan clutched her hands to her chest. Whether she was actually touched or just putting on a show, I wasn't sure, but I could only hope her display was sincere. "So, are you two engaged? I don't see a diamond."

I shook my head. "We're not. At least, not yet. We're not rushing things. But this man and these little girls are my future, and I need someone in my family to see that and realize it's a good thing." Tears shone in my eyes, and I willed them to stay put. "Tanner? Please."

We might have fought like cats and dogs as kids, and I might roll my eyes at him now; but I only had one brother, and he was it. He cocked his head to the side and looked from me to Tyrell, then to the girls. With a nod, he took a deep breath. "So, Tyrell, tell me about working at the news station."

I released a pent-up breath and closed my eyes for a moment. This was my brother trying. I knew that, and Tyrell seemed to recognize it as well. He launched into telling Tanner and Morgan about the station, about his crazy co-workers, and everything else. Morgan had wanted to be an anchor, so she regaled us with stories of her internship in college.

The children ate. Jonny cried. Sami accused Saffi of stealing a french fry, and we all tried to appease all three children with crayons and sippy cups and, finally, ice cream. We all talked and even laughed a little bit, and by the end of the night, I felt like something was resembling normal. A little bit, at least.

When we all left the restaurant, Tanner hugged me. The girls hugged Jonny. Tanner and Tyrell even shook hands again. I walked Tyrell and the girls to their car. He buckled Sami while I buckled Saffi, and we smiled at each other as the girls jabbered on about Jonny. I walked to his door and lingered a moment.

"Thank you for coming. It means a lot to me." Tears once again threatened, but I shook my head, hoping they would stay put.

A strong hand caressed my cheek. "Hey, Dream Girl, anything for you. You know that. I know your family is important to you, and hopefully, your brother sees how important we are as well."

He leaned over and kissed me thoroughly, and even though we heard the girls begin to giggle at us from inside the car, Tyrell did not let go right away. When he did, he kissed my forehead and pulled me closer. "I'll see you soon."

"You'll see me in the morning at drop-off." I laughed.

"But that's so far away."

"I think you'll survive."

"See you then."

Tyrell

T WO WEEKS HAD PASSED, and I still had a job, so I was grateful. I never did air my confrontation with Mr. Gloss—at Ashley's request—but in truth, I had no desire to ruin someone. I didn't have it in me, and I'm pretty sure that made me the bigger person.

While things with her parents had been strained at best, Tanner was making an effort and had invited us all over to his house for a cookout. It was the bougiest cookout I had ever been to, but he had tried.

I had a sit down with Sabra, and we worked out the girls' custody without attorneys yet again, but I still had her put everything in writing and had it notarized just in case she decided to pull more stunts. She spent several days with the girls before heading off to Atlanta for three months. The girls asked about her for about a week after that, but then it tapered off to only mentioning her on occasion. They both seemed happier.

Ashley cleared out the account her father had been depositing money in. Wouldn't you know it—there was just about one hundred fifty thousand dollars in it. She put fifty grand into an account for each of the girls.

"I can't let you do that."

She eyed me as she handed over the banking information. "You can, and you will. Call it whatever you would like, but it's my gift to your family."

I didn't ask what she was going to do with the other fifty thousand, but a few days later, my mom had scheduled to get a new roof and to redo her kitchen. By the time she was off the crutches, she would have a brand-new kitchen to cook in.

"You don't have to buy our affection, Ashley, honey." My mom fretted over her as she would do with me.

Ashley laid her hand over my mom's. "I know, Gigi. I'm not. You and Tyrell have been some of the only people to love me without strings or expectations, so I'm happy to repay you in this way. No matter what."

Mom made a motion for Ashley to come closer, and Ash scooted her chair over. Arms wrapped around Ashley, and Mom kissed her head. "I love you like you're my own, Ashley."

This seemed like a perfect time to me. I had been waiting for the perfect moment to come up, hoping I would know it when it did. And this—this was it. "Why don't we make her an official Harris?"

Sitting up, Ashley blinked a few times in confusion. "What?"

I moved from the couch to the floor in front of Ashley and reached in my pocket. I thought I would be nervous, but I wasn't. Complete calm washed over me. This was right. "Ashley, would you be willing to take on not just my name, but my family as well? Marry me."

The girls had been sitting in awe when I got on the floor and now began to shriek around us. Mom clapped and began to sing. I looked to Ashley, tears swimming in her eyes. She didn't look at the ring at all. She only looked at me.

"Yes. Yes, absolutely." She launched at me on the floor and almost knocked me over. Kisses peppered my face just as much as the wetness from her tears.

It took a moment, but I finally got her to sit up and get the ring on her finger. It wasn't the biggest diamond in the world; in fact, it wasn't even a diamond. Instead I gave her a rose quartz in a rose gold setting. It was a perfect fit.

I kissed her soundly, even though my mother and daughters were watching. "I love you."

Before she could respond, the girls jumped on our laps. "We love you, too, Ashley!"

"You get to be our stepmom!"

She hugged Sami close, and my daughter buried her face in Ashley's neck. Saffi sat with me and studied her sister. She must have decided Ashley wouldn't bite because after a moment, Saffi joined her sister in Ashley's lap.

"You ready for all this, Ashley?" Mom laughed from her chair.

She put one arm around each girl and laughed. "Absolutely. I've dreamed of nothing else." While the girls played with her hand and admired the ring, Ashley looked at me and mouthed silently, "I love you, too."

Epilogue

WITH THE HELP OF a professional bridesmaid (did you know there was such a thing?), I planned a beautiful wedding to the man of my dreams. Upon realizing I actually did love Tyrell, my parents came around, and my father walked me down the aisle. But I would no longer be under their thumb or dipping into their bank accounts.

Sabra had come back from her stint as a reality star and was suddenly a changed person. She agreed to letting Tyrell and me have primary custody without having to go to court. She would be going back and forth from Savannah to Atlanta, where she was trying to make it as an actress—or, at the very least, trying to get on more reality shows. It sounded right up her alley, and we got to keep the girls at least three weeks out of every month, so I was thrilled.

In fact, Sabra had apparently done her homework on Gloss Enterprises and my family. After realizing how much they were worth, she wholeheartedly blessed our relationship. I can only imagine she thought it would somehow boost her own status in the world.

When I walked down the aisle to become Mrs. Harris, I thought life couldn't get any better. I had the man of my dreams; I had two beautiful daughters, who had started calling me Mashy (get it? A mix of Mom and Ashley), and I lived in the most beautiful city in the world.

Alonso & Piper

Enemies to Lovers

Alonso

I'M NOT SAYING I was glad that Jennifer Marcingill left Action News, but I was glad Jennifer left. She was uptight and dull as a rock. I know that I look like a first-class jerk saying that, but really, everyone was thrilled. Just none as thrilled as I was.

As Jennifer's cameraman and producer, I spent the last five years by her side every day. That's eight hours a day, at least five days a week. Together we chased down stories, put together packages, and ate some terrible food. You would think we'd be close, but no. She was aloof, and I am a goof.

Still, she had tears in her eyes at her farewell party as she hugged me stiffly. She reminded me of someone's old aunt that hugged you for no reason. I told my pal, Rex, I had only come for the cake, but I knew how to be a gentleman when necessary.

I knew I needed to give the woman a proper send-off as she retired from journalism in Savannah.

When she exited the building, the real party began. People's faces visibly relaxed and the conversation got louder and more animated. The entire floor took a collective sigh, happy to send Jennifer Marcingill off to live in Florida where she would probably never see the sun or the sand.

"What are you going to do now?" Rex, who was also a producer, asked as we both claimed another piece of cake. Well-wishers began to trickle out of the break room and get back to work or head home.

"I have some evergreens to work on until they hire someone else. And Nate is going on vacation so I'll be filling in for him." I scarfed down the sickeningly sweet icing. I usually avoided a lot of sugar because it made me hyper. "Want to go play a round of pool after work? This sugar will keep me going for hours."

Rex clapped me on the back. "Aw, man, you know those days are over for me. Lil wants me to pull night duty with the baby."

I nodded in understanding even though I did not understand in the least. "Hey, yeah. Another time."

Plate discarded, Rex left the break room with a wave. I, too, tossed my paper plate in the trash and made my way back to my edit bay.

I worked steadily until the eleven started, then I checked everything one last time before shutting my equipment down.

I stood and stretched, my muscles aching from sitting in the same position too long.

"AO! The new hire will be here next Tuesday." My boss, Tyrell, bellowed at me as he came around the corner towards the editing rooms.

In the studio, I was known simply by my initials, AO. I never thought my name—Alonso Ortiz—was particularly difficult to say, but the nickname had been created and I answered to it easily enough, so it stuck.

I stopped and leaned on the door frame that had never held a door in my five years of being with Action News. "They hired someone already? Please tell me it's a man."

His pearly white teeth flashed in a devilish grin as Tyrell shook his head. "Hate to break it to you, AO. Female. But she's young and pretty."

I couldn't help the groan that escaped my lips. "Young and pretty means nothing if she doesn't know how to do the job. How green is she?"

The last thing I wanted was to work with a twenty-two-year-old girl fresh from college. Enough of them interned from local colleges and they got younger and younger each year. I had no desire to play babysitter to a little girl for a year before she moved on to another market or left to get married and have kids.

Tyrell laughed. "She's been in the field for several years. She's a Savannah local, been in Virginia for a few years, but wanted to come home. I think you'll like her." My boss raised his eyebrows.

My friends were always trying to fix me up with their cousin or their girlfriend's sister. Just because I was almost thirty and unattached did not mean I needed to find some woman to attach myself to. It was not in my five- or ten-year plan. I planned to keep it out of my plans until I was too old for people to bother me about finding someone anymore.

I shook my head. "No thanks. Especially not if I'm working with her. At least she's not green."

"You packing up?"

I nodded.

"I'll walk you out."

I disappeared back into the dark room, now lit only by the glow of several LED button lights. I checked that everything was shut off. Rex's desk had a framed photo of his wife Lily and their new baby Lex, as well as a wedding photo. My desk, by comparison, was void of anything personal aside from a coffee mug that said, "Coffee. Because meth is illegal." I grabbed my keys from the drawer and came back out to Tyrell.

"Want to head to P's and Cues?" Tyrell, Rex, and I used to play pool together every week.

"I kind of have a thing." His expression got soft and he looked off into the distance.

"Who is it this time?" I jammed my keys into my pocket, lamenting our days of playing pool and staying up all night.

"Ashley still. She said she made me dessert." His eyes wagged at me. He had been seeing Ashley for a few months now.

"Has she met the kids?"

"Last week, AO, I told you. Remember?" Tyrell had two kids but had never been married. If he introduced them to this girl, it was getting serious.

"Right, right. Well, have a good night." I pushed through the heavy steel door, Tyrell behind me. He went left to his car while I went right to mine.

It was pitch black outside, which tended to be the case when you left work at almost midnight. Jennifer had left after the six o'clock news when everyone had bid her a public farewell on camera. It was usually a skeleton crew for the eleven, with packages being pre-recorded and only the anchors and a few others behind the scenes left at Action News. Tomorrow we will do it all again.

The next day I walked into work with a genuine smile on my face. I would be filling in for Nate, one of the other producers, and staying in-house the whole week. I don't mind chasing stories, especially if they're interesting, but a week of working behind a computer sounded like a dream to me. I could churn out video packages in my sleep and I liked the anchors much more than the woman I had been trailing behind for years.

"I heard your new Jennifer is coming in tomorrow to do paperwork." Rex didn't even look up from his computer when I entered the doorless room the next afternoon. His headphones were around his neck as he played with a video of a woman talking, children playing behind her.

It took a minute for me to register what Rex was telling me. The new girl was coming in tomorrow. "Definitely not my Jennifer, and I don't want a new one of her. All I want to know is if she's as clueless as Jennifer was."

Rex paused his screen and turned to me. "Jennifer wasn't clueless, just dreary. Lifeless. This girl will be in her prime, AO. I bet she's a firecracker."

I didn't need a firecracker, either. Just someone who worked hard and stayed in their lane. "Did Tyrell say when she was coming?" My keys slid easily into my desk drawer as I sat down and looked over the daily schedule.

"I didn't hear. Want me to put in a good word if you're not here?"

I looked to my right at him and gave him my biggest cheesy grin, my unruly hair flopping over my eyes. "No way. Let her be surprised by my finesse and charm."

Rex ran his hand over his balding head. "Maybe this one won't constantly chide you about your hair."

My hair was as unruly as I was. Wild and untamed curls erupted from all over my head, and it had driven Jennifer mad. At first, I kept it longer just to mess with her, but then I became famous for my hair. And when I went out, the girls I met always wanted to run their fingers through the thick, black tangles. I wasn't about to say no to that.

Much like my hair, I was not a disciplined person in many respects and I knew it. Sure, I was easy to work with, but being focused was difficult for me. I loved my job, though, and did the best I could every day. My career was my life.

After a while, Tyrell came to ask Rex a question. Rex leaned back and put his hands behind his head. "Man, I had no idea having a baby would be so tiring. I have no idea what you just asked."

Tyrell put his hands on Rex's shoulders and shook him. "Wake up, man. I need that parks and rec piece ASAP. Tell Lil to get up at night."

Rex turned around. "You tell her that. I'm not. She's sleep-deprived, moody, and she needs a shower. I am not throwing myself to the wolves."

A grimace crossed my face before I could stop it. "She hasn't showered?"

"She's holding Lex twenty-four-seven, man. Just wait, AO, one day you'll understand." Rex ran his hand through his scraggly beard.

"No way. Not me. Y'all can have your wives and kids and commitments. It's not for me." I stretched out, my long legs crossed at the ankle as if I was on the beach. "You two used to be fun but now you have all this, this baggage. I'm the last one left."

Tyrell shot me a pitying look. "You are missing out, AO. The love of a good woman is all you need."

Ignoring the comment, I asked after my new reporter. "What time is she darkening my doorstep?"

"She's not darkening your doorstep for a week still, but she's coming in to talk upstairs. I think she'll be here at noon if you want to come play nice." Tyrell winked in my direction.

I enjoyed sleeping in then hitting the gym after I got up. I didn't arrive at work until three in the afternoon and I liked it that way. "I will be just rolling out of bed at noon, so no thank you. I can wait."

Attention back to Rex, Tyrell rapped his knuckles on the door frame. "I need that package pronto."

With a nod, Rex brought the headphones to his ears and got back to work. Tyrell disappeared, leaving me wondering what Kool-Aid they had drunk to think that a woman was all they needed in life.

All I needed in life was a good job, my apartment, and my freedom. All of which I had. Family only complicated things. I knew that because my parents had divorced when I was ten and instead of them fighting over who got to take me and my sister, they tried pawning us off on one another. Finally, when I was out of school and working, I took control of life and left my selfish parents out of it. Romance and family were messy and I didn't need a mess in my life.

I pushed the thought from my mind and brought my attention back to a story about a new high school opening in Chatham County. Our anchor Russ Raity had already done the voice over and loaded it. With a sigh, I sped through B roll footage of schools to fill the time needed.

Piper

THE STUDIO LOOKED THE same as it had when I interned at Action News years earlier. As a college student at the Savannah College of Art and Design, I had landed a coveted internship the summer before my senior year. The reporter I shadowed, Jennifer Marcingill, had helped me make a wonderful package that had gotten me hired at a small station in Virginia fresh from college. Now I was replacing her after her retirement. It was like I had come full circle.

I had been born and raised in Chatham County, Georgia. Savannah was my playground. Getting away had been a dream fresh from school, but my family needed me and I needed them. Coming home was a breath of fresh air that I desperately needed.

I checked my makeup in the mirror and reapplied my lipstick – Kiss'n'Tell – before taking a deep breath. I felt my now chin-length wavy hair, a bold and spontaneous move I had made upon moving back to Georgia, and hoped it wasn't off-putting. Nothing I could do about it now, I told myself as I exited my car. "You got this, Piper. You are a talented and excellent journalist. Show them what you're made of."

With a nod, I strode up to the front door of Action News and yanked the door open. I went up to the desk like I owned the place.

"Can I help you?" A gruff woman with a thick southern drawl stared at me from behind a desk.

"Hello. I'm Piper Campbell, I'm here to see Mr. Andrews." I picked up my chin and flashed my big grin, my signature look.

The woman behind the counter did not care. She halfway rolled her eyes and picked up the phone beside her. "A Pepper Campbell is here to see Mr. Andrews."

"It's Piper." My voice was a whisper and she didn't hear me. But it was okay because she pointed up the stairs where an older man opened the door and beckoned to me.

"Miss Campbell, come on up. Welcome to Action News." I returned his smile and hurried to the stairs, my low heels clicking on the tiled floor. As I reached him, he put out his right hand. "I'm Heath Andrews. It's nice to meet you in person."

Shake firmly, but don't squeeze, I reminded myself. People don't like women who come across as too strong. At least not at first. "It's my pleasure, Mr. Andrews. It's wonderful to be back in the building." I followed him down the hall to his office.

After a briefing of my duties and expectations, I was introduced to an attractive man named Tyrell Harris who took me downstairs to show me around.

"I'm the production manager, a bit of a do everything and anything guy. If you ever need anything, I can help. But your cameraman and producer is more than capable." He flashed a bright white smile in my direction.

"Is my producer here?" I hoped to meet him—or her—before I started work the next week. Building a rapport was an important part of the job and I had loved my cameraman and producer back in Virginia, he had envisioned himself as something of a father figure to me.

"Afraid not. He doesn't come in until three, which is when you will be coming in as well." He held a door open for me and I scooted past his large frame and waited.

Disappointed, I was determined to make a good impression on this man. I would be working with him as well. I smoothed my business dress down and prepared my professional expression.

He took the lead again and I followed dutifully. The halls looked similar to when I had been there almost seven years prior. The walls were still a dusky gray, the carpet the color of rust. When we began to pass desks I tried to recall Ms. Marcingill's old producer.

"Is Ms. Marcingill's producer still here? I was her intern several years ago." I had to walk quickly to keep up with the man's long strides.

"Well, AO has been her right-hand man for about five years now. Before that was Joe, but he moved." Tyrell stopped in his tracks and I had to halt my steps to keep from running into him.

"Oh. Did you say his name is 'Hey Yo?'" Surely I heard that wrong. Perhaps it was an Asian name I had misunderstood.

Sure enough, Tyrell laughed. "Oh, that's rich. I'll have to tell him his name is Hey Yo now. No, AO. Like the letters. A and O."

That made much more sense and I giggled. "Thank goodness. I've heard some crazy names, but I'm glad it's not Hey Yo." I rolled the letters A and O around on my tongue. They were a strange combination.

We went over to an empty desk that faced into the open newsroom. "This will be your desk, Miss Campbell."

"Please, call me Piper." I looked him in the eyes and noticed Tyrell's smile made it up to the dark brown pupils staring back at me, a sign of a genuine person.

The desk was basic, nothing overly exciting. But I had wall space behind me with plenty of room for my SCAD degree and the award I had won for reporting in Virginia. I would also bring a picture of my family and my cat.

"What do you think?"

I bounced on my toes with excitement. "It's just right. Now, what can you tell me about AO? Is he older? My previous producer thought he was something of a father figure to me he was about twenty years older than me."

The quick chuckle from before turned into a full belly laugh. "AO? A father figure?" He wiped his eyes. Clearly, this AO was not a father figure. "AO is an excellent producer. Very professional, but he's very much a confirmed bachelor and he's younger than me."

I couldn't tell how old Tyrell was, but if I had to guess I'd say he was in his early thirties. That meant AO would be close to my age if he was younger. Tyrell said he had been working with Jennifer for five years. I stared blankly at the man still shaking his head with laughter before me.

With a wave, he led me away from my new desk and introduced me to a handful of people, including the anchors of the five o'clock news. I had been following them on social media for a few weeks to learn about them. Karry Draper, divorced mom of two teens who had attended the University of Maryland and had been an anchor for eight years, was a lovely lady with a light smile. And Sam Greenfield, a silver fox with grandkids who was still fit as a fiddle, was about as disinterested in me as they came.

That was okay. Soon they would know me. I would become a permanent fixture in their world and perhaps one day I would take over their position. I had plans.

Tyrell took me to HR and got my badge. It was outfitted with a magstripe that would get me into the employee parking lot and the always-locked back studio doors. Then he led me back down the gray hallway.

"Thank you so much for the tour, Tyrell. I look forward to seeing you again next week." I shook his hand as he stopped at the lobby door to show me out.

"It was nice to meet you, Piper. I think you'll fit right in here at Action News."

"Thank you. I think so, too." My confidence was boosted by his words of encouragement. I stepped through the door and back into the lobby, my heels again making noise on the floor.

I looked at the unpleasant woman at the desk and scrunched my nose at her. "I'll be back next week!"

A confused stare looked my way but she didn't say a word as I crossed the lobby floor and exited the building. It would be different this time. Not like when I was an intern and a classmate of mine tried to ruin my career. But that was in the past. Now I was here and ready to make my mark.

Back at home, I sorted my outfits by color. I kept the basics in a variety of colors so I could easily mix and match. Savannah was a mix of old-world style and trendy happenings, and I needed to make sure I looked the part.

I had moved back in with my parents until I could find a place on my own. I hoped to be there less than six months. Already my mother was hovering over my every movement.

She had opted for early retirement and now had all the time in the world for me. I adored her, but space was needed.

"Did you see the studio?" She sat on my bed and folded scarves.

"Of course, Mom. It's much the same. The woman at the desk was unpleasant, but I won't be going in the front door anymore." I glanced at my ID card that lay on my dresser, just waiting to be clipped to my lapel.

"What does Sam Greenfield look like in real life?" My mother, Mary, had been nursing a crush on the Action News anchor for twenty years. "Is he really as foxy as he appears on camera?"

I grabbed my notebook and jotted down my first week's outfit combinations before answering her. "Yes, Mom. Looking at him is like looking at Michelangelo's David. He's tall and trim and smelled divine."

I didn't need to see her face to know her eyes were wide and her mouth slack. "You smelled him?"

I rolled my eyes before turning to my mother. "Yes, I did. I walked up to him, grabbed him by his Armani suit, and sniffed up his whole body." My face was completely expressionless as I watched her contort into shock.

"Piper Marie, really. That's not funny." An exasperated huff escaped her lips and she stood. "I'm going to Amalia's to get a wedding gift for your cousin. Do you want to come with?"

Shaking my head, I declined. I loved my cousin Amy, but I had no desire to be told yet again that I was approaching thirty with no ring gracing my left hand. I didn't need a ring from a man to be happy. Henry had seen to that.

A ring had been on my hand for about six months. My boyfriend of two years, Henry Peddler, had proposed to me on Valentine's Day with a lovely diamond ring. Excitement had given way to horror when I learned he had gotten a girl he worked with pregnant. Not to mention the fact that he completely abandoned the girl without insurance or any help. I had given her the engagement ring, told her to sell it, and dumped Henry quicker than a Kardashian. I also happened to do a segment on deadbeat dads that won an award. I might have sent a copy of it to Henry.

That was why I had moved back home. I had to get out of Richmond, out of Virginia. When the job at Action News came up, I jumped at the chance and put in my notice with Channel Seven and moved back to Savannah. It was a fresh start all around.

I changed into leggings and a tank top and grabbed my yoga mat. I needed to clear my head. Thank goodness my parents were still members of Savvy Seven and had allowed me to join under their gym membership. A class was starting in thirty, I had just enough time to get down there and ready.

After scanning my card, I made my way over to the yoga room. A class was just letting out, so I stood to the side and waited with two older women and a wiry man holding mats. That's when I heard the voice.

It was a voice I would never forget. It had been the bane of my existence for two years in college, belonging to a man I had thought I would never see again after he graduated a semester before me. A chill went up my spine as his familiar baritone voice grew closer and louder.

I pulled out my phone and turned away, just in case he saw me. I watched as the guy who had nearly ruined my career before it began came into view, laughing and talking with someone else. I turned more, hoping he wouldn't recognize me.

"I'll catch you later man," the other guy said.

"I'll whoop you tomorrow, Kenny." Then he disappeared around the corner and was silent.

But there was no mistaking that tall frame, the tanned skin, the lilt of his voice. Alonso Ortiz was still in Savannah.

Alonso

Piper Campbell was back in Savannah. And I would be babysitting her for the foreseeable future. I walked into work Monday afternoon and was greeted by a name plaque on Jennifer's old desk that read Piper Campbell in a clear, professional font. There could only be one Piper Campbell at Action News. I swallowed hard and prayed that there was some other young reporter with that name.

Hadn't she moved somewhere up north? I had mostly lost track of her after I graduated from SCAD, but the alumni newsletter had said something about her getting a reporter position in another state a few years ago.

If the people at work thought I was goofy and disorganized now, they hadn't seen anything compared to me in college. I partied too hard, I talked too loud, it was a miracle I had graduated at all.

I graduated a semester late, but I graduated. Piper and I interned at Action News together and shared a handful of classes. She, for whatever reason, hated me. Which was fine, because I thought she was a stuck-up snob in school. An extremely sexy and well put together snob, but still.

"Whatcha doing, AO?"

Tyrell snapped me out of my memory as I stood with my palms flat on the desk now bearing Piper's name. I stood and turned to him. "Please tell me Piper Campbell isn't a leggy girl with long, dark curls."

It took a second for Tyrell to answer. "Um, okay. I will not tell you that. Because she was a leggy girl with short, dark hair."

I pulled up a picture of her from Instagram. Long, pale legs folded up under herself with long, dark hair cascading over her shoulders as she stared into the camera. "Please, please, please tell me this is not the girl who is coming in today."

With a glance, my friend nodded. "That would be the woman. I take it you know her?"

The urge to pound my fist on the desk was strong, but I stopped myself. Instead, I ran my hands through my already untamed curly hair. "I do. We went to SCAD together. She hated me."

"I'm sure that's water under the bridge now, man. You're not stupid kids anymore, right? You're both working professionals." He led me to my edit bay.

My eyes falling on Rex, I begged him to swap with me. "I can't work with her, Rex. How about I take Russ off your hands and you get the new girl?"

Without missing a beat, Rex shot up a hand to stop me. "Do you really think Lil will be okay with my working with a fresh young girl day in and day out while she's at home crying in expressed milk?"

I blinked. What kind of milk? Could you get milk expressed to you from Door Dash? Whatever. "Please. I know her. It won't work out."

Tyrell interjected. "Face it, AO, you're going to have to get along with the hot new reporter." He laughed and walked away, leaving me red-faced in the darkened room.

It was a good thing the room was dark. Despite her snobbery, I had nursed a crush on Piper Campbell for the two years I knew her in college. She was poised and organized and sure of her place in the world. I was chaotic, loud, and as unconfident as one got. When we got the internships at Action News together, I had been thrilled. Until I nearly ruined her career over a stupid prank.

I still remembered what she was wearing that day. A pastel pink dress with a dark sweater over it. She had been working on her audition package and I offered to help her. She had reluctantly accepted. Except I replaced her already edited footage with B-roll of squawking ducks and stampeding cows. I didn't delete her package, just swapped it out. I thought she would check it one last time before presenting it to her advisor, we would laugh about it, and I would swap it back for her original footage. A silly prank.

Piper didn't do the last check. And her advisor - a large woman with the unfortunate surname of Duckson - thought the piece was a direct insult from Piper to her. I confessed my foul and gave Piper the correct version. I even told Duckson that my footage about a farm got mixed up with Piper's story on childhood poverty. It kept her from receiving any disciplinary action, but the damage was done.

"I will never forgive you as long as I live, Alonso Ortiz! I can't wait to get far away from Savannah and you." She practically spat at me. Tears streamed down her cheeks and her long, dark hair stuck to the wetness.

"I'm so sorry. You know I would never want to hurt your career goals." I pleaded with her as she stormed across campus.

"You don't take anything in life seriously. One day you'll need to actually focus and do work, Alonso. You can't keep playing jokes like you're ten anymore. Grow up." With a huff, she spun on her heel and took off in the opposite direction.

That prank might have caused big problems for her, but it saved me. Her words were the push I needed to see a therapist, get my ADHD diagnosis, and start sorting my life out. I learned how to focus after that fiasco, and I had Piper to thank for it. Not that I had ever actually thanked her. Though maybe now that I had the opportunity, I should.

She was back in the city and back in this newsroom, and I knew it wouldn't go well. I didn't follow her on social media,

but I knew how to find her. I didn't figure she would appreciate my trying to be her friend or follower or whatever. Best to
stay under her laser-eyed radar.

The last time I had checked up on her Instagram, she was
sporting some sparkly hardware on her left hand. I wondered
if her fiancé had moved with her to Savannah and if he had
managed to tame the overly organized beast that was Piper
Campbell. I pulled her account back up and looked through
her pictures. The engagement photos were notably gone and
it looked like she had trekked back to Georgia on her own.

So not only was Piper back, but a broken-hearted Piper
was back. Just great. I should make up my will because there's
no way I could survive working with her. The next few days
waiting for her to walk into the studio would be exquisite
torture. My last days of freedom, and possibly of life.

Come on, AO, you're being quite dramatic. Certainly she's
forgotten all about you like Tyrell said, right? You can start on
a clean slate and reintroduce yourself all over again. Maybe be
friends. Maybe more than that...

Whoa, those old feelings knew right where they had left off.
I needed to push her from my mind for now. There was work
to be done. Rex strolled in and settled a few feet away in his
office chair, getting to work on a package for Russ. We didn't
talk, which suited me fine. I needed to focus on a piece for
Karry Draper.

Thanks to Piper and her rage, I was on medication to help me focus, and that's exactly what I did for the next several hours.

The days flew by quicker than I would have liked and before I knew it, it was Monday night. The next day would bring Piper Campbell back into my life, and I was not ready for that. I thought about running away, but then I remembered I was approaching thirty, not twelve. I would have to face the music like an adult. A groan escaped my lips as I walked past the desk with her name on it on my way out of the building.

I looked her up again on social media when I got home. Sure enough, there she was in front of the Action News building in a selfie that was captioned, "Ready to go back home tomorrow and start as a reporter for Action News. I grew up watching Karry and Sam. and now I get to work with them every day." It included some overly sugary hashtags that made me roll my eyes. But Piper herself looked killer.

And if looks could kill, tomorrow would be my death sentence.

The next morning I went to the gym early because I couldn't sleep. My trainer and pal Kenny laughed at me. "You have a crush on a girl you haven't seen in years. And a girl who hates you, no less!"

"Oh, hardly. She's a high-maintenance mess of a girl who is likely to claw me to death the minute she sees me." I grunted as he added weight to the shoulder press. "Besides, I have no desire for romantic relationships, remember?"

He hung his arms on an empty machine next to me and laughed. "I get not wanting a relationship, AO, but surely you want someone to warm your bed every so often."

Of course I did, I was a red-blooded male after all. I was glad I was already red from exertion so Kenny didn't see the heat creep up my neck. But I wouldn't admit that to him. One-night stands were not my thing, just as long-term relationships weren't either. And Piper Campbell wouldn't be warming anything of mine. Ever. Even if she was incredibly attractive.

A few more reps had my muscles screaming. I wasn't a big guy, I always tended toward being skinny, so the little bit of muscle my body managed to hang on to made me happy. The workouts also helped me keep my focus at work. Exerting physical energy gave me more mental clarity. I planned to work a little extra so I didn't cause a huge blunder in front of Piper.

We moved on to the treadmill and Kenny excused himself for a minute. The pace he had set for me was not getting my blood pumping like the thought of seeing Piper was. I upped the speed and incline, making my body work harder.

The thought of Piper lighting up upon seeing me was what made my heart race though. I shook the thought from my head. She would be more likely to bite my ear off Mike Tyson style than welcome me with open arms.

Besides, she was completely off-limits. She was a new co-worker, so I would see her every day. We had a history of bad blood. And I had sworn off looking for a relationship. Three perfectly good reasons that the thought of her should make my blood run cold. But it didn't.

Piper

I TOOK A DEEP breath as I pushed my shoulders back and elongated my spine. I was wearing my favorite plum-colored suit with the cream mock turtleneck under it. Action News wouldn't know what hit it when I walked in the door. I swiped my card at the door and it audibly unlocked for me to push through. The grin that crossed my lips could not be helped as I inhaled the scent of a mid-afternoon newsroom.

The room was bustling with activity as I walked in, my plum pumps soundless on the worn carpet. I had thought maybe someone would greet me at the door, but nobody raised an eyebrow. I tightened my grip on my briefcase—more professional than a backpack—and strode to the desk that I would now occupy.

Already a nameplate was on the corner with my name displayed. I moved behind the desk and put my case in the chair.

I pulled out a potted succulent and a picture of my cat Taco and placed them behind the nameplate. That made the desk more inviting. A small cut-glass tray for hard candies would complete the space.

"Piper, good to see you. I was just going to get your laptop. Want to walk with me?" Tyrell picked up the picture of Taco and chuckled. "Love the cat."

"That's Taco. It's a palindrome. Taco Cat." It was a strange name for a cat, but I couldn't help it when I adopted him from the shelter.

"Right." Tyrell put the photo back and looked at me expectantly.

"Oh. Sure, I'll walk with you. I'd love to meet a few more people. Is Mr. AO here?" I tucked my case under the desk and joined Tyrell.

"He'll be here by the time we get that laptop." Then Tyrell winked at me. I glanced around, trying to figure out if I had missed an inside joke.

Laptop in hand, Tyrell helped me set it up on my desk. I was turned around when he announced that my producer was approaching us. I turned, expecting to find...well, anything other than what I saw.

My throat went dry and my stomach dropped. Surely Tyrell was wrong. This was not the man I would be working with. It couldn't be. "Alonso." I finally croaked out his name. My mouth was drier than the Sahara.

He was older, of course. His hair curled wildly around his face and he wore a few days' stubble on his cheeks and chin, just as he had last week at the gym. Alonso's expression was hard to read, a forced smile and squinted eyes. His hands were jammed into the pockets of his khakis, the muscles of his forearm flexing on his tanned arms. He was even more handsome than he was in college, but that was beside the point.

"Piper Campbell. Welcome back to Action News." His voice was soft and quiet. He didn't try to shake my hand, which was probably a good thing. I might have tried to bite it off.

Tyrell tried to act oblivious to the tension that erupted between us. "I hear you both used to intern here."

Turning to him, I held my hand up. "I'm sorry. Are you telling me that AO is Alonso Ortiz and this is my producer?"

His dark eyes got wide. "Yes, I am."

Before I could respond, Alonso interjected. "Yes, isn't that something? I've already talked with the higher-ups about it and we're very fortunate to get to work together. Again."

Sensing the need to vacate the area, Tyrell excused himself and left me staring warily at Alonso.

"What? How?" I sat in my chair and put my head in my hands. The calming breathing exercises I did for yoga were not helping. He was going to ruin me and this job had to work out. I couldn't go back to Virginia.

His voice grew closer. "I'm sorry, Piper. You're stuck with me. When I found out it was you, I knew you wouldn't want to work with me and I asked about pairing you with someone else. That was a no-go."

I looked up to see him in a chair across from me. His elbows rested on the opposite side of the desk. A cursory glance around showed that nobody was eyeing us, thankfully.

"You were Ms. Marcingill's cameraman?"

"For five years, yes. Before that, I worked with a small company in the city." His jaw flexed and his eyes sought mine. "I know this might not be ideal, Piper, but I am not the same stupid kid I was back when you knew me. Actually, it was your words that helped kick my butt into gear."

My eyes narrowed as I stared at him, but no words came to me.

There was agony in his eyes. I could see the pain in the dark recesses. "I hurt you, and I'm sorry. I started going to therapy, I got a diagnosis and I've been working on being more professional. Much more professional. You turned my life around and I'm going to try not to screw yours up."

I wiped my hands on my thighs and his eyes followed the movement. "Maybe I can talk to someone. There are other producers here, right?" I stood, wondering who the right person would be to talk to.

"I've asked. I've asked the bosses and the other producers. If we're both working here, we're together." He sat up and looked at me, his wild hair all over the place, matching my feelings perfectly.

Nodding, I forced a pained but pleasant expression to my face. "Right. I guess it is what it is. Don't expect me to make this easy for you. One bad move and I'll have you out of here within minutes."

He rolled his eyes. "I'm sure you'll be taking notes on my every move."

Not a bad idea. I pulled out a notepad and pen. "I'm ready."

"There's a budget meeting in a few minutes they want you at. Jump in with both feet." He stood and rubbed his hands together. I really tried not to notice that there was not a ring on his left hand.

I followed him into a boardroom full of people, including anchors and reporters, Tyrell, and a few others I had met the previous week. There was one chair left, and a guy I had met before offered it to me. I nodded as I took it and put my notebook and pen on the table.

Mr. Andrews clapped his hand together as a few stragglers came in. "Before we start, everyone meet and welcome Piper Campbell. She's a Savannah native, but she's been in Richmond for the past few years. We're happy to have you, Piper." He did not offer me the chance to speak, so I simply nodded toward him.

I tried to look alert and attentive, but inside I was seething to have Alonso behind me. Over one hundred thousand people in Savannah and I ended up with him as a partner. How was it possible that he managed to hold down a good job at a great station like this for five years? Surely he had zero ethics or drive.

Even with his speech to me about getting his act together, I couldn't see him being a responsible adult.

"Piper, ready to get your feet wet?" A laugh escaped Mr. Andrew's mouth and it took him a minute to recover. I wondered what was so funny about my news story.

I grabbed my pen and looked to Mr. Andrews as he calmed. "Of course."

"We got a call about some kudzu over a telephone pole that looks like the outstretched arms of Jesus. Apparently. And it's a blessedly s-l-o-w news day. So you and AO will head out there and see it, talk to the people who live around there. Supposedly there's a church a stone's throw away who claims it's a miracle."

A kudzu Jesus? Really? Mr. Andrews moved on to a school board meeting, drama over a restaurant, and of course, politics. The story was fluff, but I suppose it is my first day and maybe they were trying me out. Perhaps this was a sort of new girl initiation. The meeting wrapped and I followed Alonso out of the room.

We loaded into a white SUV with Action News emblazoned across the sides in bold red letters along with a graphic of lightning and the face of anchor Sam Greenfield.

The car was silent as we set out and I tried to think of what to ask people about an invasive plant that looked like a deity. Not much came to mind.

"So what have you been up to the past few years?" Alonso tried to smile as he drove.

It would serve him right if I gave him a cold shoulder, but it wouldn't be professional. "I have been in Richmond, Virginia since I graduated, working for an affiliate up there."

"That's nice. Virginia is nice."

Closing my eyes, I reciprocated the question. "You've only been here five years, Tyrell said. Where were you before that?" I held back from asking if he had been incarcerated.

The corners of his mouth raised and his cheeks pinked. "I had some family stuff to deal with, but I worked at SCAD in the media department."

"I don't recall seeing you." My eyebrows knit together. I would have seen him if he had been on campus, especially if he was in the same buildings I was in.

"I was there." He didn't offer me any more insights and I didn't ask. Alonso's life was his, and I certainly didn't care.

I needed to run through my vocal exercises, but I didn't want to do it in front of the enemy. At the location of the so-called kudzu Jesus, I got out of the car and quietly started going through my exercises. For years I had recited "She sells seashells by the seashore" and "Peter Piper" to warm my voice up and help with my enunciation. It was silly, but it worked.

"Did you say something?" Alonso's eye narrowed as he looked at me.

Heat rose on my cheeks. Had I been that loud? "No. Just doing my warm-ups. Set up wherever, I'll go find someone to interview." My voice was harsh and rough, but I didn't care. I just wanted this day over with.

Alonso set up his camera and I knocked on the office door of the church across the street. The secretary was all too happy to come out and tell me about the miracle that looked over their building. As passers-by slowed, we asked for their take on the scene, and many were happy to oblige us. After about thirty minutes we had everything we needed for a quick package and loaded back up in the car.

"Want to stop for a bite?" Alonso rubbed his stomach for effect.

It wasn't quite time to eat in my book, but we approached a deli and I thought it sounded better than anything else. "Three Alarm Subs?"

"You read my mind." He laughed as he pulled into their drive-through. One bacon swiss club for him and a turkey avocado wrap for me and we were back at the studio. I held the bag of food and glared at the floorboards as he drove.

I sat at my desk and ate, then freshened up my face. My official Action News introduction would be live on the five o'clock in just a few minutes. Tyrell had me follow him and he set me up in a chair next to Karry Draper.

Cameras were rolling and the intro began. Sam and Karry were all smiles as they told the cameras what was coming this hour. Then Karry stopped and turned to me. "But first, we have a new member of the Actions News family to introduce. Piper Campbell is our newest reporter and she's a Savannah native. Piper, welcome."

Sam tossed in his welcome before I spoke and I spotted Alonso standing to the right of the camera. His beaming grin almost made me falter and I had to look away from him. "Thank you so much, Karry. I grew up watching Action News and I interned here in college, so this is a dream come true for me. I'm happy to be back home." I smiled at the camera, looking past it, but Alonso had disappeared. I held my pose until we were given the signal and Sam began talking about school budget cuts.

That was it. I was excused from the studio and made my way out as quietly as possible. I didn't see Alonso as I gave Tyrell my mic and tiptoed through the door. The giddy feeling in the pit of my stomach from knowing he was watching me didn't sit well, though. My head argued with the rest of me and reminded me that Alonso Ortiz was the enemy.

Alonso

Two weeks of strained conversation was taking its toll on me. Oh, Piper and I could be pleasant, but simmering beneath the surface was tension thicker than my abuela's chicken tortilla soup. And Connie Ortiz's soup was thick.

In front of the staff, we were cordial, told jokes about old professors, and worked almost seamlessly. Alone in a car or edit bay, there were no words spoken, no pleasant looks passed between us, nothing. It was worse than working with Jennifer Marcingill. At least she thought I liked her. Neither Piper nor I were under the impression that there was anything other than civility between us.

It stretched beyond the office, too. She had joined my gym. My sanctuary, my safe place to get away from work - she was there. She did yoga classes and ran on the treadmills. Piper had amazing curves that were usually hidden under her cardigans and blazers, but they were on full display when she was wearing a tank top and leggings. And I couldn't manage to look away. My gaze was drawn to her voluptuous hips and long legs.

Even though we didn't get along, I found myself drawn to her. She had an easy smile when she wanted to smile. Rex, Tyrell, and everyone else were smitten with her. It was like she was everyone's little sister. Except my body didn't see her as a little sister. My body saw her as an attractive woman it wanted to know better.

I had to keep telling it no.

Piper was a natural in front of the camera. Of course, I had known that when we were in school. She lit up the second I gave her the signal that we were rolling.

We stood in front of the local hospital disagreeing on where to set up the camera. She wanted it in front of the ribbon. I said there were too many people and to go in from the side. I usually won these arguments by simply hitting record and giving her the signal.

"And we're live in three." I showed her three fingers, two, then one. I pointed to her.

The scowl turned instantly. "I'm Piper Campbell for Action News, here at the ribbon cutting for the new children's hospital wing at Savannah Regional Hospital. The funding for the new wing was donated by the McFarland family and matched by donations from the Amick Research Center." She kept talking and stepped out of the way as the ribbon was cut.

Afterward, the scowl returned. "You play dirty, Alonso. I wanted to be set up more forward."

The smirk couldn't be helped. I leaned on the car. "You have no idea how dirty I can play, Piper." I wanted to stop myself from flirting with her, but I couldn't. I was drawn to her. I needed to rein it in. "But that was a better angle, you'll see."

She rolled her eyes at me. "You know, I've been in this business just as long as you, and I think I know what my good angles are. Hurry up and let's get some interviews before they all leave." She stomped off, her green dress billowing out behind her.

She was so adorable when she stomped.

Whoa there, where did that thought come from? I shook my head and grabbed the camera to follow after her.

After speaking with an over-dressed woman, Piper thanked her profusely. The woman took Piper's hands in hers. "Oh, honey, you two are so sweet. You'll make it, I can tell."

"Pardon?" Piper's professional, toothy smile faltered and her eyes cut over to me.

"The way this young man looked at you, honey. You are an adorable couple. I can tell he will do anything for you." She waved a hand in the air like she matched up people all the time.

"Oh, no, ma'am. We're just co-workers." I knew my eyes were wide. A couple? Hardly. "I have to look at her, that's my job."

"Hey." Piper whipped her head toward me, her eyebrows knit together. She turned back to the woman. "We're not a couple, but thank you so much for the interview. It will be on at five and six."

I hoisted the camera back on my shoulder to carry it back to the car, a pile of wires and cords in my other hand. "Must be nice to only carry the mic." Piper waved to a few people as she casually came back to the car.

She blinked several times. "I'm sorry, do you want me to carry the camera? I wouldn't think you would trust me with it. You treat it like a baby."

It was ridiculously expensive equipment, of course I treated it with care. I gingerly placed it back inside its case before I turned back to her. "That camera would be like twenty-thousand to replace, and I don't happen to have that sitting around if I break it, so yes, I treat it with respect."

"That's more than you do for me."

Her words felt like a slap in the face. I did everything I could to treat her with respect, especially given our past. I shook my head and stared at her slack-jawed. I had no words that wouldn't be incredibly offensive, and my abuela would skin me alive from her grave if I uttered them. So instead I turned and got into the driver's seat, cranking the car and revving the engine.

Piper got into the passenger side and slammed her door. As she buckled up she sighed, her head down. "I'm sorry."

Well, that was just as shocking as the last thing she had said. "What?"

"I'm sorry, Alonso. Tomorrow is my birthday and Henry had the nerve to text me today and tell me happy birthday." Her voice was shaky. "I don't know if I'm more pissed that he got the day wrong or that he texted me at all." A weak attempt at a laugh escaped her lips, but I didn't miss the quick swipe she made under her eyes.

I handed her a napkin. "I'm sorry. That sucks." I didn't know what else to say. I didn't have much experience with crying females. My mother was a wreck of wild emotions, my abuela was always stoic, and my sister was perpetually happy around me. So honest to goodness tears were foreign to me.

"Thanks. I just, I thought I'd be getting married in a few months. And now I'm not and I can't believe he texted me on the wrong day of all things." She wiped the napkin under her eyes and looked at me. "I hope you know the right birthdays for all the women in your life."

Only my sister was left. "I do." My voice was hoarse as I thought about Maggie. She was all the family I had in the world. I looked to Piper and nodded. "I'm sorry. He's a jerk and you're better off. Savannah is lucky to have you back."

Dark eyes studied me a moment. "I don't have any fight in me today, Alonso, so I'll take it." She sat back and closed her eyes. "You better be right about that angle."

Heat crept up on my neck. "You won't be disappointed. It's a good angle." I turned my head to the road and put the car in drive.

Back at the studio I loaded up footage into my computer and went to hide in the bathroom. I found a flower delivery app and perused the arrangements that could be delivered within twenty-four hours. I found one that was all pinks and yellows, with a birthday balloon and a box of candies. It was pricey, but I was determined.

I just needed something for the card to say. From everyone at Action News? No. I selfishly wanted the credit. From your cameraman? No. Why was it so hard? Then the perfect thing came to my mind. I typed it out quickly, pleased with myself. She would know it was from me without it saying so. That would avoid anyone thinking we were a couple as well. I clicked order before I could chicken out.

Action News liked any reason to celebrate, so the next day as I strolled in, a giant tray of cupcakes sat in the break room and a paper birthday crown sat on Piper's desk. She was standing beside it, talking and laughing with Tyrell and Maria Warthen, one of the other field reporters.

Pink must be her favorite color because she wore a hot pink dress that looked like it belonged in a 1950s advertisement. Over it was a light pink cardigan that matched the belt on the dress. I stopped in my tracks about ten feet from her, my khakis wrinkled and my Action News polo several years old and sporting a stain that was tucked into my pants.

Her gaze traveled up to meet mine, and she tilted her head a little and nodded. I waved, feeling more awkward than I had in fifteen years. "Happy birthday, Piper."

"Thanks, Alonso." Her voice was soft and she half smiled. Maria kept talking and Piper turned her attention back to her friend.

As I turned to walk away, someone came in carrying a huge bouquet of pink and yellow flowers. I busied myself out of sight and watched from the corner of my eye. The bouquet was huge, a pink mylar balloon hovering over it.

The delivery person handed it over to Piper. "Oh my gosh. This is for me? That's unbelievable. They are gorgeous." She placed the flowers on her desk and they took up a good third of the whole thing.

Then the delivery person reached into his bag and pulled out the box of candies. It also was much larger than I had anticipated.

"More? Oh, thank you. Thank you so much." Piper clutched the chocolates and the delivery person left. She looked to Maria. "Do you see a card? I would guess they're from my parents, but I don't know."

The pair searched through the flowers and Maria came up the winner, card in hand. "It says, 'Happy birthday. On the right day.'" She knit her eyebrows together. "What does that mean?"

I held my breath as Piper's eyes immediately shot up and looked around the newsroom. They landed on me, half hidden in the hallway. Within seconds, her cheeks were as pink as her dress. I watched her blink several times and her lips draw together. Was she happy or upset?

Without a second thought, I disappeared down the hallway to get to my edit bay. The darkened room hid my flushed face as I sat down and put my head in my hands. Was that a foolish move? Why had I gotten the largest arrangement possible? Questions ran through my head as I took deep breaths, trying to calm my racing heart.

Before it could get back to normal, however, I heard a voice. Behind me.

I knew it was her.

"Alonso?"

Piper

My mind raced with possibilities. Maybe the flowers and candies weren't from Alonso. But nobody else would have put "on the right day" on a card. I hadn't told my mother about the text from Henry, nor had I told my best friends. It was too humiliating. It could only be Alonso.

I stood behind him a moment before I said anything. He sat in his dark office, his head buried in his hands, his hair standing out on end. Was he upset? Embarrassed?

"Alonso?" My voice was so quiet I wasn't sure he heard me until his head slowly lifted and he swiveled around in his chair.

Dark eyes shone at me and my breath hitched. The man I had spent seven years wanting to toss off a tall bridge stared at me, eyebrows raised. His lips were full and I watched him part them for a deep sigh. I was completely entranced. This was not the same man who had tried to hurt me years ago or even the man I had been furious to see weeks ago.

"Yes, Piper?" His voice was deep and it quivered just a bit. His prominent Adam's apple bobbed as he swallowed.

It was like time slowed down. I watched him stand in front of me, his long, black eyelashes closing and opening and deep brown doe eyes glistened at my own.

"You? The flowers?" I could barely form a complete thought let alone full sentences. "Why?"

My hand instinctively reached out and touched his arm. I felt his muscles flex under my fingers and he took in a sharp breath. The goofy grin I had rolled my eyes at last week now made my heart skip a beat.

"Because I thought you deserved a happy birthday. And because I needed to be the one who put that happy look on your face." His face grew a little closer and his fingers brushed my hair back from my cheek.

I blinked several times, sure my eyes were playing tricks on me, my skin feeling things that were not actually happening. This couldn't be the same Alonso Ortiz. He smelled like soap and cinnamon, and the skin on his arm was soft and supple.

"I... Thank you." I looked up to him and bit my lip, unsure what else to say. My fingers curled around his forearm and I squeezed lightly. I didn't understand why tears pricked the back of my eyelids, so I closed them and whispered again. "Thank you, Alonso."

His warm breath caused my skin to break into goosebumps and I shuddered involuntarily. Would he kiss me? Did I want him to?

No. I needed to get away from him. I hated him. He was immature, and I did not want him to kiss me let alone touch me. Maybe he was just messing with me, another one of his childish pranks. I needed to break the trance I seemed to be under, but I couldn't move. If this was a prank I would be played the fool all over again.

A voice from behind us provided the much-needed interruption. "Everything okay here?" Rex sounded concerned, as he should be given my proximity to Alonso Ortiz.

Immediately I stepped back and my chest heaved. "Yes, everything is fine." I looked at Alonso. "Thank you." I retreated several steps and let Rex pass into their shared office space.

Unaware of what he had broken up, Rex looked from me to Alonso. "AO, you good?"

"Yeah, Piper just had a problem with her contacts. All fixed now." His eyes were trained on mine, his face serious. "Happy birthday, Piper."

"Oh, yeah. Happy birthday." Rex raised his coffee cup towards me in a toast.

Forcing a smile I thanked Rex and went back to my desk. The floral arrangement was huge, a cheery display of pinks and yellows. Pink was certainly my favorite color and yellow was the color of friendship. Did he know that? The balloon bobbed under the air vent, announcing my birthday to everyone within viewing distance. I slipped the candies in a still-empty desk drawer. They barely fit.

Maria came back over. "Ready for the budget meeting?" When I stood, she added, "Did you figure out who they're from?"

It would raise eyebrows if I said they were from Alonso. He hadn't signed the card and I assumed that was on purpose. Workplace romances were discouraged and we were certainly not in a romance. We were barely working towards liking one another.

No, I couldn't tell Maria. "Oh, they're from a, uh, friend of mine. We've known each other a long time." Satisfied with that, we walked together to the daily budget meeting.

An hour later and Alonso and I were in the car heading out to interview a family with six children who all joined the military. It was a good news story, my favorite kind. We were silent as we left downtown Savannah and headed over to Richmond Hill.

Once the landscape opened up to more greenery, I scrounged up the nerve to ask him the one question that had been plaguing me. "Why didn't you sign the card?"

His grip on the steering wheel tightened. "You've been in newsrooms before. You know they're like a high school with the rumor mill. I didn't figure you wanted people asking questions about the two of us."

I nodded. "That's what I thought. And I appreciate that. We certainly don't need tongues wagging."

His laughter filled the car. "And I have a reputation to uphold."

The warm feeling I had just developed for Alonso dissipated. "Excuse me?"

"Everyone knows I'm the bachelor in residence. So many people have tried to set me up with their sisters or friends. I don't need a woman."

His easy grin infuriated me. But I had just the right comeback. "Oh, so you're gay? I should have known."

The car wobbled back and forth for a second as he whipped his head toward me. "What? No!"

"You said you don't need a woman, I figure that means you prefer a man." I threw my head back and laughed.

"Listen, I have friends who are gay. Kenny at the gym is in a long-term, committed relationship with Carson. But I, Alonso David Ortiz, am not gay. I definitely enjoy the company of women." He spoke so fast I couldn't help but laugh.

"Noted." I looked out the window and spoke before I realized. "Why are you a confirmed bachelor?"

The question sucked all the air from the car and I instantly regretted asking. "I'm sorry. You don't have to answer that. I know it's personal."

It took him a second before he took a deep breath and opened his mouth. "Um, I mean, my family life when I was a kid wasn't great. My parents split up shortly after my sister was born, and then my mom just left us with my abuela and abuelo. I figured if that was what happened when you fell in love, I didn't want any part in it." He brought a hand up to his mouth and began chewing on the cuticle around his thumb, a habit I had noticed in weeks past.

I was shocked. My parents had provided my sister and me with a loving home with a large extended family and pretty much everything we could need or want. It never occurred to me that Alonso hadn't been raised similarly.

"I'm sorry your parents abandoned you. Were your grandparents kind?" My voice was low and I picked at my own fingernails.

Alonso chuckled. "Oh, yeah, they were amazing. They took care of Maggie and me. Raised us right. They died within about six months of each other a few years back."

"Sorry to hear that."

"No, no, it's fine. They waited until they knew we were taken care of before they passed. It's like they knew their work was done." He scratched his head, making his hair flop all over the place. "So, since we're fessing up. What happened with your fiancé? If you don't mind my asking."

My first instinct was to tell him to mind his own business, but I realized I was okay with talking about Henry and what had happened. It was cathartic to tell it to someone who was pretty impartial and hoped he would agree with what I did.

"So, wait, your fiancé got someone else pregnant and just abandoned her?" Alonso's mouth hung agape as he turned into a residential section.

"Yep."

"And you found out, gave her your engagement ring, and dumped his sorry behind?" We pulled up to a red light and Alonso parked and stared at me.

"Also yep."

He leaned on the steering wheel and laughed. "You know how I feel about people who abandon their children. What you did—that's amazing. Like, *eres una verdadera dama machista*."

Whether he knew it or not, I understood him and his compliment at my actions. I shrugged. "I don't know about that."

Shock registered on his face. "You know Spanish?"

Laughter bubbled up and I couldn't help it. "I know enough. My best friend growing up was Latina and I hung out with her family a lot. Anyway, I just wasn't going to give him back the ring, and that poor girl was left with nothing. She was a temp secretary at his office. A five-thousand-dollar ring won't go far, but I hope it helps her."

We parked the driveway of a modest ranch home with American flags adorning the front porch. It would be perfect for B-roll. I looked at Alonso. "Thanks for listening. And for agreeing with what I did. Not many people agreed with me."

"Yeah. I think it's awesome. He got what he deserved." He winked at me and swung himself out of the car. I sat stunned for a moment, mainly because I wasn't sure why my heart began to race and I could feel the heat creep up on my cheeks in reaction to his wink.

You do not like him, Piper. Come on. It's Alonso. Arch enemy. Except, he's been incredibly decent, and he sent you all those flowers. Maybe you need to change your mind about him. Maybe.

"Piper?"

I jumped when he called my name. I was still sitting in the car, willing my pulse to return to normal. "Right, yes." I fluffed my hair and climbed from the car, ready to interview a family with a long and rich military history.

Ninety minutes and three glasses of sweet tea later, we left an incredible family. My cheeks hurt from so much smiling and laughing. With the car loaded, we slipped into our seats to head back to the studio.

"Um, I hate to ask AO, but can we stop at a gas station?" I put my hand to my stomach. I didn't want to ask to use the family's bathroom, though I'm sure they wouldn't have minded. I didn't want them to think I was snooping.

"What?"

I grimaced. "I had too much tea and I need a bathroom. Please?"

He licked his lips. "Yeah, I got that. But you called me AO."

"Everyone calls you AO." I furrowed my brow and crossed my arms.

"But you don't. You call me Alonso. And I kind of like that."

Pink crept up my neck and I turned from him. "Oh. I could call you Senor Ortiz. I much prefer Alonso myself. I thought your name was Hey Yo when Tyrell first mentioned you."

He pulled into a gas station and parked. I ran in and when I got back to the car, he looked at me. "What are you doing after work?"

"Nothing. It will be late, and it's my birthday." I checked my phone for the time even though it was right in front of me on the dash clock.

"Want to grab a bite and play pool?"

"With who?"

"Me."

The smile that spread across my face was instant. There was no way I could have hidden it. "Yeah. Sure. As long as it's your treat."

"What? I bought you those flowers." His Chesire cat grin was just as wide as mine and I knew he was playing with me.

"How many times do you think I turn twenty-eight?"

He bit his lip and my insides melted a little. Maybe I was thawing to Alonso Ortiz.

"Okay, birthday girl. My treat."

Alonso

It used to be that Tyrell, Rex, and I would go out every week and play pool, eat bar food, and unwind from work. But then Rex got married and they had a kid. And Tyrell had been dating Ashley for about six months. All of which meant my Friday nights at P's and Cues were over. Going alone was nearly always a bad idea.

I'm not sure why I invited Piper to go out, except that when she blushed and looked at me with her doe eyes from under incredibly long eyelashes, I only knew I wanted to spend more time with her. This was my twenty-one-year-old self's dream. Of course, now we were coworkers so any sort of funny business was strictly off the table. But I had a feeling Piper and I would enjoy some flirting back and forth.

After work, I went up to her desk and tapped my fingers on it. "Want to meet there or take one car?"

She scrunched her mouth up and wrinkled her nose. "Where is it?"

"Over in Midtown."

She squinted her eyes, perhaps trying to pull up a map in her mind. "I'm over at Whitemarsh. I think I'll just meet you."

Whitemarsh Island was one of the ritziest neighborhoods in Savannah. How did she afford to live there? Even with a generous signing bonus, she wouldn't be making enough on her own to afford a place on Whitemarsh Island. I was a little stunned until she giggled at me.

"I see that look. I moved back in with my parents until I can find a place on my own. I just need the time to go out and apartment hunt." She locked up her desk and stood, pulling a small purse onto her shoulder.

"Oh, there are a few places open for rent by me." I might have sounded a little too eager to offer that information.

"Where is that?"

"Starland. I live in a loft above a tattoo parlor. In fact, my tattooist, Joel, works there." I pulled my shirtsleeve up over my left shoulder to show off a quarter sleeve he had recently done for me. "Do you have any tattoos?"

Piper's cheeks pinked immediately. "I do. But none you'll ever see." With that, she strode past me. "Text me the address of this place and I'll meet you there."

Within ten minutes we were parked and walking into P's and Cues. It felt good to walk in with a gorgeous lady on my arm, even if she wasn't mine. The place was part gastropub and part dive bar with pool tables. We slid into an empty booth and both awkwardly looked around everywhere but at each other.

A bubblegum chewing waitress with bubblegum-colored hair approached us. "What can I get you?" She winked at me then looked at Piper. "Oh, you're Piper Campbell! I know you from Action News."

Used to being recognized, Piper put on what I had learned was her professional smile. It was wide but didn't reach her eyes. "I am, thank you. Thank you for watching. This is my producer Alonso Ortiz."

She leaned on the table and smacked her gum. "What a name. Alonso Ortiz. Whatcha drinking Alonso?"

The waitress was eyeing me, which I usually would have enjoyed, but not with Piper sitting across from me. It wasn't like having my guy friends around where we competed for the attention of a good-looking female.

I cleared my throat. "Ladies first." I needed to distract Bub-blegum and also my abuela had taught me to always let ladies go first. Chivalry wasn't dead.

Piper beamed at my offer to let her order first. "I'll have a sweet tea and I'll take a half-dozen boneless wings in the siracha honey please."

"Tea and a half-dozen in siracha honey." She didn't write the order down, but blew a bubble with her gum before turn-ing to me. "And for you, gorgeous?"

Out of the corner of my eyes I saw Piper grimace. Was she jealous? I suppressed the smirk that threatened to cross my lips.

Maybe I would play with Piper a little. Leaning in closer to Bubblegum I winked at her. "You know, darlin' I would love a Corona and I'll also take a half-dozen wings, with bones, in the siracha honey. Honey."

A wink and a nod later and Bubblegum sauntered off. Piper sat across from me, her arms folded and looking off at the pool tables. Her cheeks were pink and she was puckering her lips.

"Want to play?" Her question surprised me. I thought surely she would comment on my interaction with the waitress.

"Sure." We went over to an empty table and Piper immediately began to rack the balls. I chose a cue and watched. She expertly sorted the pool balls and slid the rack forward and back a few times.

As she grabbed a cue and chalked it, Bubblegum sidled up to me. "Your drinks are on the table." She touched my arm, her long nails that matched her hair traced the outline of a muscle. Goosebumps raised up on my skin and I took a cautious step away from her.

Piper scowled. Was she feeling jealous? I certainly didn't mind flirting, but I didn't know if I was ready for her to feel jealous. Even if I had spent two years in college drooling over her. She lined up her cue and broke the set.

Within five minutes she had sunk three balls and removed her cardigan, revealing the adorably pink, figure-hugging dress underneath. It showed off her curves and had me sweating, and not from the heat. After my pitiful attempt at taking a shot, she spun around, her skirt flying up to mid-thigh, and aimed.

Piper leaned over, giving me a view down the front of her dress, and shot her large doe eyes my direction.

She looked at me, her dark eyes sparkling under her lashes, while she took her shot. I had called her a dama machista before, but at that moment she possessed all the power in the world and I was helpless to stop her. My senses went into overdrive and I felt an intense need to wind my hands up in her hair and kiss her.

But before I could blink, she handed her cue to a burly guy waiting his turn for the table and proclaimed the table his. She walked up to me and whispered in my ear. "Our wings are ready, Alonso."

Never did I think a statement about wings would turn me on so much. She swayed her hips as she went back to the table, her hot pink skirt entrancing every man in the place. I could do nothing but follow her back to the table like a lost puppy.

Sitting back down, Bubblegum reappeared with an appletini in hand. She slid it in front of Piper. "This is from the gentleman at the bar. He says he's a fan."

Piper thanked her and peered toward the bar to see who her mystery drink gifter was. I tried to look without looking, but probably only managed to look like a crazed boyfriend. Which I was not. From the corner of my eye, I saw a good-looking older man raise a glass and nod to her. She waved and nodded graciously, then she moved the drink to the interior of the table away from her.

"Are you not drinking it?"

"Oh, no. Never. I don't know what he put in this drink, and with the way Pinkie there is looking at you, I wouldn't put it past her to let him slip something dissolvable into that. I never drink what men send over to me, even if they are a silver fox." She grabbed the drink again and motioned the man before pretending to take a sip and setting it back down away from her.

"You like a silver fox?" I rested my chin in my hand and laughed at her.

"About as much as you enjoy tarts who blow in your ear like Pinkie did." She picked up a wing and bit into it.

I enjoyed flirting with women, but I can't say I was overly fond of how easily Bubblegum had slipped into that mode. For her, flirting meant bigger tips, so I was sure I wasn't the only poor soul she was whispering to.

"I'm surprised he sent over a drink while I'm with you."

She sighed. "That's how guys like that work. If you and I are together, he's just a fan and I thank him. If we're not together and I'm interested, I go chat with him. It's all a giant game of attraction chess."

A lump rose in my throat as I chewed my food. Now I had to wonder if she was interested and would possibly go home with that creep. But if she wasn't drinking his offering, I had to think Piper was smarter than that. Managing to swallow, I looked down at the table. "Will you go chat with him? Since we're not a couple?"

Piper placed her hand on mine and I felt a jolt go from her to me. As I looked up, she threw her head back and laughed. "No. He doesn't know we're not dating and I am not interested in someone who looks like he's almost sixty. So play along so he will stop looking this way."

With a nod, I lifted her other hand, the one messy with wing sauce, and I licked the sauce from her index finger. Eyes wide, Piper's breath hitched. I grinned my Cheshire cat grin as I popped another finger into my mouth. At least Piper's nails weren't talons like Bubblegum's. Speaking of, the waitress stopped short with a pitcher of tea and huffed when she saw us.

Removing her hand, Piper glanced toward the bar. "Yeah, um, I think that did it. He's not looking anymore. And neither is Pinkie." She grabbed a napkin and began wiping her hand under the table.

"Care to reciprocate?" I wiggled my messy fingers in front of her.

Not one to back down from a challenge, Piper grabbed my hand, cocked her head to the side, and licked the sauce from my own fingers. One by one. Without taking her eyes off of mine. I had never been so turned on in my entire life. Every inch of my body felt like a live wire ready to sizzle.

After that, we finished eating in silence. The silver fox had disappeared and Bubblegum stuck to silent refills of Piper's tea. I asked for a glass of water after finishing my single beer. "Actually, do you have any cake? Chocolate? It's her birthday."

Piper beamed as the waitress went to check on their desserts. "That's sweet of you. And how did you know I liked chocolate cake?"

"I have a sister. Chocolate is always the favorite."

"Tell me about her." Piper leaned closer and sipped from her straw. A huge hunk of chocolate cake appeared before us with two forks flanking it. "Thank you."

We both grabbed a fork. I thought perhaps to divide the cake in half, but since we had already had each other's fingers in our mouths, I guess it didn't matter at this point.

"Maggie is my sister. She's three years younger than me and I've always been incredibly protective of her. When our dad left she wasn't even a year old, and less than a year after that our mom left us with our grandparents. I was five, almost six at the time, and we had been through way more than we should have. But Abuela and Abuelo were the best parents we could have asked for. They made sure all our needs were met. They worked hard to send me to college and always doted on Maggie. She's a spitfire of a girl now, full of sass. But she's very bubbly and fun."

With an easy smile, Piper noted, "She sounds like you."

"More the other way around. She keeps me grounded, humble, and full of laughs." I shook my head. Maggie would adore Piper. She already watched her on the news every day. It was part of her ritual to see where I work even if I wasn't on camera.

"It sounds like you're close. Does she live nearby?" Another gob of the cake was speared by Piper's fork.

"She does, actually. She lives in a long-term care facility about two miles from me. She has Down Syndrome, so while she can't be completely independent, the facility helps her be as on her own as she can manage." It wasn't usual for me to offer up Maggie's differences to people, but I had a feeling Piper would handle it well.

And she did. Her face lit up. "That is wonderful. I would love to meet her one day." Piper's hand brushed mine again and again my skin felt that jolt.

"She's your biggest fan."

"How about Sunday? Can we go visit Sunday?"

All of my thoughts of being a bachelor for life started to fade. Women were always scared off by Maggie. Well, not her herself, but the thought of her. Of caring for her, of interacting with her. But here was Piper Campbell, the most gorgeous woman in the world, and she was asking to visit my special needs sister.

I nodded. And we finished the cake making plans for Sunday.

Piper

Growing up, I had a cousin with Down Syndrome named Hazel. We had been incredibly close as kids and I cried for days when her family moved to Boston. Hazel had been about five years older than me but we were the same size. She loved to play with dolls and pretend we ran a restaurant. So when Alonso said he had a sister with Down Syndrome, I lit up like a Christmas tree. I was practically giddy Sunday morning as I waited for Alonso to pick me up at my parents' house.

"You're going on a date with the boy who ruined your project?" My mother just didn't understand what I was doing.

"No, Mom, it's not a date. At all. He has a sister with DS who is a fan of mine and I said I would go see her. You know how close Hazel and I were." Even now, years later, I could feel the tears threaten as I thought about Hazel.

About five years ago Hazel had died in a car accident. I mourned for weeks. Before her passing, we talked on the phone often and we followed each other on social media. Yes, she had social media. She was quite tech-savvy, my Hazel.

"Well, regardless, I'm glad you're finally over that stupid prank he pulled." Mom stood in front of me and tried to fluff my hair. I had to wave her away.

Alonso's car pulled into the driveway and I debated running out before my mom could grill him like she would have when I was fifteen, or seeing if he could play the gentleman and come up to the door. Before either of those happened, my dad appeared from the garage and walked up to the blue sedan. From behind the curtain, I watched Alonso get out of the car and shake my father's hand.

Dad was imposingly tall, but his overly friendly demeanor made it hard for anybody to fear him. Growing up most of my friends were a little afraid of him for his size, but they quickly learned he was a teddy bear - it was my mother who was the imposing force in my life.

Hands were shaken and my father laughed. I bit my lip as Alonso laughed in return. My stomach did flip-flops. I had to remind it that this was not a date. Why did my mother and my stomach think this was a date?

Dad walked Alonso up to the front door and they chatted. When the door swung open I slid down into the couch and grabbed a magazine from the table. Of course it was all about men's prostates. Maybe he wouldn't notice.

"Piper, honey, your friend is here." They came in behind me and I stuffed the magazine into the couch cushion.

"Already?" I sounded out of breath. I hoped they didn't notice.

Of course, my mother came back into the room right then. "What already? You've been staring out the window for twenty minutes, Piper Marie."

Kill me now.

"Alonso, this is my mother Mary. And you met my father, Tim." I could feel the heat on my cheeks as Alonso smiled at me.

"Yes. Mrs. Campbell, it's a pleasure." He extended a hand for my mother who took it for a dainty handshake. Alonso looked like he didn't know how to handle her delicate fingers. He looked back at me. "Shall we?"

Jumping to my feet, I was eager to get away from my well-meaning parents. "Yes! See you later, Dad. Mom." I stuffed my wallet and phone into the pockets of my jeans and hurried to the door. Alonso followed me out.

In the car he looked at me before starting the engine. "You were staring out the window for twenty minutes?"

Rolling my eyes away from him, I scoffed. "My mother likes to exaggerate. I had just glanced outside because it was about time for you to arrive." There was no way I was telling him I had been looking out for him for about ten minutes. Purely because I prefer people to run early, not late.

In no time we were at the facility where Maggie lived. Alonso had told me she was mostly independent but there was a small staff on hand to help when needed. He had wanted his sister to live with him, but with his schedule he wasn't as available as he would have liked to be for her. It had been Maggie's idea to move into the residential home with other adults who were mostly on their own but needed occasional assistance.

I wasn't sure what to expect, but I was pleasantly surprised by a building that presented as a regular apartment complex. There was a small lobby and desk with a cheerful woman behind it. She wore a staff shirt, not scrubs. Her attention elsewhere, she merely waved to us in greeting. I had thought maybe we would need to sign in. But perhaps she was used to seeing Alonso. We took the elevator up to the third floor and I followed him to the second door on the right.

"She's excited to meet you." Three knocks sounded and it was just a second before the door jerked open.

"Alonso!" The siblings didn't hesitate to quickly wrap each other into a bear hug.

Once they broke apart, I got a good look at the pretty young woman before me. Her long hair hung around her shoulders in soft waves and she wore light make-up. Maggie only came up to my armpit in height, but I could tell immediately she possessed a large personality.

"Piper!" Before I knew it, I was wrapped in a bear hug of my own. Tiny arms wrapped around my waist and squeezed.

I couldn't help but laugh at the display of affection. "It's so nice to meet you, Maggie. Your brother has told me all about you."

She stepped back and led us inside. "Well, he's been telling me about you for weeks."

I side-eyed Alonso. "Weeks? That's a lot longer than my twenty minutes."

He held up his hands as if in surrender. "Listen, she asks about you. That's all."

There went those stomach flips again. They needed to learn to go away. I turned back to Maggie and let her show me around her apartment.

Lemonade and cookies waited for us at her small table. It took Alonso seconds to sniff out the baked goods. "This looks great, Mags. You know I love lemonade."

"That's why I made it. Piper, do you like lemonade? I have bottled water, too." Maggie was a great hostess.

"Lemonade sounds perfect." We sat down and chatted while we ate cookies and drank lemonade.

I was grilled on everything related to the news station. Then Maggie grilled her brother about his relationship with me.

"We're just co-workers, Mags. She wanted to meet you after I told her about you." Alonso cast a fleeting glance my way and I saw a slight smirk cross his face before he looked away.

"Well, are you dating anyone?" This question was aimed at me. This girl was definitely direct.

I cleared my throat. "Oh, no. I'm not seeing anyone. But I just got out of a relationship. I'm certainly not looking." Parched, I took several gulps from the lemonade and refilled my glass from the pitcher. "More?"

Without waiting for any reply, I topped off both the other glasses. Alonso quickly grabbed his and took a long drink.

We chatted for almost two hours, Maggie showing me childhood photos of her and Alonso with their grandparents. We talked about her favorite shows, what music we all enjoyed, and joked about some of the silly stories we had been assigned over the years. The time passed faster than I had expected and my cheeks hurt from so much smiling.

"It's getting late, we should be going." Alonso set his glass down firmly, as if he was finalizing an edict. "Maggie, I'll be back Wednesday and we'll go shopping, okay?"

She crinkled her eyes as she smiled. "I love shopping day."

"I know. You love it—me not as much." He mussed his sister's hair and got a playful smack in return.

I giggled at their interaction. My sister and I weren't close anymore and I missed the interaction. "What kind of shopping?"

Maggie beamed. "We go to Target and we get lunch." She clapped her hands with excitement.

"Oh, I love Target. It's my favorite place."

Alonso laid his hands on his sister's shoulders. "Well, Wednesday we need to do some special shopping. Night to Shine is coming up and you need a dress."

Night to Shine is a sort of prom set up specifically for adults with special needs. I had covered it for the station in Richmond and had loved the whole concept. Events were held all across the country. It warmed my heart to think that Maggie got to enjoy such a special night.

"Oh, yes! I do need a new dress. Can I give my old one to Emily?"

Alonso's eyes crinkled much like how Maggie's did. "That's really sweet of you. Of course you can. I'm sure Emily would appreciate it."

Turning to me, a sly smile crossed Maggie's face. "Do you want to come prom shopping with me, Piper?"

Of course I did. But if that was a special time between Alonso and his sister, I didn't want to interfere.

Reading my hesitation, Alonso echoed his sister. "You have to come now. I am so lost when it comes to fancy dresses."

Lucky for him, I happened to be a fancy dress expert. Most recently I had been doing wedding dress shopping. Thankfully, no purchases had been made before I discovered Henry's deception.

Eager for a happy occasion, I readily agreed. "I would love to join you. Thank you for inviting me, Maggie."

She beamed, clearly pleased with the outcome of the day. We said our goodbyes and got back into Alonso's car.

Alonso took a deep sigh and looked my way. "If you can't make it Wednesday, it's fine. I know that was kind of putting you on the spot."

"Are you kidding? Women love dress shopping for any reason and I am no exception." I was already picturing what colors would look best on Maggie's gorgeous skin. But then I thought maybe Alonso didn't want me to be a third wheel. "Unless, that is, you don't want me to come with you. I understand that it's a special time for you and your sister. I can easily bow out if you prefer."

Truth be told, in the five minutes since I had accepted the invitation, I was already looking forward to the shopping trip. Maggie was fun and easy to talk to. And as much as I hated to admit it, my loathing for Alonso Ortiz was changing rapidly into something completely different.

His response was subdued as he looked at me and scratched his chin. "No, no, I would love for you to come with us. Maggie clearly loved you. And..." He paused, shook his head, and brightened his smile. "And, um, I could use the help with all that girly stuff. So yeah, come with us."

A lump lodged in my throat and I couldn't figure out why. Was it his more serious tone? The way he looked at me? Was it how I thought he was going to say he wanted my company? All I could do was nod in agreement. I looked out the window and sat silently until he dropped me off at home.

"Thank you for taking me to meet your sister, Alonso."

"Of course." And he drove away, flying down the street as if his tailpipe was on fire.

Alonso

Dress shopping was not my idea of a good time, but I would do anything in the world for Maggie. I also pushed her to do things for herself. When other kids at school made fun of her, I taught her to insult them in Spanish. Abuela had been horrified at the words that came from Maggie's young lips. But, I had to think that my tutelage was what allowed her to live mostly independently and to think for herself.

I picked Piper up again and together we went to get Maggie. We made polite small talk as we drove through Savannah. Piper graciously allowed Maggie to sit up front. She had even brought my sister a tall, glittery tiara to wear while shopping. Naturally, Maggie had loved it and was all too happy to wear it as we wandered the mall.

In the first store, a saleswoman approached Piper. "Can I help you miss?"

"No, but you can help my friend here. She's the shopper today." Piper stepped to the side so Maggie would shine. The puff of pride I felt was oddly warming and I had to ask myself if it was pride in Maggie or in Piper. Of course it was in Maggie. Naturally.

The woman's fake smile fell, an action that did not escape the notice of myself or Piper. "I see. Feel free to shop around and let me know if I can get a dressing room started for you." She then whispered to Piper. "Is she going to be a bridesmaid for your wedding? How nice of you to include someone like her."

Shoulders rolled back and Piper's head whipped toward the rude salesperson. "I'm sorry, ma'am, but if you can't treat all three of us like actual people, we will happily take our business and money elsewhere. Do you realize I'm a reporter with Action News? Maybe you've seen me. I would love to do an exposé on ableist shops in Savannah and you will be at the top of the list!"

The woman stood stunned, her face bright red. Before she could begin to apologize, Maggie stepped up to her and repeated a line from one of her favorite movies. "You work on commission, right? Big mistake. Big. Huge. I have to go shopping now."

And together my sister and Piper walked away from the woman and I could do nothing but follow in their wake.

Outside, the two girls hugged. "That was amazing, Maggie. I am so proud of you."

Maggie struck a pose and kissed the air. "I know what I'm doing. Ali taught me well."

Piper turned to me. "Ali?"

I shrugged. "Childhood nickname. Alonso is hard for a toddler to say." I patted Maggie on the back. "But for the record, I am proud of you, too. People like that need to be put in their place."

"Now, can we really go shopping?" Maggie took Piper's hand and started to pull her toward another store.

Armed with five dresses to try on, Maggie hid away in a dressing room, aided by an overly helpful saleswoman. Piper had helped pick out colors that would look good on her skin tone and shapes that would flatter Maggie's body. Both things I knew nothing about.

"I need to thank you for what you did back there. Not many people would stand up for Maggie like that." I cleared my throat and shoved my hands in my pockets. My palms were sweaty and my stomach was in knots.

"She's a person, not a pet. She deserves respect. I'm sorry if I got out of hand." Piper's doe eyes met mine and she tucked her hair behind her ears.

It's just a crush, AO. And only because she was nice to your sister. You do not want to kiss Piper Campbell. You're co-workers. Nothing can happen. Stop imagining what her lips taste like. I bet they taste like raspberries. I have no reason for thinking that, aside from it would be perfect if she tasted like raspberries. Stop it, AO!

"Oh, geez, I went too far, didn't I?" Piper's eyes grew larger and she rubbed her hands back and forth.

Pulling myself away from thinking about her lips, I had to reassure her. "No, no. I think you were amazing. That woman needed to be educated. And saying you would do a story - actually, that's a decent idea. We should pitch it."

My stammering was cut short by Maggie coming out in a royal blue dress that hit her mid-calf. Spinning around for us, she smiled from ear to ear. "What do you think?"

Nothing could make me stop thinking about kissing Piper like seeing my sister look so lovely. "Oh, Mags, you look great. I think that's a winner." My heart burst to see her so happy.

I looked to Piper for her input. But instead of looking pleased, her mouth was twisted to the side. "Um, it's nice. But I really think you need to try on the pink one before deciding."

I was about to have words with Piper for popping Maggie's bubble, but I was surprised when Maggie agreed.

"Yeah, I like this one, but I think the pink will show my curves better."

"Maggie!"

My sister eyed me. "Flaunt it if you got it, right?" And with that, she disappeared into the dressing room again.

The second she was out of sight we began to laugh hysterically. "Where did she learn that?" Piper swiped the tears from under her eyes.

"I have no idea. Abuela would tan my hide if she knew Maggie said that." I shook my head. I refused to see my baby sister as a sexual being, ability difference aside. No brother wanted his sister to flaunt her curves.

"Don't worry. the pink one is more princessy. But I think it will flatter her more and be a better length." Piper sighed.

"Thank you for being here. You have no idea how much it means to Maggie." I scratched my head, sure I was making my wild curls even frizzier.

"It might seem shallow to you, but back in Richmond I volunteered as a pageant coach for inner-city girls. Mostly just school pageants, but it gave them a sense of self-confidence and poise. One girl used what she learned to ace her college entrance interview and got a scholarship to Harvard."

The more I spent time with Piper the more I learned about her and liked what I discovered. "That's amazing. I never thought about pageants preparing girls for interviews."

"Girls learn etiquette, poise, interview skills, and how to promote themselves in a world that doesn't always see their worth. Especially minority and differently-abled girls. I loved working with them." Piper looked off into the distance and looked genuinely happy.

The dressing room door opened again and Maggie came out in a pale pink gown. Piper had been right, this one suited her much more. Maggie's waist was small, but the skirt was full and didn't show off all that many curves. The neckline was different and Maggie looked more comfortable than she had with the strapless dress.

"Oh, yes. Maggie, that's the one." Piper clapped her hands together.

The store attendant came out with the other dresses in her hand. "That's what she said, too. I'm putting the rest of these back." She slipped away.

Tears welled up in Maggie's eyes and she was visibly choked up.

My mind immediately went into high alert. "What's wrong, Mags?"

She couldn't speak. I stood up and looked from her to Piper. Piper was teared up as well.

Piper took my hand in hers to calm me. "She loves it so much she's speechless, Alonso. They're good tears."

Utter confusion tore through my head. I was panicked for my sister who wasn't actually panicked. And my hand was being warmed by the heat from Piper's hand. My body was in overload and it took a moment to come back to my senses.

I turned back to my sister. She nodded. "I. Love. It." Her words were broken up by smiling sobs.

My hand was still in Piper's. Did she realize she still held me? I didn't move, didn't breathe for fear of her taking her hand away. Should I grip her hand in return? My pinkie twitched and I felt that jolt I had felt before when we had occasionally touched. Piper's hand leaped back as if burned and she tucked it under her thigh.

The saleswoman reappeared with a smile. "And?"

I rubbed Maggie's cheek. "Wrap it up. We're taking it home."

Over lunch, we laughed and talked. Maggie filled us in on all the goings-on in her building. Some of the residents were dating and two were caught canoodling—Maggie's word—in the back of the recreation room. Giggles erupted from her as she told the story.

"Surely people are allowed to date." Piper's laughter faded as she thought a little more about the situation.

Maggie rolled her eyes. "Well, yes, but they're not supposed to get to second base in a public area!"

I was getting way too many shocks from my sister on this trip. First the overly girly crying because of a dress and now she's talking about people groping each other. "You've never done that have you, Mags?"

A pointed look turned to me as my sister's dark eyes turned serious. "Why would I tell you if I've gotten to second base? You're my brother. Ew."

Piper laid her hand on Maggie's. "He's just looking out for you the way a big brother should. He wants to make sure you're safe."

Another eye roll came my way. "No, I have never gotten to second base, Alonso. Thanks for reminding me." She turned to Piper and crinkled her eyes before blocking her face from me. "But I wouldn't mind if it happened!"

Laughter burst from Piper so loud that a few other patrons of the restaurant turned to look at us. Of course, I had heard my sister, who was not exactly great at whispering. I wanted to be upset with her, but it had been a while since I had gotten to second base myself and I wouldn't mind it happening again sooner rather than later. I laughed with them.

Suddenly it occurred to me that Maggie was treating Piper like one of her best girlfriends. Something a completely normal twenty-something woman would do. And all I had ever wanted for Maggie was for her to live as normal of a life as she could. Part of that was having crushes on boys and possibly kissing a few.

Maggie was completely smitten with Piper, I could tell. Part of me worried what would happen if things soured between Piper and me, but then I remembered we weren't dating. We were just coworkers. My singleness was completely on purpose.

It was then that I remembered something my abuelo had said to me. Relationships built on nothing but passion will fizzle out and leave things in a bad place. But relationships built on friendship and respect - that's where the passion builds over time instead of dying a miserable death. He had looked at Abuela and winked at her. They had that relationship built on friendship and respect. When they passed, they had been married for fifty years.

My parents' relationship, on the other hand, had been built on nothing but a passion that quickly died out. They had tried to stay together for me, but in the end, they both had given up on each other and their children.

Maybe not all relationships started as a burst of flames only to be doused when reality hit. Maybe, just maybe, they could start as a little warmth and grow into a roaring fire that would last.

And maybe I could convince Piper Campbell to turn her icy feelings towards me into a little warmth. After all, we could only get warmer from here.

Piper

THE IDEA ABOUT ABLEIST businesses had been a huge hit with the bigwigs at Action News. As it happens, Mr. Edward's nephew was autistic and had experienced his share of ableism in stores, so it was something he was all too happy to have us tackle. I even gave credit for the idea to Alonso, who had looked at me with surprise.

After several phone calls and finding some great resources, I told Alonso we were heading back to his sister's place.

"What? Why?"

"I'm doing an interview for the piece on ableism. And you can ogle that desk clerk." Wagging my eyebrows, I grabbed my bag and made sure I had my phone.

A scowl crossed his face. "Wendy? Really?"

I burst into laughter. "Okay, maybe it's more like she ogles you."

Alonso scratched the stubble on his chin and winked at me. "Jealous?"

My nose scrunched up automatically. "Hardly." And yet, that wink did things I was not prepared for. I dug in my purse looking for nothing until I could regain my composure.

"Oh, well, in that case, maybe I should get her phone number." He pretended to slick his hair back, which only resulted in his curls springing all over the place and my heart fluttering a little.

The ride was quiet, and I found myself contemplating the change that had occurred in my heart recently. I hated Alonso Ortiz. For years. But after the past several weeks, I found that not only did I not hate him, but I kind of liked him. A lot. My heart rate would increase and my body would flush when he called my name. His infrequent, work-related texts caused my breath to hitch.

But he's my co-worker and not only are inter-office romanced frowned upon, but I would have to still work with him if we broke up. When we broke up. Because he was adamant about his confirmed bachelorhood, so there would be a breakup at some point. So why bother?

When I shook my head at my own inner-conversation, Alonso looked my way. "You okay, Piper?"

My cheeks flushed as he said my name. "Um, yeah. Sorry. I was just arguing with myself in my head." My attempt at a chuckle came out more like a choke.

"Who won?"

"What?"

"Who won the argument in your head?" He smiled wide, showing off his perfectly straight teeth.

Embarrassed, I looked down, unable to hide the grin that crept onto my own face. "Well, I guess I did."

He slapped my knee. "Well, then, good job."

We both started to laugh as we pulled into Maggie's apartment complex. She was waiting for us outside, wearing the tiara I had gotten her and an adorable halter maxi dress.

With a kiss, Alonso greeted his sister and asked why she was so dressed up.

"For the story, dummy." Maggie rolled her eyes.

Looking for a shady spot, I pointed to where I wanted to set up. "Over there, please."

"Where's your interviewee?" He truly looked like he had no idea.

Maggie and I both looked at Alonso with confusion. I put my hands on Maggie's shoulders. "She's the star on the piece. I want her to tell everyone about that nasty saleswoman. No names, just share her experience." I crossed my arms and tapped my foot as I waited for him to pick his jaw up off the ground.

"No." He stared at me, his face expressionless.

"No? Why?" Maggie tilted her head to the side. "I want to be on TV."

Grabbing me by the shoulders, Alonso pulled me aside and whispered to me. "Piper, people will make fun of her. They'll judge her."

His concern for his sister was evident. But his understanding that she was a woman who deserved to be treated normally was clearly lacking.

"Everyone on the news gets judged. But Maggie faced this discrimination firsthand just recently. And she offered to be interviewed. It was her choice." I crossed my arms and stood firm.

"Not my sister." He was being incredulous and overprotective. Maggie was entirely capable of doing the interview, she wanted to do it, and he was stopping it?

Maggie approached us and pointed her finger into Alonso's chest. "Ali, I am a grown woman. You are being just as bad as that saleswoman. You think because I'm different I can't do this. But I can. Stop holding me back."

Shame filled Alonso's face and he hugged his sister close. "You're right, Mags. I was holding you back. Because I love you and I never want to see you hurt. But you are grown and you can make your own decisions. I'm sorry."

Then the wisest words I had ever heard came from Maggie Ortiz. "Everyone gets hurt from time to time. But being an adult means you pick yourself back up, dust yourself off, and keep going. I can do that, Alonso. You just have to let me."

We set up for the interview and Maggie was flawless, just as I expected she would be. Paired with another interview and some statistics, we had a compelling piece that I couldn't wait to share. I just hoped the woman from the store caught it.

Lunch with Maggie was a given and she was certain she was about to get her fifteen minutes of fame. I adored every minute with her and promised to call her once the piece was ready to air.

On the way back to the studio, Alonso sighed and looked at me. "I'm sorry."

"What for?" I eyed him, unsure where this apology was coming from.

"For not seeing my sister as a capable adult. She's still just a little girl in my mind. But you see her as a grown woman and I know she appreciates it."

I patted him in the arm. He was a good brother. "She's the one you need to apologize to."

"I did. But I wanted you to know I've seen the err of my ways. But she's all the family I have left and I just want to protect her. I've lost everyone else. I can't lose Maggie, too."

My heart ached for him and his sister. They had experienced a lot of loss. "I can't imagine. My sister and I aren't close at all, but I would still be devastated if something happened to her."

"How did you pick yourself back up and keep going?" He looked over at me as we sat at a red light.

"What?"

Through a grimace, he mumbled. "How did you pick yourself back up after you ended things with your fiancé?"

Oh. How had I done that? "I had to. It wasn't easy, but what choice did I have? I didn't want a husband who was so nonchalant not only about having a girl on the side but getting her pregnant to boot. Life must move on, and I'm proud to say I've survived one hundred percent of my bad days so far. I have a good track record."

"So it seems." His grin was a little dull, but still there. I thought Alonso seemed a little more introspective as we made our way into the parking lot.

Back at the studio, we parted ways and went to our respective desks. After about twenty minutes, though, Alonso texted me.

Alonso: Come see Maggie's piece. She's amazing.

Piper: Told you so.

Alonso: You sure did. Thank you.

Piper: You're welcome.

I stared at the phone for a moment, a smile playing across my lips. The unsteady stomach flips returned and I was hesitant to push them away for once.

Maria approached my desk, her long hair neatly pulled over one shoulder. "Girl, who put that smirk on your face? It must be a man."

I quickly put my phone in my desk drawer. "Oh, no. Well, from a man, yes, but it's just about a story I'm working on. Nothing that exciting."

"A group is going to P's and Cues after work to play pool. Want to join us?" She tapped her navy blue nails on my desk.

"Oh, maybe."

Leaning in closer, she whispered. "Could you ask AO to come? He's so hot. Maybe we can play strip pool."

Never had my heart leaped in my chest like that. Even when I found out Henry had cheated on me I had not been this shocked. Maybe I had subconsciously known that things with Henry wouldn't have worked out. But I had absolutely no claim on Alonso Ortiz, and I knew it.

Swallowing hard, I nodded to Maria. "I'll mention it to him."

"Thanks, girl. I'd love to get my hands on him." She winked and went off to her own desk. I watched her sit down and reapply her bold, red lipstick.

Knots filled my stomach. Alonso wasn't mine in any sense of the word, so I had no right to the feelings I was having. But I knew jealousy when it reared its ugly head. Maria was my friend and she deserved happiness. And maybe Alonso was my friend now. Maybe. And he deserved to find someone, if he wanted someone.

I remembered I was supposed to see Maggie's piece, so I made my way to his edit bay. "How does she look?"

"She's on fire. Thank you for doing this." Alonso's eyes pierced my own, a warmth in them I could not help but notice.

"Um, Maria said a group is going to P's and Cues tonight and said everyone is invited. She, um, told me to pass the word along, so..." I stammered. I was not usually one for stammering.

"Are you going?"

"I'm not sure."

Without another word, Alonso pulled up Maggie's part for the story and showed it to me. She was poised and well-spoken. It wasn't long, but it was well done.

"She's going to love this. I think it's perfect for the story." I shook Alonso's arm with excitement.

His hand fell over top of mine as a smile lit up his face. In the span of a breath both our faces stilled and we became hyper-aware of our hands on each other. My breath hitched as my eyes searched his. What was this? What was going on?

Alonso licked his lips and I had an urge to taste him. I wondered what he tasted like. Cinnamon and spices, maybe. That Mexican mole sauce I knew he loved. The need to find out was incredibly strong.

"Come tonight? To P's and Cues?" His voice was low, almost a whisper.

Unable to tear my eyes from his, I could only nod. I felt his forearm flex under my hands.

The air around us shifted as Tyrell's voice bounced into my head. "Hey, AO..." He stopped upon seeing me. Alonso and I broke apart quickly. Tyrell laughed and raised an eyebrow, but continued to talk. "Hey, AO and Piper, pool tonight at P's and Cues. I think Ashley and I are going to go."

Ashley was all Tyrell talked about, seeing as they were newly engaged. I had met her once and she seemed sweet, if not a little shallow. But she came from old money and enjoyed the finer things in life. Alonso, it seemed, was to be a groomsman for his friend.

Alonso turned away from me to Tyrell. "Yeah, we were just talking about that. Maria invited Piper. I think I'll be there. Piper?" An expectant stare met my gaze, full of unspoken questions.

My smile was too wide, I knew, but I couldn't help it. "I hope so. We'll see." I stood and smoothed down my dress. "Let me know when you have the rest of that package ready, Alonso. Maybe see you later, Tyrell."

I scurried away, unsure why I felt guilty or embarrassed when I had done nothing wrong. Except, maybe, open my heart up a little more to Alonso Ortiz.

Alonso

THE CROWD FROM WORK was small, but all people I knew. P's and Cues wasn't a large place to begin with, so it always seemed cozy, and since it was just a mile away from the studio, it was convenient. I searched around for Piper. Not that I was looking for her, but she had said she would come.

Oh, who was I kidding? I was totally looking for her. I had nursed a crush on her back in college and it had returned full force after watching her interact with Maggie. A few months ago I swore I would never date someone from work, but Piper made me rethink that.

I watched Tyrell and Ashley groping each other in the corner booth. Ashley was a Savannah socialite who worked as a preschool teacher to keep herself from being bored and because her father said she had to have a job. They had been high school sweethearts who just found each other again recently. Now they were joined at the hip.

Pangs of jealousy hit me. I wasn't jealous of Tyrell, not at all. Ashley was pretty, but so not my type. But I did feel that slam of jealousy over having someone to come home to at night. Someone to share my dreams with and someone to make Abuela's mole sauce for.

I scanned the room again for Piper and saw her come from the restrooms with Maria. They laughed at something Maria had said and my breath stilled. The unbridled joy that broke out onto my face was automatic.

Piper Campbell radiated light.

Which could spell disaster for me. She didn't look any different than she had at work, but she had removed her cardigan and her hair was swept off her face with a clip or something. But still, she simply shone from across the room. And I felt completely smitten.

The pair made a beeline for me and my pulse quickened. My mouth dried immediately and I struggled to swallow. This sensation was new to me. Sure, I had dated plenty in my life, but nobody had made me feel like this before - and we weren't even dating.

"Hi, AO. You look happy to be off work tonight." Maria smiled. She sidled up to me and batted her eyelashes.

I knew she was trying to be flirtatious, but I was in no way attracted to Maria. "Something in your eye, Maria?" Yes, it was a little mean, but I wasn't going to let her think I was interested. Especially not with Piper standing next to her.

Straightening out, Maria ran her fingernail under her eyes. "Um, no. I got it." A look of defeat came across her face. "I'll be right back, Piper. Want a beer?"

Piper shook her head as she sat across from me. As Maria walked away to the bar, she spoke without looking my way. "Maria likes you. She asked me to invite you tonight."

I took a long drink while I thought over what she said. I had picked up on Maria's flirtations, but I didn't realize she was actually interested. Or that she had asked Piper to invite me. Did that mean Piper had only mentioned it to me for her friend? "She's a nice girl, but not my type."

"You don't date people from work." It was a statement, not a question. Yet, based on her tone, Piper was definitely asking me for an answer.

I shook my head. "Not usually. But it's not a rule. I would date the right person if she came along, regardless of where she works." It had been a rule up until that exact moment. But I meant it when I said I could change the rules for the right person.

"But it's not Maria." Another statement.

With long black hair and a tiny, delicate body, Maria was beautiful. And she was a great coworker and a nice person, but none of it added up for me. I shook my head. "No. It's not."

I tried not to let the sly smile that crept onto Piper's face encourage me. Was she glad Maria wasn't my type? I thought about offering her what I did find to be my type. Long-legged, sassy women with eagle eyes and a knack for coaxing a story from complete strangers. That was my type.

A pool table opened up and I challenged Piper to a game. She eyed me. "What's the wager?"

A date. The loser takes the winner on a date. Which meant that either way, I would still be the winner. But I chickened out when I opened my mouth. "Loser carries all the equipment for a week?"

"And..." She chewed her lip while she thought. "And buys lunch for the winner at least twice." Her cheeks flushed at the addition.

I only nodded my acceptance. It was almost like a date, though we ate lunch on the road often enough. Perhaps we could have more wings and I could lick the sauce from her fingers again.

When it became apparent she would be whipping my tail, I bit back a laugh. With each shot, Piper grew more animated and the smack talk got livelier. I would happily buy her lunch every day to see that smile on her face more often.

Tyrell stood beside me as she sunk another ball into a corner pocket. "Man, you're not even trying."

I turned to him. "I am trying. She's kicking my butt."

He laughed and clapped me on the shoulder. "And you're enjoying every minute, AO. I saw how you were looking at her earlier. Mr. I'm Never Settling Down. Mr. I'll never date anyone from work."

I steeled. "I like her, yes. But I'm not settling down and we're not dating."

"Yet."

A chuckle came from my friend. "When you're done getting your backside handed to you, come see me. Ashley has a story idea that's actually pretty good." He sauntered back to his table when I nodded in agreement.

When Piper beat me soundly, she whooped loud enough for everyone to hear. "You owe me, Alonso. Carry everything and two lunches this week. I am the pool master. Bow down to my pool prowess."

"I've never seen you so cocky, Campbell. But I will bow to you, O Queen of the Pool Cue." With that I bowed low, my hair flopping and almost touching the dingy bar floor. She curtsied and as I came back upright I noticed Maria look from me to Piper and back again.

At Tyrell's table, I slid in across from the lovebirds. "Ashley, you look great as always."

The bombshell beamed and blew me a kiss. I knew better than to read anything into it, the girl was a flirt. "You are the sweetest thing." She ran a manicured finger over Tyrell's cheek.

"What's the story idea, T?" I wasn't too interested in watching their table groping.

Ashley came to attention then. "Oh, that was my idea. I hired a professional bridesmaid to help me with the wedding. I thought it was a great story idea. Have you ever heard of a professional bridesmaid before?"

Professional bridesmaid? That was a thing? I scratched my chin. "I can't say I've ever heard of one, but I'm not up on wedding stuff. Let's see if Piper has heard of it."

I caught her attention and she came over to us. Piper slid into the booth next to me, her bare thigh touching my hand. I quickly retracted it, but I didn't move over more. I liked her close to me.

"Ever heard of a professional bridesmaid?" I raised an eyebrow in her direction.

"No. They have professionals now? Aren't you supposed to have friends be bridesmaids?" Ashley wasn't offended by the remark, thankfully, but that did raise a great question.

We talked for a few minutes and Piper got the contact info for Ashley's professional. The whole time I could only concentrate on the fact that Piper's long, toned leg was firmly pressed against mine and I had the desire to place my hand on it to see if I would feel that spark I had felt the last time we had touched. I refrained, keeping my hands on the tabletop and feeling like a fool the entire time.

Maria left early, which was a relief because she was reading far too much into the unspoken words between Piper and me. Tyrell and Ashley also left because Ashley needed her beauty rest. I couldn't help but wonder how much of her beauty was applied with a sponge. A few others from the office lingered, but I wasn't close with them. Piper moved her things over to my table and sat across from me sipping on a tea.

My thoughts turned to the night of her birthday when we had licked the sauce from each other's fingers. I kept my eyes trained on the slender digits "Are you hungry?"

"Hungry? No. We ate an hour ago, Alonso. Didn't you get something?" She tilted her head to the side.

Of course I had ordered something. A huge burger. And I had eaten every bite. I wasn't hungry, I just wanted to have that experience again.

I snapped out of my trance. "Of course, yes. You know me, always hungry." I rubbed my stomach.

Piper tucked a piece of her hair behind her ear with a slender finger. "You know, I could go for more of that chocolate cake if they have any. Where's Pinky the waitress?"

With another slab of cake between us and two forks, we laughed as we fought over the large swirl of chocolate buttercream sitting in the middle of the cake. She may have won the pool game, but I wasn't giving up on an extra dose of sugar. Much to her disappointment, I won that battle and scooped up the icing. As I licked it off my fork, I offered her the leftovers. She made a face, sticking out her tongue, and I did my best not to lean across the table and kiss her.

That night I tossed and turned as I tried to fall asleep. Piper's radiant smile appeared every time I closed my eyes. Which made my heart beat faster. Which kept me awake longer. But when I finally fell asleep, she filled my dreams as well.

I dreamed that her long legs were intertwined with mine and she had one of her signature cardigans draped over her shoulders like a 1950s schoolgirl. We ate sauce-laden wings and after she went to lick the sauce from my fingers, she kissed it off my lips. I wanted to smear more sauce on my mouth so she would keep kissing me.

Suddenly, we were reporting on a story about playing pool and the dangers of it, how it made people fall in love. Piper looked into the camera and said many men had fallen for women who had beat them in a game of pool. Shaking my head, I said I wasn't in love and Maria showed up and disagreed with me. She said I was in love with Piper and not her and that I should have played pool with her instead. Finally, I explained that I didn't love Piper because she had beat me at pool, but because she was the most amazing human being I had ever met.

Then, in the dream, I got down on one knee and professed my undying love for the world to see and asked Piper Campbell to marry me. All while Tyrell held the camera and Karry and Sam reported the whole thing live.

The only thought in my head as I woke up drenched in sweat: I love Piper Campbell.

Piper

I HUNG UP THE phone with the professional bridesmaid and shook my head. It was unreal what some people managed to do for a living. But Ashley was right, this was a unique story. And I looked forward to Alonso treating me to a meal after we talked to this girl.

"Load up, Alonso. We're heading over towards Tybee." I grabbed my pad and paper as well as my recorder and stuffed them into my giant bag. Sure it could double as an overnight duffel, but it fit all my stuff in it.

The bottle of water stopped at his lips. "What's on Tybee?"

"That bridesmaid for hire is that way. Not on the island, but over that direction. Maybe you can take me for some shrimp and grits when we're done." I did a little shoulder dance in my excitement. I loved shrimp and grits.

I stopped when I noticed the look on Alonso's face as he watched me. His eyebrows were raised and he folded his arms. "You're a little over-excited about some tiny dead invertebrates."

I gave him a deadpan glare and blinked several times. "They're delicious dead invertebrates."

The laughter that erupted from him was so loud, several people stopped and turned to us. Alonso doubled over as his eyes began to water and I started to giggle as I watched him. Within a few seconds, I was full-on belly laughing as well, having to grip the desk to hold myself up.

Once we had calmed and the rest of the office had dismissed our juvenile laughter, I walked with Alonso to grab the equipment. We still wore huge smiles on our faces.

"You really do have a great sense of humor, Piper. That's the reaction I wanted from you back in school. That's what I always loved about you - your laugh. Definitely your best feature." He bent down and hefted the camera bag onto his shoulder before grabbing a fresh battery pack from the charging station.

Alonso chuckled again and walked off, leaving me standing in his wake.

I was stuck right where I stood. That's what he's always loved about me? He's always what?

Maybe it was just an expression, but anyone who has studied communications knows that only ten percent of it is what is said. The other ninety percent is non-verbal - how it's said, the facial expression, the setting. And Alonso saying that's what he's always loved about me, the heaviness of his voice, the look in his eyes, said way more than he could have had intended.

And me? I was stunned. Over the past few months, my hatred for all things Alonso Ortiz had certainly shifted to comfort and liking. He was a great co-worker. He was a fabulous brother to Maggie. And yes, he was becoming a pretty good friend. But more than that?

I was brought back to the night before when he said he would date someone from work if it was the right person. I had taken it as innocuous flirtation. But maybe it was more. Maybe the longing to feel his lips on mine - a longing I had shoved down - wasn't as flippant as I had been thinking. He had stared into my eyes when he said it. Had he meant me?

Inter-office dating was frowned upon, I reminded myself. He was my partner and producer. If things didn't work out, then what? It's not like our jobs were a dime a dozen. We would still have to work together. Best to continue squelching the desire to feel his lips and his hands on me. Best to keep things strictly above board.

My head was decided, but my heart burned as if I had thrown it into a volcano. I had gotten over Henry, I could get over this heady crush on a co-worker. Finding my feet working again, I turned slowly.

Alonso had backtracked for me. "If you want shrimp and grits, Campbell, we have to actually leave the building."

In the car, we sat silently. Not that we jabbered every day on the way out to stories, but we talked often enough. Everything felt awkward, though perhaps that was just my perception. Alonso beat his hands on the steering wheel to the Lady Gaga song on the radio, seemingly oblivious to the turmoil going on in my own head.

At a red light, he turned to me. "So how long has this lady been in the business?"

"Huh?"

"This professional bridesmaid. How long has she been doing it?"

Oh. That. "I think she said about five years. She kind of fell into it and has been going strong since. She has a website, she's in a professional bridesmaid's network. And she sent me contact info for a few of her clients. She said she averages two weddings a month."

"And these people pay her?"

My comfort level was returning to normal. I could talk about work, especially fascinating stories, all day long. "Yes. She also runs an online boutique, but she said being a bridesmaid is her primary income."

Alonso laughed. "Man, how did I miss all these cushy jobs?"

"You'd make a fine professional bridesmaid. I can see you in a long, pink, ruffled dress. Mermaid cut." I couldn't help the jab. He made it so easy.

He fluffed his curls. "Pink? Honey, no, I do better in jewel tones." His voice was high-pitched and he batted his eyelashes as he spoke.

I burst into laughter and he followed suit. I was glad we were at a long red light. Not many men were secure enough to make that kind of joke at their own expense. Henry certainly wouldn't have allowed it. I had laughed more with Alonso in the past few months than I had in three years with Henry Peddler.

But, like Scarlett O'Hara, I couldn't think about that now. Or ever. Alonso was just a friend. A co-worker. Forget that his smile made me want to melt on the spot. We had work to do.

The professional bridesmaid, Amaya Journet, was the most gorgeous woman I had ever seen. She was petite and had olive skin and long, glossy, black hair. I immediately felt frumpy and gangly next to her. It didn't help that Alonso practically had to pick his jaw up off the floor.

Jealousy had never been a huge problem for me, but it was rearing its ugly head as Amaya showed us into her office and studio space. Her face could light up the Tybee Island Lighthouse on its own. And there was Alonso, camera in hand, following her like a puppy.

"I pulled out some of the bridesmaid dresses I've worn. Believe it or not, I've worn a few dresses twice." Amaya showed us over twenty dresses on a clothing rack in hues of blue, pink, green, and even one in neon yellow. "The cost of the dress is built into my price package, so while it looks like I'm paying for the dress myself, the bride has already paid me for it."

"Fascinating. I'll set up the camera to use the dresses as a backdrop." Alonso set to work setting up while I turned in a circle to see the rest of the room.

"You also make jewelry?" For some reason, this was the only question in my head.

"I do. Custom silver pieces with semi-precious stones. I can show you once we're done with this interview." Amaya's face was animated and her smile genuine.

The green-eyed monster who had apparently come with me for this piece was tucked away in my giant bag as I pulled out my notepad and recorder. "Great. Let's get started."

She was one of those people you wanted to hate but couldn't. Amaya the bridesmaid was just too nice. There was no other way to say it. She was flawless on camera, and I was thankful to be off camera while I interviewed her. I was much taller than her and my tailored dress looked like a gunny sack. After answering several questions, we set up for my opening shot.

I fluffed my hair and reapplied my lipstick while Amaya brought us both bottles of water. She and Alonso chatted and I tried not to let jealousy back out in the open. Why did I feel this way? Alonso and I were not a couple. I barely liked him. Okay, I really liked him, but still, I had no ownership of him. And I didn't want it. Did I?

We decided I would walk into the frame in front of the dresses, holding a bouquet of fake flowers. When Alonso gave me the signal, I walked in front of the camera. "We've all heard the phrase 'always a bridesmaid,' but Amaya Journet takes that to a whole new level as a professional bridesmaid here in Savannah. Serving dozens of brides every year, Amaya has made a career of being best buds with brides all over the city."

We recorded it again just in case, and Alonso took some B-roll footage because you can never have enough footage.

"This is so much fun. You must love being a reporter." Amaya sat back, her eyes wide with fascination.

"Stories like this are fun. I love bringing good news to people." I took a sip of the water she had brought out.

"That's why I do this. Weddings are happy and I want to be around happy people. There's enough strife in this world." Amaya was beautiful, friendly, and wise, it seemed.

"That's a beautiful sentiment." I checked the clock on my phone. We had time for those shrimp and grits if Alonso would just hurry.

"Are you two together?"

The question caught me off guard. "Um. No. Just co-workers. We've known each other a long time, though."

She leaned in close and kept her volume low. "He keeps looking at you." Her voice was even and matter of fact.

"I'm the one on camera. He gets paid to look at me." I shrugged, ignoring the implication of her comment. He had said the same thing about getting paid to look at me on our first day together. Not that I remembered.

She leaned in closer to me. "You know what I'm saying. I can see it in your eyes, too. You both keep stealing glances when the other isn't looking. If you ever need my services in the future, I'll give you a discount."

Alonso turned to us. "Ready, Piper?"

I jumped up from where I was sitting. "Absolutely." I turned to Amaya. "It was a pleasure. Thank you so much for meeting us on such short notice."

After our goodbyes, we loaded back up in the car and I thought over what she had said. We both stole glances at one another. So while I was checking him out, he was checking me out. But the decision to keep things platonic has been made. Nothing can happen aside from friendship.

We stopped to eat, but I was too busy mulling over everything to enjoy my shrimp and grits. Things were moving too fast and I had no idea where they were going. And I had to figure out if I wanted things moving at all. On one hand, this was Alonso, the guy I had hated for years. On the other hand was Alonso the thoughtful co-worker who had a mile-wide smile and dimples for days.

After we finished, Alonso looked at me and frowned. "Was your shrimp and grits not up to par? You didn't look like you enjoyed them."

I shook my head. "Oh, no, they were excellent, actually. I just have stuff on my mind."

"Anything I can help with?" He opened the car door for me and allowed me to slide in. After running around the car, he got into the driver's seat and looked at me expectantly.

I tried to smile. "Oh, no. I'm sorry. I'm fine. Thank you for buying."

With a nod, he started the car. "Any time, Piper."

Alonso

"WE'RE SAD TO ANNOUNCE that Karry Draper will be leaving us at the end of the month." Mr. Andrews smiled as he held out his hand to Karry at the budget meeting. "Karry, you've been a part of the Action News family for twenty years. I can't imagine this place without you."

A round of applause for Karry began and I watched as she wiped tears carefully under her eyes. I didn't understand why women did that. Why not just wipe your whole eye? I looked to Piper and wondered if she did the same thing.

Standing, Karry addressed the room. "Mike and I have decided to retire early. And since our daughter is in Nashville, we're heading that way. I will miss you all terribly."

Mr. Andrews leaned into the table. "This means we'll have an opening for an anchor. We like to promote from within, but we're open to bringing in someone from the outside as well.

It's an exciting time at Action News. Now, let's get rolling for the day."

Budget meetings were a necessary evil. Nobody liked them, but everybody went. And emails were just too slow or easy to miss, so in person they were, every day. Stories on politics, a shooting, an unfortunate drowning. Sadly, things that made the news had become mundane for me. I hadn't been surprised by a murder in years.

"Piper, what are you working on?"

My attention turned back to Piper who sat beside me. She straightened and tucked her hair behind her ear. It was adorable the way she did that every time before she began to talk. Why was I noticing this? I was supposed to be a life-long bachelor, why was I thinking I could fall in love with her?

"Yesterday we spoke with a woman who is a professional bridesmaid. We should have it ready for tonight." She turned toward me with a raised eyebrow.

Right, we're at work. Nodding, I confirmed. "Yes, I should have it ready within an hour of sitting down."

Mr. Andrews jotted it down on his legal pad. "Great. I also want you to run out to the Soup Kitchen. A local Girl Scout troop is volunteering there. Quick feel-good piece."

We nodded in unison and the agenda moved on.

As we left the meeting, Piper fell in step beside me. "If you want to finish that bridesmaid package, I'll call the soup kitchen and the Girl Scout person and arrange to go out there." She waved a paper with a phone number on it.

"Perfect. Give me about an hour." My mind was already on the next step of editing as I stepped away from Piper and toward my edit bay.

Maria stopped me before I got too far. "AO, would you do me a favor?"

My mind on my footage, I bounced from one foot to the other. "Um, sure?"

"Can you put together a package for me so I can apply for the anchor position? And would you recommend me?" She batted her eyelashes and adjusted her shirt so her cleavage was well in view.

I had worked with Maria for two years but didn't know her well. Of course, I had noticed her flirting in recent months but I hadn't thought much of it. "I'm a little busy, Maria. Can't Rex do it for you?"

"You're way better than Rex." She pressed against me ever so slightly. "Please?"

It was easier to just go along with it for now. With a sigh, I held my hands up in surrender. "Do you have the footage you want? I can take a look. But probably not today."

She squealed. "Oh, thank you, AO. You're the best. I'll bring it by your desk later." With that, she scurried away on impossibly high heels.

Within an hour, I had a visually appealing, if not a little boring, package for Piper on the bridesmaid. I texted her that it was ready for her voice over and seconds later she appeared in my doorway.

"Give me ten minutes and I'll knock this out and we can leave for the soup kitchen." She plopped down in Rex's chair and pulled a set of headphones in front of her.

"Perfect. Hey, Maria wants me to edit a package for her to apply for anchor." I cued up the video as I told her what Maria said. I wondered if she thought Maria would be good as anchor.

"Well, I would agree that you're a better editor than Rex, but isn't that a little underhanded?" Piper fiddled with the headphone wire as she looked at me, her dark eyes searching my own.

"It kind of feels that way, yeah. And she wants a recommendation." I sat back in my chair and put my hands behind my head.

Piper stiffened. "You're not going to give her one are you?"

"I don't know her that well and we haven't worked together much at all. You don't think I should give her one?"

"I mean, you're going to give me a recommendation, aren't you? I realize I'm newer here, but I've been doing this longer than Maria has." Piper blinked several times as she spoke and a stray piece of glitter sparkled with the movement.

Sitting up, warmth crept through my body. Did Piper want the job? Then she wouldn't be with me every day. The thought didn't sit well with me. I liked working with Piper. We had good chemistry and I realized the potential for more chemistry. Perhaps if we weren't working side by side every day, it would make it easier for us to go out socially. Or give me room to breathe so I could get over this crush and stop fantasizing about what her lips taste like.

"I don't know, Piper." It was a non-committal answer and a cop-out, but it was the truth. "Record your V. O. and I'll be back in a few minutes." With that, I stood and left the room.

We got in the car to head to the local soup kitchen and Piper's door slam did not escape my notice. She crossed her arms as she sat back and huffed.

"What put you in a mood?"

She turned to me and glared. "You did. You don't think I deserve to be an anchor?" Anger showed plainly on her face, but I could see the hurt behind it. Her eyes were glossy and her lower lip poked out.

"I didn't say that, Piper." I pulled out onto the main road, glad to not have to look her in the eye.

"You didn't have to. Go ahead and recommend Maria. She's got the hots for you and I'm sure she would 'reward' you for a recommendation."

I nearly slammed on the brakes at that comment. "Piper, seriously? Do you think I would do that? Clearly, you don't know me as well as I thought." I shook my head, glad I was now sitting at a red light. "One, I value my job and take it seriously. I know I like to have fun, but I won't recommend Maria for a chance to roll in the hay with her. Second, I won't be guilted into recommending you just because you're my partner and you think it's expected. I didn't even have time to think about it before you both were demanding I put in a word for you. At this point, Campbell, I'm out of the equation."

It was silent as we drove to the soup kitchen. Once there, Piper began her tongue-twister warm-ups. They had been endearing the last time I heard them, but now they were just grating my nerves.

How could she assume I would automatically give her the recommendation? Then again, helping her get this position would help me get her out of my head. I had no desire for commitment in my adult life and she had me questioning that. Removing her from my day-to-day life would surely remove any foolish notions that I needed her in my arms. So what if she was smart, sexy, great with Maggie, and one of the kindest people I had ever met? Well, kind to everyone except me.

We worked seamlessly and silently for the next hour as we did the story on the soup kitchen and an adorable group of Girl Scouts. One of them even had Down Syndrome, a little redhead with bright blue eyes. Piper and I were both drawn to her and she looked at Piper as if she were a movie star instead of a field reporter. Piper's patience and obvious care for the girl broke down the bitterness I felt.

She'd be a great mom one day. I stopped in my routine and pondered that thought. Why did I care if Piper Campbell would be a great mother one day? I wouldn't be there to see it. That thought made me feel a little sad. Perhaps I would see it on the periphery, as a co-worker. Piper and whatever man was lucky enough to get her, with their children at the company picnic. With her looks and my coloring, our children would be much better looking than any from some other guy.

Whoa. Where did that thought come from? My heart pounded furiously and my palms were sweaty. I could see what our children would look like in my mind. It was thrilling and terrifying at the same time. I needed to get her the anchor job so I could get her and these thoughts out of my mind.

"Alonso? Why did you stop?" Piper's annoyed voice snapped me out of my imaginings.

I was standing in the doorway with my equipment halfway taken apart, a camera hanging precariously in my hand. "Oh, sorry. I got lost in thought." I carefully placed the camera on the ground. "Piper, if you want a recommendation for anchor, I'll give it to you. I'll type it up tonight and send it to Tyrell and Andrews."

Now it was her turn to stop mid-stride. Pink tinged her cheeks for a moment before she jumped up and down. "Oh, Alonso, really? I could never thank you enough." Then she bound over to me and wrapped her arms around me.

The little Girl Scout made a kissing noise. "Is he your boyfriend?" Looking over, her little red eyebrows waggled up and down in our direction. She reminded me so much of Maggie. I bet she could get away with a lot of sass at home, just like Maggie did.

The tight squeeze released and Piper quickly stepped away. "Oh, no, Bailey. He's just a co-worker who agreed to help me with something."

Bailey stepped closer to Piper and motioned for her to come closer. Piper leaned over. With one cupped hand, Bailey attempted to whisper in Piper's ear, but everyone within twenty feet could hear her. "He should be your boyfriend. He's really cute."

The adult in charge of the girls finally stepped in. "Bailey, stop that. Leave Ms. Campbell alone." She held out her hand and Bailey obediently went to her side and took her hand. "I'm so sorry."

Back at the studio, I sought out Maria to tell her I would not be able to give her a recommendation. "I think you're great at what you do, but you know Piper is my partner and I told her I would write one for her. If you really need help with your package, I can see if I have time, but I really think you need to ask Rex or Dooley."

With a nod, Maria swallowed hard. "I totally understand. I'm disappointed, but that's okay. The right person will be chosen for the job."

"That's a great way of looking at it." I patted her hand and said goodbye, heading back to my edit bay to work on the soup kitchen package.

A few minutes before eleven, both Piper's stories were ready and loaded to run. If she wanted the anchor job, this was a good day for Mr. Andrews to be watching her work. Both stories were excellent and Piper seemed to be on fire in front of the camera. With my work done, I stayed at my desk and wrote the recommendation for her. With it emailed over to Mr. Andrews and Tyrell, I began to pack up just as the bridesmaid piece began to air.

Hm, that's not the package I made earlier. I swallowed hard and blinked several times as I stared at the screen.

Oh no. Not again.

Piper

The color drained from my face. What was going on?

The clip that was supposed to be my interview with the bridesmaid had been replaced with footage of me applying makeup in the women's room while doing vocal exercises.

"She sells seashells by the seashore. If Peter Piper picked a peck of pickled peppers, how many pickled peppers did Peter Piper pick?" Eyeliner went around my eye while my mouth made a wide O shape. I picked at my teeth and made a sucking sound. My eyelashes fluttered and I sighed heavily while looking at myself in the mirror before flipping the light switch and it got dark.

How? Why? Hot bile rose in my throat. That video had been shot before we left for the interview this afternoon. Had Alonso set up a camera to record me? In the women's dressing room no less? Why would he do such a thing?

Memories of college and my ruined story flashed in my mind as Karry laughed awkwardly.

"Oh, Piper, I don't think that's what you meant to show us. Let's come back to that in just a moment, hopefully with the right footage." Karry turned her body to the camera as she shook her head. "The Savannah Children's Choir held a concert this afternoon for residents of the Sunny View Retirement Home. Here's Maria with the story."

When Maria's package rolled, I ripped off the mic and fled the studio. Without thinking I headed straight to Alonso. He was in his edit bay, shutting things down.

"How could you do this to me again? And with a possible promotion looming? I thought we were friends! I thought you said you would help me!" Hot tears rolled down my cheeks. He did it again.

Eyes wide, Alonso shook his head. "I don't know what—"

"You didn't like the idea of me being promoted to anchor so you sabotaged my package on purpose. Again! You haven't changed one bit, Alonso Ortiz. I will be taking this to Mr. Andrews first thing tomorrow and getting another cameraman. And I don't care if you get fired in order for that to happen."

I grabbed the closest thing to me, a well-used coffee mug, and threw it on the ground so it shattered into dozens of ceramic pieces. I turned on my heel and ran to my desk, grabbed my things, and fled the building. Alonso called out after me, but I didn't stop.

In my car, I realized I was supposed to stay and present the correct story, but I didn't care at this point. My career might be over anyway, thanks to Alonso and his need to constantly be a prankster. I slammed my hand on the steering wheel, they could run the right piece without me. I drove back to my parent's house as I tried to keep the tears at bay.

Ringing erupted all around me as my car picked up the Bluetooth. Alonso Ortiz popped up on the screen. No, thank you. I tapped to reject the call. I didn't want or need his explanations. A hot tear slid down my cheek. I will not cry over this. Crying solves nothing. I will come out stronger and Alonso Ortiz will lose his head like one of the Red Queen's playing cards.

I slammed every door as I went through it. The car door, the front door, my bedroom door. Yes, I was acting like a teenager again, but I didn't care. This was devastating. Not just to my career, but also to my friendship with Alonso.

Over the past several months, my hatred for him made a complete turnaround. We were friends. We might have been more than friends if he wasn't so set on being a bachelor for life.

Oh. Maybe that's why he did it. Was I getting too close? I had wanted to kiss him and I'm pretty sure he wanted to kiss me as well, but maybe I was wrong. Did I read too much into his friendliness? If so I am doubly, no, triply mortified. But still, for him to humiliate me in that way...

More tears ran down my cheek when a knock came at my door. "Who is it?"

"Piper, honey, are you okay?" My mom's voice drifted softly through the door.

I swung the door open, then flopped onto my bed like I would have done as a teenager ten years prior. "No. I'm not. Did you see it? How bad was it?" I stared at the ceiling, preparing myself for her to tell me it was the worst thing she'd ever seen on television.

A sigh escaped her lips. "It wasn't that bad. Embarrassing, sure, but really it just showed you're human like the rest of us. It's not career ending, which is how you're acting."

I propped myself up on my elbows. "Mom, I sucked my teeth on television. I don't even know how that was recorded. And I really don't know how he could do this."

"Who?"

I flopped back again, angry tears burning my skin as they rolled back into my hair. "Alonso Ortiz."

"Wait? The same guy who did this to you in college? The one who's been hanging on you like a lost puppy for weeks?" Mom sat down next to me and smoothed my hair. "I see how he looks at you, Piper. I don't see how he could do this."

"He's the one who creates my packages. He's the one who knows my warm-up routine. And he's the one who admits to being a prankster." I slammed my fist on the soft mattress, but it only bounced. I wanted to break things.

Silently, my mother continued to smooth my hair. My mind raced with thinking if it would have been anyone else. I'm friends with everyone, or at least friendly. I had never seriously offended any of my coworkers that I knew of. And given my history with Alonso, I didn't see how it could be anyone else.

"I think I just need to be alone with my thoughts for a while, Mom. Thank you." I squeezed her arm in lieu of a hug.

"Of course, honey. I'm here if you need me." After kissing my head, she stood and exited, closing the door softly behind her.

Once again, my phone began to ring and I pulled it from my pocket. Alonso again. I sent it to voicemail and turned my phone off. I didn't need to deal with him or anyone else for a while. Without even changing, I pulled my quilt up over myself and fell asleep.

My dreams were full of deception. My mother laughing at me and pointing. Henry flaunting an unknown woman with a round belly, telling me she was better than me. Sam and Karry tripping me on set and snickering about it. Then Alonso, exposing me for the world to see, devil horns growing through his hair and his eyes glowing red.

The next morning was my regular yoga day, but I couldn't face a room full of people, or chance running into Alonso. I opted to go for a run instead. The rhythm of my feet on the pavement as my angry and determined playlist came through my earbuds pushed me forward. Again, I tried to search my brain for why Alonso would do this to me again after how well we were getting along.

My phone rang, jarring my thoughts and bringing me to a halt. It was Tyrell. I answered it, ready to spout off every reason why Alonso should be fired.

"Tyrell, if you defend him I will hang up faster than Ashley can spend money." I was rude and I knew it. I would have to apologize.

A huff came through my earbuds. "Piper, I'm not defending anybody or anything. I know you're upset. Can we chat?"

I sat on a nearby bench and bounced my legs. "Yeah, we can chat. I'm sorry. I didn't mean to be so rude. Did I lose any hope of getting that anchor position?"

"Let me lay it down. The video that aired was obviously not your doing. We're looking into that. But it wasn't your fault at all. What is your fault, however, is your reaction. You could have handled that with dignity, and you didn't. You ran. If you've lost your chance at being anchor, it's because of that. Not what aired."

Tears formed in my eyes and mixed with the sweat, causing my eyes to close. I held my head in my hands. "I really mucked things up."

"Mr. Andrews doesn't know you stormed off, but he will if Karry or anyone else who was in that room talks to him before you do." Tyrell hesitated. "He didn't do it."

I knew who he was talking about and I ignored the comment. "I'll come in early and talk to Andrews. In fact, I will email him as soon as I get home and then come in early and talk to him. I want this job."

"Why do you want it so bad?"

"At this point, if nothing else, to get away from Alonso Ortiz." I stood, my eyes still closed. I had to use my shirt to wipe my eyes and try to see again.

A sound came from Tyrell, but then he stopped before finally speaking. "I'll see you later, Piper. It will all work out."

"Thanks." I hung up and wiped my eyes again before heading home.

I checked my voicemail on my way back. I had three messages from Alonso. Curiosity got the better of me and I listened to the first one.

"Piper, I saw the whole thing. I swear it wasn't me. I'm not the same person I was back at SCAD. I would never want to hurt you like this. Please call me."

Not the same person? I scoffed as I hit the second message.

"Piper." His voice was firmer. "Listen, I know you're upset, but you're upset at the wrong person. The right package aired just fine. Why did you leave like that? Everyone is talking and it's not good. You need to call me."

I was going to lose the promotion and I hadn't even had the chance to apply yet. I groaned as I reluctantly pressed play on the third voicemail.

This time his voice was clipped and hard. "Piper, seriously. I'm sorry this happened, but it was not my doing. I can't believe after all this you would actually think I could do this to you. I thought... You know what. Never mind. Clearly, I was wrong."

My chest tightened to hear his voice so full of anger. But then, didn't I have the right to be angry? He had played me for the fool yet again, and I had every right to be beyond outraged. I had started off working with him checking every package before it aired, but I had slacked off recently because I thought he was as sincere as he claimed. Oh, how I was wrong.

Showered and dressed in my plum power suit, I headed to the studio and straight for Mr. Andrews' office. His secretary, a sweet motherly type named Barbara led me into his office.

After being invited to sit across from him, I launched into my tirade. "Mr. Andrews, last night's debacle was orchestrated and executed by one person—Alonso Ortiz. If you're not aware, he pulled this exact stunt on me while at school. I refuse to work with him further. I could also press charges against him and the station for spying in the women's room." My heart pounded, my toes curled, and I fought the urge to bang my fist on his cherrywood table.

With one eyebrow raised, Mr. Andrews stared at me a moment before licking his lips. "Ms. Campbell, if you're done with that, I will tell you that Alonso emailed me late last night, well before I knew what was going on. He has an alibi and has assured me he is not the culprit of last night's snafu. Now, we're looking into it. However, I understand you not only left the newsroom but left the building altogether. Would you care to explain that?"

The color drained from my face and my throat felt suddenly arid. "I'm very sorry, sir. I was so embarrassed, I didn't know what to do. In my panic, I simply fled. It will never happen again."

He leaned forward in his sleek office chair. "See that it doesn't, Ms. Campbell. I'll let you know when we find out who messed with the video last night. Until then, have a nice day."

I was dismissed. With a nod, I left and made my way down to my desk. I needed to find Alonso. I didn't see how it wasn't him who sabotaged me, but if he had an alibi, I wanted to hear it.

Alonso

Maggie's irritated voice berated me. "How could you let this happen, Ali? Again!"

I pinched the bridge of my nose and sighed. "I didn't. I loaded her complete, correct package into the system and then left my computer and my phone to talk to Tyrell until the cameras rolled."

"You have to fix it." It was a demand, not a suggestion. "Piper is the best thing to ever happen to you. Besides me, of course."

"You will always be my number one, Mags." I rested my head on the back of my chair and closed my eyes. Exhaustion loomed since I hadn't slept the night before, trying to figure out what had happened. "I wish I knew what happened, I just know I didn't have anything to do with that footage—from a room I've never been in—being on-air last night."

A voice from outside my office snapped me to attention. "Then you better figure it out, big shot."

Piper. My eyes flew open to see her in her dark purple suit, hands on hips, head cocked to one side with a scowl on her face. She towered over me, and I told Maggie I would have to call her back before abruptly hanging up on her.

"I tried to call and explain."

She rolled her eyes. "I know. I wasn't in a headspace to listen. All I know is I said I wanted to be anchor to you and only you, and the next thing I know, I'm making weird noises and sucking my teeth for the world to see." She stepped forward and pointed a finger at me. "I will end up as a meme or on one of those embarrassing news YouTube videos!"

How she was still blaming me was beyond my comprehension. My own ire rose. "After all these weeks and months working together, do you really think I would do this to you again? Have you not seen that I have changed from that stupid college kid? I would never jeopardize your career, or mine for that matter, with an on-air prank like that.

"I loaded your package, labeled 'P. Campbell Bridesmaid Package,' and then left all electronics on my desk to see Tyrell. He can tell you there's no way I did this. And the package I uploaded was still there, everything just as it was supposed to be." I stood and looked Piper in the eyes, internally begging her to believe me.

"So what happened?" A look of defeat came over her and her eyes fell to the floor. I could see goosebumps rise on her arms.

I threw my hands up. "I have no idea. When I saw what was running, I immediately checked and what I loaded was there, but so was another file. 'P. Campbell package, use this one.' That was what aired. And it was loaded from one of the daytime intern's computers. He had left about five hours earlier."

Piper bit her lip, it was what she did when she was think-ing. I loved to watch her, wondering what her lip tasted like, longing to be the one biting it. But not now. Hurt, disbelief, and fury filled me. I had spent months going out of my way to prove myself to her, to apologize for what had happened in the past. And she still thought the worst of me.

Well, if Piper Campbell wanted to be rid of me, I could make that happen. "Did you talk to Andrews yet?"

The hair that had fallen forward was tucked back. "Yes. I just came from there. He said they were looking into it." Her voice was low, defeated.

"Did you tell him you wanted a new cameraman?" I stared at her, making her fidget and refuse to meet my gaze.

"N-no."

"Well then, I'm going to go demand a switch. I won't work with someone who can't trust me." I pushed past her, not caring that I shoved her shoulder into the doorjamb. "See you later, Campbell."

But I didn't go straight to the bigwig's office. I went to the men's room and sat in Sam's make-up chair for a minute, my head in my hands. After several deep breaths, I looked at myself in the mirror. The room was dark, as the overhead light didn't provide much in the way of illumination. I leaned forward and flipped on the mirror lights. and studied the room behind me.

The ladies' room was beside the men's and I could only assume it matched. Bathrooms and sinks behind, a dressing and make-up area in front. The dressing area was partitioned off with a heavy curtain for privacy. Where had that video been shot from? It was a little grainy, so I imagined it was from a cellphone.

I positioned myself where I thought Piper had been standing. The video showed her from the side and her mirror image reflected back. I needed help.

I grabbed Rex. "You got to come to the bathroom with me."

"Whoa, AO, I didn't think we were that close."

"I'm trying to figure out what happened last night. Just come with me." I pulled him into the men's room and sat him in Sam's chair. "Now, lean forward and look at yourself."

Rex turned and looked at me. "You've got it bad, AO."

"What?"

"You've fallen for her, man. Everyone can see it. Maria even said something to me about it yesterday." Rex looked at me through the mirror and wagged his eyebrows while puckering his lips.

Maria. I told Rex to stand still while I hid behind the dressing room curtain. I left a crack between the wall and the fabric and aimed my phone. Sure enough, it gave me the right angle for the video that aired. I videoed a few seconds' worth of Rex playing it up before coming back out.

Rex turned and looked at me. "I thought you were a confirmed bachelor, AO."

The thought that I was falling for Piper came to mind, but then the hurt that she didn't trust me outweighed those feelings. "I'm reconfirming, Rex. Relationships are too much work and bring nothing but trouble."

My friend clapped his hand on my shoulder. "Anything worth having is hard work, man. And the trouble is all worth it in the end when you have someone who gets you and knows why and how you tick. It's a risk, sure, but the reward... Man, the reward is so much more." With that, he exited.

Back at my desk, I pulled up the video of Piper in the dressing room. I froze the frame and zoomed in. Sure enough, a high-heeled shoe was poking out from under the curtain. It was a dark color, which could be any of the women who worked at Action News. The glint of camera phone glass flashed momentarily on the video and I froze it again. The face was too grainy to make out, but sure enough, pale skin was visible.

A text alert came through my phone and I glanced down. Maggie's name popped up.

MAGGIE: DID YOU FIX IT?

ALONSO: NOT YET.

MAGGIE: YOU AND PIPER BELONG TOGETHER. YOU HAVE TO FIX THIS.

My little sister was playing matchmaker now? I knew she was too attached to Piper.

ALONSO: SHE DOESN'T TRUST ME. YOU CAN'T HAVE A RELATIONSHIP WITHOUT TRUST. BESIDES, I DON'T NEED A WOMAN.

MAGGIE: DON'T BE STUPID, ALI. SHE MADE A MISTAKE JUST LIKE YOU DID. AND YOU DO NEED A WOMAN. I'VE SEEN YOUR PLACE. AND PIPER, SHE'S LIKE A PERFECT MATCH.

ALONSO: I'LL CALL YOU LATER, MAGS. TE AMO.

MAGGIE: ADIOS.

Before I could put the phone back in my pocket, I noticed a missed text from Piper. I debated erasing it before reading it, but I couldn't. I had to know what she said.

PIPER: I CANNOT SAY HOW SORRY I AM FOR NOT BELIEVING YOU. I SHOULD HAVE CALMLY COME TO YOU BEFORE MAKING ANY ACCUSATIONS. IF YOU DON'T WANT TO WORK WITH ME ANYMORE, I COMPLETELY UNDERSTAND. BUT TRULY YOU ARE THE BEST CAMERAMAN AND PRODUCER I'VE EVER HAD. YOU MAKE ME LAUGH AND THAT'S SOMETHING I'VE MISSED OUT ON IN THE PAST FEW YEARS. NO MATTER WHAT HAPPENS, PLEASE KNOW THAT I'M SORRY FOR MY BEHAVIOR.

PIPER: IT'S BEEN TWENTY MINUTES. YOU MUST BE RE-
ALLY UPSET WITH ME. I ASSUME YOU'RE WITH ANDREWS.
I'LL TALK TO TYRELL ABOUT GETTING US SWITCHED. I
THINK I MIGHT APPLY AT CHANNEL SEVEN.

What? Apply at Channel Seven and leave Action News? The idea of not just losing Piper as my partner, but losing her from my life was terrifying.

I fired a text back to her.

ALONSO: STOP! DO NOT DO ANYTHING AND FOR THE
LOVE OF GOD DON'T APPLY AT CHANNEL SEVEN. YOU'D
HATE IT. I THINK I FIGURED IT OUT. COME TO MY EDIT BAY
NOW.

PIPER: OK?

A minute later she tentatively stepped through the doorway. "What's going on? You don't hate me?"

I raised an eyebrow in her direction. "Hate you? Can't I be mad at you without resorting to hate? Do you hate me?"

She shook her head. "No."

"Being upset doesn't mean hate, Piper. It just means you're upset. And believe me, I've been plenty upset that you didn't trust me, but I understand. And I think I figured it out." I motioned to the seat beside me and she took it, her arms wrapped around her middle.

I cued up the video and showed her the high-heeled shoe and the glint of the camera. She held a hand up to her mouth as she watched.

"Who was in there with you?"

Shaking her head, she looked at me. "I had no idea anyone was in there. I was in front of that mirror for a good ten minutes, they must have hidden the entire time."

I laid my hand on her arm and felt the goosebumps pop back up. "The question is, was this intentionally planned, or was this spur of the moment? Regardless it's bad, but that's something I think you need to know."

She looked from me to the computer screen. "Have you shown anyone else this?"

"No."

Piper's mouth opened, but then she shut it again. I could tell she was changing gears as she bit her lip and moved her hair. "First off, Alonso. Please, please forgive me. I had no right to accuse you. You've been nothing but professional here at work, and a friend both at work and outside. I was wrong."

"Forgiven. As long as you've finally forgiven me for all those years ago."

She nodded shyly. "Second. I think this might have been Maria. She was wearing dark shoes. And she had already announced her intentions to apply for the anchor job."

"She was not happy when I told her I wouldn't be giving her a recommendation. I think you're right." I leaned in closer to Piper. "I think we need to tell the powers that be. They can follow up on that."

"Alonso?"

"Piper?"

"Can we—can we try again?"

I brought my face within inches of hers. "Only if I can do this first." My hands went to her cheeks and I lowered my lips to hers, kissing her softly. She tasted like cinnamon and coffee and the combination gave me a rush of heat and caffeine. I brought her closer and tasted more of her as she groaned under the weight of my lips.

Breaking apart, Piper looked at me with heavily lidded eyes. "I um, I might need to try that again. Just to make sure we're on the same page."

"With pleasure." I moved my chair behind the wall so we were hidden, and brought Piper onto my lap. She leaned into me and wrapped her arms around my neck as I claimed her lips, working my way down her neck and back up the other side.

"I thought you were proud to be the last man standing?" She giggled.

"Now I'm proud to be the man who gets you, Piper Campbell. Now, no more talking."

With that, I pressed my lips to hers once again and forgot all about being a bachelor, ready to take on the role of claimed man.

Epilogue

We ride in silence toward Tybee Island, our hands entwined. I steal a glance at Piper as we sit at a red light and give her hand a squeeze. She squeezed back. From the backseat, Maggie sighs. I hadn't told her what was going on, just that I wanted her to take some pictures of us on the beach.

A picnic lunch sat in the trunk and a velvet box sat uncomfortably in my pocket. I'm shocked Piper can't tell my palms are sweating. Or maybe she can and she's just being nice. I'm terrified—too terrified to say anything. I'm glad we're at the "comfortable silence" stage of our relationship.

We arrive on the island and trek out to the beach. The picnic basket is heavy and bulky in my arms, but it's not weighing me down as much as the box in my pocket. I've mucked up too much in Piper's life already to risk anything happening to ruin today.

Maggie carries the blanket behind Piper, who has a pitcher of lemonade and a box of tres leches in her hands. She's wearing a pair of peach colored shorts and a royal blue top, her hair is falling on her shoulders in soft waves. She looks like perfection. Who am I kidding? She is perfection.

"Does this look good?" Piper points to an open spot on the beach. It's October, but there are still people dotting the sand and soaking up the warm rays of Indian Summer. The spot has a great backdrop of the Tybee Lighthouse, which is exactly what I wanted.

"Looks good." I shrug. Acting casual isn't exactly my strong suit, but I try.

Maggie spreads the blanket and plops down. I sit, the slim box is hard and heavy against my thigh and I shift it so Piper won't notice. We both kick off our shoes.

Piper sits and primly removes her sandals. "Grab the plates, Mags, and I'll start serving up lunch. I'm starved."

I know she'll hate me if she ends up with lettuce between her teeth for pictures, so I stop her before she can grab the basket. "Wait!" I clear my throat. "Wait, I wanted you to see something first." I stand back up.

Piper eyes me suspiciously. "See what?" We know Tybee well enough that there's not much unique to see.

I want to roll my eyes but I don't. "Mags, will you take a picture of us in front of the lighthouse?"

Maggie lights up. "Sure." She loves to take pictures.

I hand her my phone and set it to video. "It's doing a video, just let it record, okay?"

"Okay."

When Piper stands, we back up so the lighthouse is at our backs. We're facing the beach and I feel like my heart is going to literally burst from my chest like it might in a horror movie.

"Ali, whatever is in your pocket is poking out." Maggie makes a face.

Piper furrows her brow and looks to the square shape in my back pocket. "If Maggie has your phone, what's that?"

It's now or never. I gulp.

I get down on one knee in the sand and take the box from my pocket. A shell stabs me in the shin, but I power through. I will not ruin this moment. "Piper, I know we've had our share of cuts and edits over the years, but I want to make this a permanent production. I love you so much. Marry me?"

The box is open and I'm staring up at the woman I love. Piper puts a hand up to her mouth as shock registers on her face. "Oh my gosh, Alonso, yes! A million times, yes."

I knew she would agree, yet I'm still blown away. I know the smile on my face stretches from ear to ear and my heart is thudding harder than a production of Stomp. She actually accepted my proposal. I don't think I'll ever come down from this high.

With a shaky hand, I pull the antique diamond and emerald ring from the box and slide it onto her left hand. It had been my abuela's ring and know she's smiling on us from heaven as I give it to Piper.

Piper crashes onto me to hug me and we topple over into the sand. But I don't care because Piper Campbell said yes.

There's sand embedded in my hair now, and I'm pretty sure my shin is bleeding—but this is the happiest I have ever been in my life.

Recording forgotten, Maggie jumps up and down. "We are getting married!"

"You have to be my maid of honor, Maggie." Piper adds Maggie into our hug. This is one of the reasons I love her so much.

"I love you, Piper." I kiss her to the point that Maggie disengages from the hug and tells us we're gross.

"I love you, too." She nuzzles in close to me. "I never would have thought it at the beginning of the year, but Alonso, you make me the happiest woman alive."

Who would have thought that I, Alonso Ortiz, the last man standing, would find himself blissfully engaged to a woman like Piper Campbell?

Amaya & Orlando

Workplace Romance

Amaya

THE GROOMSMAN NEXT TO me breathed heavily on my neck. *Ugh, gross*. Regardless, the show must go on. As a bridesmaid-for-hire, dealing with overly enthusiastic groomsmen came with the territory. I noticed the indention left by his removed wedding ring. *A liar and a cheat*. He reminded me of Kyle. Wouldn't you know it, this guy's name was Coyle. They were like a matching pair. *Creepy Coyle*. A chill ran over me and my stomach turned.

I moved a half-step away from him as I cued the adorable flower girl and ring bearer down the aisle. Their father was waiting at the end for them, making it an easier task. Somewhat. Halfway down the little girl declared she was out of flowers and began to pick the flowers back up. Thankfully it was quickly remedied with a hand tug from her brother.

The bridesmaids were in order and had their instructions. I checked that each bouquet was facing the right direction and all bra straps were hidden. I took my place, Creepy Coyle next to me. It took real effort to try not to touch him, but he used his sweaty, meaty hand to pat my own. With a final look of reassurance to the bride, I walked down the aisle to take my official place as bridesmaid.

After more than one hundred weddings, there wasn't anything I hadn't seen. The phrase "always a bridesmaid" literally described my life. Especially since nobody was beating down my door to put a ring on it. In fact, I had named my business Always a Bridesmaid. It was on my cards.

I donned the dress of a bride's closest friend and held their hand through the entire process of wedding planning from dress shopping to bachelorette parties to getting the bride and groom off on their honeymoon in time. I knew when the flower girl was going to pee. I knew if a pregnant bride was going to vomit. I knew if the groom was hungover. Over five years in this career, I had experienced just about every kind of wedding there was. I was also pretty proud that more than two-thirds of the couples were still married.

When everything had gone off without a hitch and the couple was pronounced husband and wife, I retreated up the aisle and made sure the guests were filing out to the reception area while photos were taken. Photos. Again. My cheek muscles could win a bodybuilding contest. They were on point.

Forgotten programs sat on chairs and I picked them up as I looked around. The wedding location was picturesque. The Promenade was a favorite for Savannah weddings with its tall white columns and gorgeous hallways perfect for a dress to be on full display. I also loved the gardens with all the colors and the butterflies flitting to and fro. It was run by a family who had owned the estate for over a hundred years.

This wedding held the ceremony in a room referred to as the chapel as it closely resembled a church. It helped many a grandmother feel better about a wedding not being in an actual church. Stained glass windows adorned one side and the chairs had a certain pew-like quality.

If I ever got married, I wanted it to be at The Promenade—outside in the garden atrium. It was the perfect location for photos. There were indoor and outdoor ceremony options, and the staff was wonderfully accommodating. It was synonymous with the word *Savannah*. There wasn't a corner of the place that wasn't picture-perfect.

I should get a discount for all the business I've brought them over the years. I was on a first name basis with the owner at this point. However, Cordelia Daniels was retiring and her son would be taking over. While I knew Cordelia, I had not met her son yet. Would he make changes? Major changes? I hoped not. Nearly fifty percent of my weddings were held at The Promenade and I liked things the way they were.

While family photos were taken, I wandered the hall a little to check on cocktail hour. The venue staff was always meticulous and quiet, and I watched as a few servers strode silently from kitchen to cocktail area with silver trays in hand. When I realized they were not in their usual black shirts and blazers, I began to panic a little. They had always worn the black uniforms, looking professional and blending into the background.

My cheeks warmed as I searched for Cordelia, but I couldn't wander too far as I had to oversee the photos. *What's done is done. I can't make them all change clothes.* With a sigh, I closed my eyes and ran a mental checklist of what was next in my head. Pictures. Make-up touch-up. Cueing the DJ and the bridal party entrance. Make it all seamless.

I ran the magenta chiffon of my skirt through my fingers, enjoying the texture. There were times, though, I would love to not be in a bridesmaid's dress. Next weekend was one of those weekends. It was wide open and I planned to spend a day on the beach at Tybee Island. Quiet and low-key. Maybe I would call my sister, Linaya, and see if she wanted to join.

Footsteps snapped me to attention as expensive shoes sounded on the tiled floor. I looked up in the direction of the sound and saw a man emerging from the back of the house. He wore a dark gray suit with a blue tie that was pulled loose. His wingtip shoes went quiet when he saw the wedding party ahead of him.

Our eyes met for the briefest of moments. His were a dark chocolate brown surrounded by full, thick lashes. He smiled at me for a second before someone called my name.

"Amaya, we're ready for you." The photographer, a thin fellow named Jacques, called to me. We had worked together on close to two dozen weddings and we were on friendly terms.

I hurried over as silently as I could so my heels didn't clang on the floor. I joined in where Jacques told me to stand and smiled brightly. These photos would be looked at by the couple for the rest of their lives. A few brides had stayed in touch, thinking me a true friend after the ordeal of wedding planning, but most did not. I wasn't friends with any of them. Not that I didn't like them, but it was purely a working relationship for me.

This bride wouldn't think we were friends. She had a small circle while her groom had a larger one. She had needed one more bridesmaid and a wedding planner. I was able to fulfill both roles. And the bride had paid well for both.

Creepy Coyle came up to me for more pictures and was all too eager to put his arm around my waist. He definitely reminded me of my ex-boyfriend Kyle. Handsy, rude, and about as misogynistic as they come.

"So how do you know Suzette?" Again, he was breathing on me. We were close to the same height, and his breath was moist on my ear. I shuddered.

"Arm down groomsman at the top." Jacques was a professional and he looked out for me if there were sleazy guys.

As Creepy Coyle put his arm back down, I forced a pleasant expression. "Suzette is an old friend. I'm happy to be part of her day." It was a lie I was used to telling. "How do you know the groom?"

"Hodge was a high school friend of mine. We were roommates for a while, too."

When we were done, Creepy Coyle followed me down the steps. He had been following me like a puppy since we'd met at the rehearsal dinner. "So what are you doing after this? Think you might want to grab a drink?"

Some guys just didn't get the hint. He tried to catch my arm, but I yanked it away before he could touch me. I had tried to avoid him the night before without much success. I walked over to the flower girl and fluffed her hair, hoping having a child nearby would get him to vacate my personal space.

I never wanted to act like a snob, but sometimes it was necessary. "I'm sorry, but I have plans."

A snort came from the guy. "Plans? How about you make plans with me? I have a hotel room only a block away."

Getting propositioned was an ugly side of the job. Groomsmen or guests would end up drinking too much and hit on anything unattached. And since I was working, I didn't have a date. And without a date, I appeared to be fair game to lots of inebriated men.

An unfamiliar voice spoke up behind me. "Hello, sweetheart. Are you done with pictures?"

I whipped my head around to see the handsome suit with the gorgeous eyes standing there. Was he coming to my aid? Or was he talking to the groomsman? Obviously not. He raised his eyebrows to me and I instinctively stepped closer to him.

"Oh, sorry, man. I didn't realize she had a date." Coyle shook his head and walked off into the crowd.

Was I supposed to be thankful or insulted by his intervention? I shook my head to clear it. "Thank you. I appreciate your help, but I could have handled that. I've dealt with his type before."

His laugh was deep and velvety. "I'm sure you have. But at least now he won't bother you anymore tonight."

"Why? Are you going to stay by my side all night? Surely you have a date?" I didn't see anyone lingering by looking for him. But then, he had come from the back of the house. "Are you even a guest of this wedding?"

With a sigh, he put his hands up. "Caught red-handed. I'm not. I work here."

My eyebrows shot up. "You're Cordelia's son." The one who would be taking over. I swallowed hard and grabbed a bouquet that was thrust at me as the mother of the flower girl picked her up and ran her to the bathroom.

The commotion didn't faze him. "You know Cordelia?"

"I've known her a few years. I've been in several weddings here before." I glanced over to the newlyweds who were still taking photos.

A sly smile crept across his face, but his eyes remained cool. "So you've heard of me?"

If this guy was taking over as the head of The Promenade, I needed to tread lightly and be on my best behavior. "I only know that you're taking over here when she retires soon. Oh, remind me to talk to you later about the hideous green polos the staff are wearing."

He chuckled, at what I wasn't sure. "Allow me to tie up a few loose ends and I will join you for a dance if you're willing. I can check in on you from time to time in the next few hours."

For a moment I wondered if he was a creep like the groomsman, but something in my intuition said he was a good guy. I gave a subtle nod. "I would appreciate it. I love to dance."

"I'll be back." He moved toward me for the briefest of moments before deciding against it and winked at me instead. He turned and disappeared down a hidden hallway. This time his shoes were quieter.

I turned back to the bridal party and Jaques. As they finished up, I went to the DJ and told him to start calling the guests into the ballroom. The light background music changed to a heavy beat, beckoning to the people gathered.

The bridal party was called in by pairs, so yet again I was next to Creepy Coyle.

"Where's your date?" He looked around.

I suppressed an eye-roll. "Don't worry, he's here." We were called and I ran in ahead of him. Now I just needed to avoid him for the rest of the night.

After the couple was introduced and had their first dance, dinner was served. I finally had a moment to sit down and breathe while I inhaled the meal I had helped Suzette pick. My curls has fallen, my make-up had melted off, and my stomach protested at how fast I was eating. But this was part of the job description and I loved every moment of it.

The room was immaculate with the bride's chosen colors of mauve and dusty lavender everywhere. The slate-gray walls were neutral and kept the huge room feeling more intimate. Cream-colored columns were decorated with balloons and fresh flowers.

My eyes kept going to the door looking for the young Mr. Daniels. *This is nuts, why I am looking for him?*

When he slipped back into the ballroom while dinner was wrapping up, a giddy feeling bubbled up in my stomach. He strode through the room, his eyes scanning the crowd. While I had the advantage, I studied the man. He was taller than me, but not overly tall. His dark hair was cut close but had a hint of wave to it. He filled out the suit nicely, it was perfectly tailored.

Once his eyes found me, limp hair and all, a huge grin broke out on his face. I couldn't help but return the smile as I felt the heat creep up my cheeks. He approached and held out his hand right as a slow song began to play through the DJ's speakers.

I bit my lip as he led me onto the dance floor where two other couples swayed cheek to cheek. In that moment, I wanted nothing more than to be held in this man's arms.

Orlando

THE PHOTOGRAPHER HAD CALLED her Amaya. It was the perfect name for the beauty with long, almost raven-colored hair. When I had spotted her loose curls across the room, I had to stop myself from skipping over to her. Skipping. I'm over thirty. My days of skipping were long over.

But the days of dancing were still going strong. I had loathed the dance lessons that came with the equally unliked charm school lessons when I was twelve. But both now came in handy for business functions. And pleasurable ones as well, it seemed.

When she took my outstretched hand, a slow jazz number began. Perfect timing. It was almost as if the DJ had been tipped to play it. I would never tell. Two other couples came to the floor, both older, and they danced close together. *I would love to still be in love when I'm that old.*

Unable to help myself, I pulled Amaya close, but tried not to make it too intimate as I began a basic box step. She followed my lead effortlessly. I should tell her I've seen her here before in a few different bridesmaid's dresses, but that could wait. She must be quite popular with her friends. The silence between us was perfection, there was no need to talk, the conversation in our steps spoke volumes.

She held her body close to mine, a sign that she was comfortable and didn't think I was too adverse. I cracked a simple joke that made her laugh and her eyes twinkled with flecks of gold. When the music reached a crescendo, I twirled her around and Amaya neither fumbled or mis-stepped. There was a certain grace about her.

The music ended and the DJ announced it was time to cut the cake. Both bride and groom were ushered forward, and Amaya broke free from my arms without a glance back as she hurried to the cake table. What was going on with her? Sure she was a bridesmaid, but did she have to run the show as well?

I fell back from sight and settled against a wall as people gathered around and began to cheer. Amaya grabbed two small towels and waited with them. The groom pushed a small amount of icing on the bride's nose while she flung an entire piece onto him. Once the laughter died down, the towels were handed to the couple and Amaya helped them both clean up.

When I came to her aid while the sweaty groomsman had been hitting on her, I hadn't thought beyond getting the creep away from her. But now my thoughts were definitely going beyond the moment, the evening, and further still. How had two minutes of conversation and a dance turned me into a fourteen-year-old with a massive crush all over again?

She returned to my side, a wary smile on her lips. "Sorry, I'm a working bridesmaid."

"A what?" What was a working bridesmaid? I tilted my head.

A nervous giggle escaped her lips. "I mean, I'm helping them with some coordinating and things. I'm supposed to make sure Suzette stays clean from icing, I'm helping her get changed for the honeymoon later. Things like that."

She spoke with her hands and was quite animated. It gave her an air of innocence, like a child who was too excited to speak. But as I looked her over, her body was definitely all woman.

Her explanation made sense. She was assigned tasks to help out. "Oh, I gotcha."

I must have looked perplexed because she laughed. "I'm a wedding coordinator and hired bridesmaid. So this is literally my job."

A professional bridesmaid? I had never heard of such a thing. "How long have you been doing this?"

In a surprise move, she pulled a bright pink card from her cleavage and thrust it at me. "Five years. Amaya Journet, Always a Bridesmaid." She stuck her hand out and I shook it. She had a strong grip.

"I'm Orlando. Amaya is a lovely name." Unable to help myself, I picked up a loose curl from her shoulder and ran my fingers along the silky strands.

She shrugged. "Thanks. My mom gave it to me. I was named after both my parents – Emil and Anya. They kind of smushed their names together."

Another slower song began and the bridal couple took to the floor. Amaya looked over to them and bit her lip. I wanted to bite it myself. "Another dance?"

She hesitated for the briefest moment before grabbing my hand. "I'll give you half a song, then you have to help me set up for the bouquet toss."

It was kind of sexy that she was suddenly bossing me around like that. I could feel the blood thrumming in my veins.

When the dance ended, the bride raised an eyebrow to Amaya and she excused herself to perform her professional duties. I told the DJ it was time for the toss as Amaya grabbed a small bouquet from behind a table. Ladies gathered around, ready to pounce.

After that, it was time for the couple to depart. My eyes stayed on Amaya as she picked up the bride's train and trailed behind her. They disappeared behind one of the many doors along the hall.

The sweaty groomsman approached, drink in hand, and raised a finger. "Hey, uh, sorry about that before. I didn't realize she was attached. Cute thing like her, I'm not surprised." The man had a receding hairline, bushy mustache, and the obvious lines from where a wedding band had been up until recently.

Wedding guest or no, I rolled my eyes. "What do you do?"

"I'm in sales," he said. "You?"

Of course he was. "I own five businesses, have houses in Savannah and Atlanta, and made ten grand while we've been standing here."

Without another word he walked away, his face pale and drawn.

A few minutes later, the bride reappeared now dressed in a simple, white, knee-length dress. She joined the groom so they could get ready to leave for their honeymoon. Looking past her, I watched Amaya exit the room with a giant dress bag that she hung up before running – in heels no less – to the front where she began passing out containers of rose petals to the guests.

She was engrossed in her task, and I thought I should go back to my office, but I couldn't tear myself away from watching her. She was absolutely mesmerizing. I had noticed her a few weeks back when she had been a bridesmaid in a different wedding, but actually talking to her...it was like she possessed a certain kind of magic.

Of course, it was also the first time I had been single in several years. For three years I had thought I was in a committed relationship with Tori. It was too bad Tori didn't feel that way in return. She had decided to move to Portland after I said I wanted to come back home to Savannah. I ended up returning alone.

"Watching how the business works, son?" My mother came up behind me and laid a hand on my arm.

I looked in her direction and nodded. "Yes, I guess so. I was actually dancing with one of the bridesmaids. She mistook me for a guest."

"Ah, Amaya, right?" She winked as I felt heat creep up my neck. "She's a wonderful girl. Quite the entrepreneur. And she's here at least once a month, usually more."

My mother was the type who loved love, and she wanted me to find it before she became old. She was petite with silvery-blonde hair that only made her look more regal than anything else. She dressed impeccably, had gumption galore, and was Savannah royalty.

"Did you need something, Mom?"

She shook her head. "No. I like to watch happy couples ride off into the sunset. The wedding might be over, but their lives are just starting."

While her own marriage to my father hadn't worked out, my mother was a perpetual romantic. She always believed in the power of love and romance. I was something more of a skeptic.

Amaya came towards us with lightning speed. "Bride forgot her bag. I'm meeting them in the back." She sped past, again never wavering on the three-inch heels.

"She works hard." I watched her backside sway side to side as she disappeared again. It was a decidedly nice backside.

Another wink came from my mother. "So do you, Orlando. And you're both in the wedding business."

"Mother." I shot her a look that I hoped said to not meddle, but I laughed instead. Cordelia Daniels was a romantic through and through. And besides, I was not necessarily in the wedding business. I was taking over, yes, but I had it in my mind to sell the place.

"I did not say a thing. Just that you have similarities." She patted my arm, laughed a little, and took off down the hall with a wave.

Servers began piling up used plates and clearing things as the party began to wrap up. A few guests returned to the dance floor. The party had booked the ballroom for another hour. Figuring my chance to see Amaya again was over, I turned and nearly smacked right into her.

"You waited? Did I see Cordelia out here?" She looked around.

"She came out to check on things." I waved my arm around in a sweeping motion.

"She's so sweet. And so wise. You're lucky to have a mother like her." She looked at the dainty watch on her wrist. It was a real watch, not a smart one. "Sorry, I'm on the clock for thirty more minutes. I have to get a few things done. Thank you for dancing with me. I'm sure I'll see you again some time."

"Of course. See you around." What else could I say? I barely knew the girl, even if I had a mind to get to know her better.

She once again sped off, not giving me time to even think about getting her number. Thankfully I was fairly certain it would be in my mother's office. Amaya was like a hummingbird always flitting around. *Did she ever stop to rest?* I would have to find out.

Amaya

The next weekend I loaded up my little compact car, picked up my sister, and headed to Tybee Island for a day of relaxation. I didn't get to see Linaya as often as I liked since she was a student at the Savannah College of Art and Design, or SCAD, and my own weekends were usually booked.

As we spread a blanket on the sand, Linaya began to fidget and could not settle in one spot. I considered asking what was wrong, but it was usually best to let Linaya speak on her own time.

I decided to stick to a neutral topic. "How's school?"

She was quick to answer. "It's really good. I'm ready to graduate. Only a few more classes." Linaya was majoring in fashion design. I had no idea what would come of that degree, but our parents seemed assured that she would find a profitable career.

Not that I had room to talk. I managed to get an English degree and now I was a professional bridesmaid. It was a good thing I had taken some business classes because those had been well worthwhile. Who knew what would happen in a few years when I was too old to be a bridesmaid for everyone in the world.

At only twenty-one, Linaya was still headstrong and trying to find her way in the world. I had to laugh inwardly at the thought. I was only twenty-six and still trying to find my way in the world as well. I'm not as headstrong. Linaya did everything full-steam ahead like a train while I was a little more flighty, like a bird.

"I met someone." Linaya's words rang out into the air twenty minutes after we arrived.

That's why she had been looking nervous. I took a deep breath and held my gaze at the book in front of me. While the words were now unfocused, I didn't want to look surprised. "Oh yeah?"

"He's older."

"Okay."

"He's thirty-five."

Now I turned to look at her, but I kept my face as calm as I could. The sunglasses I wore hid my widened eyes. Inwardly I was shouting, *Thirty-five? You're still a baby and he's probably divorced with kids! THIRTY-FIVE?*

"He's a professor."

It kept getting worse and worse. No wonder she looked so worried. There was no way our parents would approve and the way we were raised, your parents had to approve of anyone you might bring home. Our paternal grandmother was from Thailand, and while our father was born in Georgia, some of those Thai customs were still held close. Especially when it came to dating.

Not to mention my own disastrous dating life. Kyle the creep had two-timed me for six months, which was eight months too long. It was only when his other girlfriend showed up at my doorstep pregnant that I learned the truth. He had been a smooth talker and I had wanted to believe him. What a fool I had been. I didn't want my sister to become one as well.

"Linaya. What on earth?" I flipped my book upside down and peered over my sunglasses. "Is he your professor?"

She laughed. "No. All my professors are women or gay. But his office is next door to one of my professors and we kept bumping into each other and one thing led to another..." Her voice trailed off and her gaze shifted out over the ocean.

"Mom is not going to approve and you know it." Shaking my head, I could envision Anya Journet pitching a royal fit over her youngest daughter dating someone so much older.

"Which is why I want you to meet him first and let Mommy and Daddy know that you like him." She flashed a brilliant white smile at me and brought her hands together to plead.

Scowling, I pulled my sunglasses off. "I already don't like him."

"Please, Amaya. He's a great guy. He teaches American Literature so you should love him. We can do a double date." Big, doe eyes batted at me as she begged.

Which led me to one question. "Who would I take as a date?"

One person came to mind. The same face that had been occupying my dreams for a week. Orlando Daniels. But I had barely met him, how could I ask him out on a date? I supposed I could call up The Promenade and leave him a message. What if he said no? What if he said yes? Could I face him when I was working if things didn't work out between us?

"Amaya, where'd you go?" Fingers snapped, popping the image of Orlando from my mind.

"Sorry, just trying to think who I could ask out for a double date. I met a sweaty balding groomsman with a wedding ring mark last week." I shuddered at the recollection of the guy who had a distinct ring mark. "Speaking of, this guy you met doesn't have a wedding ring does he?"

Linaya sighed. "I knew that was coming. He's never been married, if you must know. And no kids attached. His name is Josiah Whitman and you can look him up easily enough."

I assured her I would indeed look him up and she begged me to find a date and let her know when I could meet this man. Could I call up Mr. Daniels and ask him out? A double date would give us some buffer. And he seemed like the type who could hold his own with a professor – he had class and finesse. I guess the worst he could say was no.

He said yes. My heart hammered in my chest when I called him at The Promenade and pretended to ask for the perfect "meeting the new boyfriend" restaurant. When I told him I needed to hang up and find myself a date, he offered to be my plus one. So, technically, I hadn't asked him out at all, but that was a minor detail.

We agreed to meet separately. It made sense in case things didn't go well. Or I needed to grab my sister and run away from a lunatic guy. I wore a light pink swing dress that skimmed mid-thigh. It showed my tanned and toned legs, which I thought to be one of my better assets.

Mr. Daniels, I supposed I should think of him as Orlando, came around the corner as I approached the door. "Amaya, perfect timing." He leaned in and kissed my cheek lightly.

I blushed like a schoolgirl, but I tried to cool my gaze. "Mr. Daniels. I mean, Orlando. I appreciate you coming. It saved me from calling half of Savannah asking for a favor."

With a wink, he offered me his arm. "The most beautiful bridesmaid in Savannah needed a date. Who am I to turn down such an opportunity?"

Inside, my sister waved from the table. I pointed her out to Orlando. "My sister, Linaya. She's a fashion major and loves the idea of being in love. She's a serial monogamist. Apparently this guy is a literature professor, though not her professor. I'm sure that's still frowned upon, though."

"So we're feeling him out?" The smile fell from Orlando's face and was replaced by what I could only call a soccer goalie expression. Like he would rip the legs off this man if I commanded him to.

I had to appreciate his desire to protect the little sister of someone he barely knew. With a chuckle, I patted his arm. "Down, boy. I am feeling him out. You are the arm candy who looks and talks nice."

Orlando stopped in his tracks. "Wow, that's incredibly hot."

As if we were old friends, I huffed and pulled him forward while I hoped he didn't see the pink that bloomed on my cheeks. Linaya jumped up and hugged me while her new beau stood and shook hands with Orlando.

Light radiated from my sister as she took the man's hand. "Amaya, this is Dr. Josiah Whitman. Josiah, my sister Amaya, and her friend..."

"Orlando Daniels. It's nice to meet you both." Orlando pulled out a chair for me across from my sister.

I shook Josiah's hand and noticed how hairy it was. Is that what happened when a man got older? The back of his hands sprouted hair? *Amaya, be nice. Your sister likes him. Give him a chance.* I looked at Orlando's hand. It was not covered in long, coarse hairs. I breathed a sigh of relief.

As we sat, Josiah asked after Orlando's family and merely nodded at the reply. Then he turned to me and asked after my career. Linaya filled that in for him, making my job sound much more glamorous than it really was.

"Amaya studied English," my sister said as the server filled our water glasses and brought out tiny puffs of bread.

"Did you? Where?" This came from my own date.

"At SCAD. I graduated a few years ago, but while I was trying to decide what to do with such an illustrious degree, I started my business and now this is full-time for me. I love it."

"I thought you were familiar. You were in my class. American Literature two-oh-three." Josiah sat forward, studying me.

I shook my head. "No, I had Dr. Jackson for that. Though I think some TA did the actual teaching."

"That was me, I was adjunct at the time under Dr. Jackson." He turned to Linaya. "That's why I thought I knew you, you look like your sister."

My sister laughed her high-pitched nervous laugh. Things had just gotten a little awkward – well, more awkward. We ordered our dinners and Orlando asked Linaya polite questions about her future plans, which included a desire to go to New York and design costumes for Broadway. She was always into the theater, despite not having any acting skills.

After two glasses of wine, Josiah was starting to loosen up. "Boy, you two sure like out of the ordinary jobs. No regular nine-to-fives, huh? I guess you'll kick back and live the high life when you get married?"

My glass hit the table so hard I thought it would crack the stem. "Excuse me, but what do our career choices have to do with getting married? Nobody at this table it looking to get married anytime soon. Especially not my twenty-one-year-old, still-in-school sister."

The table was silent for a few beats. I sent a murderous glare at Dr. Whitman while Linaya looked like a deer in headlights. The professor kept his eyes down, refusing to meet anyone else's gaze.

"Dr. Whitman, if I may, what is it your parents do for a living?" Orlando stabbed a piece of salmon and smiled politely at the professor.

Caught off guard, Josiah nodded. "My father is a CPA and my mother is a high school history teacher. But she took time off when she had my brother and I."

The rest of the evening didn't get much better. I found Dr. Whitman to be a pompous, arrogant man who was only interested in having a pretty, young co-ed on his arm. When we parted ways, Linaya looked like she wanted to cry, but had assured me she was fine to ride home with the illustrious professor.

"Well, that was a disaster." I stalked from the restaurant, Orlando on my heels. I spun to face him and he nearly smacked into me. "I'm sorry. This isn't your problem at all. You were very kind to come with me and I do appreciate it."

He raked a hand through his hair and smiled, my heart leapt just a little. "It wasn't a total disaster. If anything, maybe your sister will realize this isn't the guy for her. But ultimately, she's an adult and can make her own decisions."

"She's not an adult, she's a little girl." I pictured my sister with ebony pigtails as she ran around the living room with her favorite mermaid doll.

"You said yourself she's twenty-one. That's an adult." Orlando flinched as I shot him a look that could ignite flames. "Maybe she's not that mature, but that only comes with experience, you know?"

I lowered myself to a bench on the sidewalk and groaned. "Sometimes being the big sister sucks."

"Hey, I'm a big brother, I get it." He sat next to me and looked like he wanted to pat my knee but he hesitated.

I looked up at him, searching my mind for information that wasn't there. "I didn't realize Cordelia had another child."

"She doesn't. My father and his second wife had children. Brett is eighteen and thinks he knows everything, and Lily is fifteen." He licked his lips, causing me to lose my focus on my sister.

I bet he tasted divine. The honey glaze on his dinner might have lingered and I desperately wanted to find out and distract myself from my sister's current inferno. Perhaps I could start an inferno of my own.

Distance, I needed distance before I did something I shouldn't. Getting to my feet, I stepped away from him. "Well, I should get going and let you get back home. I do appreciate your coming with me tonight."

"Anytime, Amaya. We should do it again soon."

I rushed to my car before I could do something truly stupid.

Orlando

I HAVE NEVER DATED people I work with, so this left me in a conundrum. I really liked Amaya. And while we didn't work together, we did work together. She wasn't my employee. We didn't stare at each other all day from across the office – I've been there and it was incredibly smothering. But I would certainly see her often enough.

Plus, my mother wanted me to offer her a job as an in-house event coordinator. She could still be a professional bridesmaid for those who want it, or just a regular coordinator. Now that we were doing more and more private events, Mom thought it required us to have our own person on staff.

What my mother didn't know was that I'm not completely sure I want to keep The Promenade. Sure, it's a lucrative business, but it's not the business I know. I know corporate mergers and takeovers, not formal gatherings for weddings and parties. I was so out of my element. And I would hate to hire Amaya just to sell the place and her end up out of a job.

And I didn't date people I worked with.

My brain told me that, but when I saw her coming down the hall with a couple hot on her heels, my breath hitched. She wore a black knee-length pencil skirt and an emerald green silk blouse. She looked professional and sophisticated and I desperately wanted her to turn around so I can see her walk away in that skirt.

She spoke openly with the woman beside her, the man clearly tagging along. They must be a couple she's working with. I had no reason to go down the hall, but I found myself looking straight ahead as I barreled toward them.

"Oh, Mr. Daniels. May I introduce Misty Allen and her fiancé Connor Harwood? They're considering The Promenade for their wedding next year." Amaya's mouth turned up into an easy smile and her eyes sparkled in the low lights.

The urge to cup her face in my hands was overwhelming, so I stuffed my hands in my pockets. Then realized I would need to shake hands, so I pulled them back out again. "A pleasure. I do hope you like the look of things."

The groom shook my hand and looked desperate for a guy to commiserate with. The bride offered me a limp hand and barely looked my way. Instead, she marveled at a piece of art on the wall. "Oh, this is gorgeous."

It was one of my favorite pieces in the place. "My mother commissioned that from Geoffrey Bucklier. Have you heard of him?"

The woman's mouth dropped open. "Heard of him? He's my favorite artist, I would kill for one of his paintings."

Amaya crinkled her nose. It was adorable, not that I noticed. "Misty, did I tell you that Geoffrey's daughter Ingrid was married here seven years ago? Sadly, I was not in attendance, but that should attest to the beauty and prominence of this venue."

It was a fact I didn't even know. I only remembered my mother telling me she had commissioned the piece. The bride squealed in delight.

"Why don't you all go into the ballroom right here? I will be right behind you," Amaya offered. The bride scurried in, the groom bored behind her. When they were out of sight, Amaya turned to me. "Thank you. That is a great selling point. She's a socialite if you couldn't tell."

"High profile client, then?"

She nodded. "I get them on occasion. And sometimes they don't want it to look like they had to hire a coordinator. And the guy's only request was that his brothers be groomsmen and he has four brothers. She has a sister and two best friends, so she needed a fourth. It will be a huge wedding."

Unsure what to say, I nodded and made my excuses to let her get back to her clients. She briefly touched my hand as she said goodbye and I could feel a spark come from her. Was it an electric shock? No, these floors weren't carpeted, there was nothing to cause it. Maybe it was just from her own electric charm.

Back in my office, I made a few phone calls and looked over the schedule for the next several months. Every weekend was booked with weddings, anniversary parties, corporate events, and more. The business was making money but largely sat unused during the week. There had to be something more that the space could be used for. Maybe we could rent it out to small businesses. I understood practicality, not all this whimsy.

Which is why I was considering selling the entire place once my mother retired properly. I was a corporate man, not a party planner. I knew nothing about running an event location except how to pay for the catering. I had spoken to three interested parties already and planned to show them The Promenade in the coming weeks to gauge their interest.

My mother flitted into my office. "Orlando, darling, did you see that Amaya Journet is here?" She perched on the arm of a chair opposite me.

"I did indeed. I told the bride with her that we had a Bucklier. She was duly impressed." I lifted my coffee cup for a drink of the lukewarm liquid.

"Such a sweet girl, that Amaya. You could speak with her today about working here. I would love to have her join the family."

Coffee sputtered from my mouth as I choked. Join the family? Thankfully most of the coffee was swallowed and a little ended up leaving droplets all over my desk. I was glad there were no contracts laying on top.

"Orlando! What on earth?"

I wiped my mouth with a tissue and took a deep breath. "Sorry. Mom. Join the family? What do you mean?"

Her eyes grew large. "Join us here working at The Promenade. What did you think I meant?"

Tears formed in my eyes from the coughing. "I don't..." cough, cough, "I just..." cough, cough, "Nevermind."

Slight wrinkles worked their way around my mother's eyes. "You like her, Orlando. I thought you might get on with her. She's sweet young lady."

"I'm here to assess the business, Mom, not swoon over gorgeous bridesmaids." I cleared my throat again, finally feeling somewhat normal.

"I never said she was gorgeous. That was you." She stood and looked out my office door, her face lighting up even more. "And there she is now with a vision of a bride. How did you like The Promenade?" Mom shook hands with the couple and then with Amaya.

"It was perfection. The crystal chandelier!" The bride made a chef's kiss gesture and gushed some more.

"Right in here and my son can talk with you. I have an appointment of my own to rush off to," Mom said, ushering the three visitors into my office.

I only had two chairs and Amaya immediately offered them to the couple. The woman – Missy? – took one and the guy hesitated before Amaya jumped back out and grabbed a chair from elsewhere. He finally sat.

We hashed out details for their nuptials. Everything was still done in an old black binder with dates that stretched out two years. *We'll need to update this if I keep everything going. We need a site-wide network that allowed everyone to interact and see what was happening when, from caterers to waitstaff to the cleaning crew.*

After booking their wedding and paying a hefty deposit, the couple excused themselves and left. Amaya stayed behind just outside my office door. Once they were out of earshot, she turned and looked at me expectantly.

"Did you need something else?" I again picked up my coffee mug, only to remember it was completely cold now.

She plopped herself down on one of the chairs that belonged in my office. "Cordelia said you wanted to speak with me," she said as she rotated her foot in the air, wincing as she did so.

"Is your ankle okay?"

She chuckled. "Don't laugh at me, but I can feel rain coming in my ankle. Old dancing injury that flares up in bad weather. It'll be okay." She put her foot back down, her calf muscles flexing in the three-inch heels she wore. "What did you need to talk about?"

I sat back and closed my eyes. "I need to talk about my mother's meddling, apparently." I opened my eyes to find them drawn immediately to the outline of her thigh. I shifted my gaze to her face. "She wants you to come work for us."

"Work for you? How so?"

Do not stare at her full lips, Daniels. "She would like an in-house event coordinator and she has you in mind for the job. She really likes you." Naturally, I would not mention my growing attraction for her.

Her mouth twisted up for a few seconds as she thought. "I like your mother as well, and I love doing weddings here. I don't know if I want to leave my business though."

"The idea is that you could still be a bridesmaid for hire for weddings, and help coordinate the other events that occur here." I sighed and sat forward. What would she say if I told her I planned on selling?

Amaya crinkled her nose and began to chew on her lip. My eyes were drawn to her mouth and I really wanted to taste it. A small noise peeped from her before she finally said she wasn't sure.

Seriously, she was the most gorgeous woman I had ever seen. "You can still play dress up." I smirked at my little joke.

Except she didn't see it as a joke. Dark eyes narrowed and color rose in her cheeks. "Is that all you think I do, Mr. Daniels? Play dress up? I have negotiated with the toughest caterers in the business, I have held a bride's hair as she puked both from drinking too much and from being pregnant. I have warmed cold feet and I have even stopped a wedding when I realized the bride was being abused. I do a lot more than just dress up." She stood, her face red and her chest heaving. "Good day, Mr. Daniels."

She turned on her spiked heels and strode from the room.

Well, I officially mucked that up. It's a good thing I don't date people I work with.

Amaya

MY NEXT APPOINTMENT WAS about twenty minutes away and I stewed over Mr. Daniels' words as I drove. *Play dress up. Seriously?* How would he have liked it if I said all he did was sit at a desk looking handsome all day? He pushed papers around and raked in the money. Except, someone else did the actual raking for him.

I pulled up to the bakery still muttering under my breath. When I saw my bride, however, I did my best to switch that part of my brain off and switch on the bridesmaid bestie part. This bride was shy, disorganized, and as sweet as pie. I was to be her only attendant and truth be told, I was giving her a steep discount after I spoke with her future mother-in-law about the planning.

"Sydney, honey, I'm so excited to see you! Are you ready to pick out a wedding cake?" I gave her a light squeeze when I approached her and she heaved a sigh of relief.

"I'm nervous. This looks expensive," she stammered.

Sweet Tooth Savannah's was a middle of the line shop that I brought clients to frequently. They did a good job for a decent price. I eyed the window and the six-tier dummy cake in the window was definitely impressive. "You're not getting a huge cake, though, right? And there are plenty of options to cut costs. But this is only a free tasting, so don't worry about it just yet."

She took a deep breath. "Right. Yes."

We sampled several kinds of cake, and the baker assured us he could create a beautiful small cake for cutting then have cupcakes for everyone else. Sydney was happy with the compromise and even happier with the estimated cost.

As we left, she laid a hand on my arm. "Amaya, you have no idea what a godsend you are. I know nothing about being a bride and being without a mom, you're doing all the things I would be doing with her. So thank you."

This is why I do what I do. It's not about dressing up. It's not about cake or showing off custom chandeliers. It's about making a connection with a bride who needs help, who is looking for someone to guide them through a perfect day. Helping the Sydneys of the world feel beautiful and happy on her big day, that's what it's about.

"Sweetie, I am honored to be with you for all this. Don't worry about a thing." I hugged her tight. "I will see you next week for invitations, right? And if you need anything before that, just text me."

Goodbyes were said and I made my way home. I changed into sweats and sat at my desk to organize a few things. Each couple had a folder, color-coded by the month of their wedding. I added the contract for the Promenade to the couple I had been with that morning and the cake order for Sydney's wedding.

My mind went back to Orlando saying his mother wanted me to work there with them. I stayed busy, but I could always be busier. I loved coordinating events, not just weddings. Would the job come with a regular salary? Benefits? That would be nice.

But then I would have to see that insufferable Orlando Daniels every day. Oh, he wasn't insufferable, he just put his foot in his mouth from time to time. I do enjoy dressing up and looking nice, and it was pretty clear he did, too. The way he filled out a suit with those wide shoulders and toned thighs were enough to turn my cheeks pink. Not that I had noticed his thighs under his tailored slacks.

The ringing of my phone made the picture of Orlando's thighs disappear from my mind. My sister's face appeared on the screen. "Hi, Linaya, what's up?" I cradled the phone with my shoulder while I pulled up my email.

"What are you doing Friday?" She sounded near breathless.

I didn't mean to laugh, but my Friday nights and Saturdays were usually jam-packed. The majority of my work was on weekends and Linaya knew that. "This Friday? Girl you know I have to work. This weekend is the Amick wedding."

The heavy sigh that came through nearly blew out my eardrum. "Ugh, you're always busy on weekends."

"It is my job. What's up?" I scanned the emails for anything that stood out while I waited for her reply.

My sister's voice came through sounding very pouty. "I just miss you and I want to talk to you."

With a chuckle, I replied, "Talk to me now."

"In person."

"Come over now." I laughed fully. She was good at getting her way and though she was my baby sister, she was also a built-in best friend.

"Really?"

"Really. We'll order Thai food and I have ice cream."

"I'll be there in thirty." The excitement in her voice made me smile. I loved nothing more than making my sister happy, and if she needed an in-person chat session, she had something going on.

I put my phone down and opened my emails. A dozen new inquiries appeared before me. Ever since I had been interviewed for Action News there had been a definite uptick in requests. And while not everyone wanted to book, many did. Unfortunately, many who asked couldn't afford my rates, but that's what being in demand did. It was exciting and humbling at the same time.

How would that change if I were to work for the Daniels family? What about the clientele I had already booked? I hoped Linaya would know what to do, because I sure didn't. She always brought a fresh outlook to everything.

Over bowls of pad thai and tom kha kai, we chatted on my couch, our legs intertwined between us. Linaya wore a cropped shirt and running shorts while I had on sweats. We both wore our hair in wild messy buns. A pair of glasses sat forgotten on my sister's head as she squinted at her phone.

I told her about the potential job at The Promenade and she nearly jumped from her place on the couch. "That is so exciting! When would you start?"

I shrugged. "No idea. I don't know how these things work. I have clients booked out eighteen months." I slurped on my soup. Yai, our Thai grandmother, would have given me a shocked expression at the faux pas. Slurping was considered rude. But our father, her son, thought she was so outdated, he had taught us to slurp and slurp loudly. Linaya and I still enjoyed seeing who could be the loudest.

"Quit slurping," she scolded. "Can you still work with those brides even if they're not married there?"

I wish I knew. It wasn't something Orlando and I had discussed at length. My immediate thought has been to turn him down, but it could be beneficial in the long run. One day I would be too old to be a universal bridesmaid, and having event planning on my resume would be great.

"I guess I need to talk to him more about it. There's a lot to consider."

Crinkling her nose, Linaya grabbed my hand. "Does this mean a shopping trip?"

"Let me talk with this guy first. Then, we shop." We settled into silence for a few minutes, both of us eating and occasionally making a very loud slurp. Yai would be tanning our hides by now if she heard us. Thankfully she lives several hours away.

"So I dumped Josiah," Linaya finally said, a sad expression crossing her face.

There was no surprise there, but I tilted my head and tried to look sympathetic. "I'm sorry, Linny. But truthfully, he didn't seem well suited to you."

"I guess not," she muttered with a pout. "I'm ready to find the right person, you know?"

I sat up straighter. I did not know, and I told her as much. "You want to go to New York, you want to design for runways. Why do you feel the need to settle down now?"

Linaya chewed on her nail while she thought. "Well, Mom married Daddy when she was twenty-one. Yai was nineteen when she married Pop. Gran was twenty-two when she married Granddad. I think my biological clock is ticking."

I put my hand to my stomach, feeling for an imaginary biological clock. At twenty-six, I did not feel like mine was ticking away like a time bomb. I rarely dated, being a perpetual bridesmaid pretty much killed my dating life outside of creepy groomsmen. My mind went to Orlando. He was the closest thing I'd had to a date in the six months since Kyle. I figured he was a little older than me and wondered if men had biological clocks that began ticking at a certain age.

My gaze came to rest on my sister's big doe eyes. "Your biological clock hasn't even begun yet, let alone be counting down the time you have left. You're young. And people don't get married as young as they used to. I mean, Gran and Yai got married in the seventies – do you know how long ago that was? That's just how it was done then. You have all the time in the world now."

Even though she heaved a sigh, Linaya smiled. "I guess you're right. Maybe I need to be looking for a guy after I graduate and go to New York."

I stood and put my bowls in the sink. Opening the freezer, I called back to her, "That's right. And until then, I have mint chocolate chip ice cream."

Orlando

Trying to show The Promenade to a potential buyer without alerting my mother was harder than I thought it would be. She said she was retiring, so I thought she would be drastically cutting down her hours. That turned out to be a bald-faced lie. She was there every day with her tailored clothes and her pearls, chatting up every person who walked through. I managed to send her to lunch with her friends for the first potential buyer, but now I had one coming in an hour and my mother was walking around with the head gardener, chatting about what new things to plant.

If things went as planned and she transferred ownership to me, I would be selling it and didn't care one lick about what flowers were blooming when. I needed to sit down with her and make sure she was going to turn things over to me, so I could then sell and set her up for a luxurious retirement and I could get back to my own company.

Though I did enjoy the more relaxed pace set here in Savannah. It was much more casual than in Atlanta. Suits were not everyday wear, I had learned. Polos and khakis passed as business-wear here and I liked that. I liked taking things slower and not feeling rushed. But it wasn't the life I was used to. And I had plans to sell. At least, I think I did.

I paused though, thinking about Amaya coming to work for us. I could see her every day. If I sold The Promenade, I might not ever see her again. Selling as quickly as possible had always been my plan, so actually looking over the books to see just how lucrative a business it was had never entered my mind. It did now. If my mother wanted to hire Amaya, there must be enough revenue to do so easily.

I quickly opened our finances program and scanned everything. People were paying an arm and a leg to use this space. The entire property was paid off, so aside from taxes, utilities, and maintenance, there weren't many expenses for the building itself. I pulled up the big numbers for the past five years. Even with the pandemic we were well in the black.

There was a lot of thinking to be done, but first, I needed to get my mother out of sight.

"Orlando, darling, I'm running to have brunch with Rebecca Gloss." My mother's small frame filled my doorway. She looked like a modern day Jackie O with her large sunglasses and flowing scarf. "I'll be back in a few hours."

Relief flooded me, but I steeled my jaw so as not to show it. "Enjoy yourself, Mom. You're supposed to be retiring, right? You've earned a life of leisure at this point."

She waved a bejeweled hand at me. "Leisure? What's that? I like to stay busy. I'll be back this afternoon." She disappeared from view, her scarf fluttering after her.

Shaking my head, I pulled up my email to check it before my appointment. There was an email from Amaya.

```
Mr. Daniels,

I am interested in hearing more about
the option that come with a job at
The Promenade. Can you give me more
specifics? Would this be full-time? Are
there benefits? What are the company
policies?

I want to give this my due considera-
tion. Thank you.

Amaya Journet
```

There were no set answers to those questions because it had all been my mother's idea. Would an event planner be needed full-time? I checked the schedule and every weekend was completely booked a year out, with only a few dates open after that. There were a few lunch and evening events as well. It could certainly warrant a full-time position.

But I was going to sell the place, right? And despite that, I didn't date coworkers and I wanted to date Amaya. Maybe I should ask her out for coffee to discuss details.

When my appointment arrived fifteen minutes early, I was happy for the distraction from Amaya. These potential buyers were a couple who had always dreamed of a beach-side event venue. The wife was immensely disappointed that we were not oceanside.

I toured them around, showing them the ballroom, several conference spaces, and ending in the gardens. The husband appeared bored, the wife grew more and more disappointed as the tour went on. She had wanted a beach-side castle and this was not it. No amount of uptalking would convince her to alter her vision.

As they left, my mother returned. "Was that a couple looking for a wedding venue?" She watched them drive off in a neon green convertible.

"They had heard about us and wanted to check it out," I told her. "But the woman wanted ocean-side, it seemed." I turned to go inside, expecting my mother to follow me.

Once we were in the shade of the colonnade, she spoke again. "I need you to set up a meeting with Alexander. We need to go over the books."

When I looked back at her, her mouth was in a thin line and her brow was furrowed. Did she know what I was doing in showing the place to potential buyers? It was best to appear unflummoxed. "Okay."

"You've been learning the ropes here wonderfully, but I want to talk to Alexander about future projections. How we can expect to do in the next five years, maybe ten years. Especially if we bring Amaya on and perhaps a chef."

In my office, I leaned on my desk and Mom took a seat. "Good idea, Amaya actually emailed me just a bit ago and wanted to know more details about the job. If it came with benefits and what the salary would be."

With a huff, my mother shook her head. "I don't know that right off. Call Alexander. See if he can come in this week."

I leaned over and kissed her temple. "I'll call right now. Don't worry, Mom."

Standing, she waved her hand in the air. "I never worry, Orlando. It gives me wrinkles if I worry."

Amaya

T HE IDEA OF WORKING at The Promenade raced through my mind the entire day while I waited for a return email. I would love to not worry about job security and being able to see Orlando's smile would be a perk. A smile crept across my face as I thought about that smile. It would be great to see him every day, but then, if we ever did date that could become incredibly awkward. Best to push it from my mind.

A reply finally came from Orlando telling me to come into his office at lunchtime two days later. I couldn't have hidden the smile that crept up on my face if I'd tried.

I strode into The Promenade before noon, my low heels announcing my arrival. I wore a short, flowy black skirt and a hot pink button-up blouse with the top two buttons undone. Before I got to Orlando's office, I undid a third button.

Yes, we would talk business, but I knew he had invited me at the lunch hour for a reason and I did not intend on giving him the upper hand. Giving my hair a final fluff, I approached his office door, which was wide open.

"Amaya, right on time," he said, setting his cell phone down. "Come in. We'll go over for lunch in just a few minutes."

I clutched my bag in my left hand while I shook his hand with my right. "Go over? Where?"

A million-dollar smile and lifted eyebrow made my insides flutter slightly. "I'm considering bringing on a chef full time. Chef Aaron Tierney has been experimenting in the kitchen. I told him I would bring a distinguished guest over to taste test."

He really was making changes if he was thinking about bringing on a chef full-time. As it was, The Promenade only had a list with a handful of approved caterers on it. An in-house chef would make things both easier and harder depending on how he handled things like dietary restrictions and allergies.

"But first," Orlando motioned for me to sit, which I did. "Let's talk shop a moment, shall we?"

"Absolutely."

"First, I apologize for my comment the other day. I did not intend to make your work sound so trivial. And I'm glad you decided to hear me out." He raised an eyebrow and I nodded for him to continue. "I'm looking at making several changes here once the business is fully mine and Mom retires. I spoke with our financial consultant this morning and the business is doing well. There are several options I'm considering – like hiring a chef or an event coordinator."

He took a moment, and I spoke up. "What else are you thinking about?"

"All in due time." He checked his phone briefly, but didn't linger with it. "If we were to bring you on, it would of course include a reasonable salary and full benefits for you. You could still do the occasional wedding outside of The Promenade, but that would have to be when there's nothing planned here, or enough time has passed that we can afford an assistant for you."

He continued to talk as he stood and motioned for me to follow, which I did. I asked a few questions and he gave me honest answers if he didn't know something right off, but the idea of a steady income and my own office was sounding quite nice. After a turn to the right, we were at a table just outside the kitchen.

Orlando pulled a chair out for me. "After you." I sat and placed my purse in my lap. Those charm school lessons certainly had paid off. Orlando took the seat opposite me.

A slight man with reddish hair came from the kitchen, his hands clasped before him. "Mr. Daniels, Ms. Journet, I am delighted to have the chance to cook for you today. I do hope you will enjoy everything I have prepared." Before we could reply, the chef disappeared and a small cart was brought out to us.

Chef Tierney went over all the items he had prepared, which was enough to feed a small army. Once he was done and we were served, Orlando asked him to join us, but he politely refused.

"I would like Ms. Journet to ask any questions she might have," Orlando noted with a pointed look in my direction.

"Of course, I would be happy to answer." The chef looked at me expectantly.

I asked him about dietary restrictions for clients who needed special meals, about allergies, and about how he would react in a few different situations. Orlando did not ask any questions himself, which made me wonder if he even knew what to ask. When Chef Tierney excused himself, we began to eat.

"This is delicious," Orlando said as he closed his eyes. "Don't you agree?"

"It's very good," I replied. And it was. The food was perfectly cooked, if a little on the bland side. "You didn't ask him any questions."

A wink came my way. "You had it handled."

I put my water glass down. "You didn't know what to ask." When Orlando shrugged and shook his head, I balked at him. "Is that why you asked me to come over? To help you interview chefs?"

"Of course not. That was only part of the reason." He laughed. "It was also partially an interview for you, so I could see if you know what you're doing. And you clearly do. You know my mother adores you and I think you have a knack for this. When, and if, you want it, the job is yours."

Not wanting to reveal too much of any emotion, I simply said, "I'll think about it," before taking another bite of my lunch.

What I was refusing to think about, however, was how much I wanted to take the job so I could spend more time with Orlando. There was definitely something there. I knew he could feel it as well. I was at ease around him and I already knew I liked his mother. Not to mention he was the most handsome man I had encountered in a long time.

After lunch, we went back to his office. "I do appreciate the offer, I hope you know. And I am going to seriously consider it. The idea of benefits included is very alluring. Even though I sound incredibly boring being excited about that." When he sat at his desk, I leaned against it facing him.

The smirk he gave me said plenty, but he quipped, "I think it's very attractive that you're considering your options and weighing the pros and cons. You're smart, you'll come to the right conclusion."

If I kept thinking with my body and heart instead of my head, I might not. But I was enjoying the moment too much to pause. I stood, sauntered to the door so he had a nice view of my backside, and turned back to him. "I'll be in touch."

Then I sashayed right out the door without a glance back at him. I hoped he was feeling just a little tortured over my exit. I know I was.

Orlando

S HE KNEW HOW TO torment me, that was for sure. Watching her walk out of my office made my heart begin to race. What was I thinking offering her a job? First, I didn't date people I worked with. And second, I wasn't sure I was keeping The Promenade, which meant I couldn't guarantee she would have a job when new owners took over. But at least then I could date her.

I groaned in my chair and swiveled around to face the wall. A mantra came to my mind. *I will not chase after her. I will not chase after her.*

"Orlando?" My mother's voice definitely cooled my jets.

I swung back around to see her standing there with Chef Tierney. I put on my game face. "Chef, thank you so much for coming out today. Your food was delicious." I pointed to the chair before me and he took a seat.

Tierney was young, maybe my age but definitely not older. Would he be capable of running a full kitchen on his own? Could he manage waitstaff? Could he work with Amaya? *Don't let him near Amaya.* I blinked. Where had that thought come from?

"I appreciate the opportunity," he said, his knee bouncing.

Mom took a seat beside him. "Chef, can you run a kitchen? Take control?" It was like she read my mind.

The young man nodded. "I'm young, I know, but I have been in kitchens since I was a kid. I was a kitchen manager by twenty-two. My resume shows I'm fully capable and I am on fire for this opportunity."

I narrowed my gaze on him and his knee stopped mid-bounce. "Can you handle serving weddings of two hundred plus?"

With a resolute nod, he cracked his knuckles. "I can, I have, and I will."

We did a little negotiating and agreed to let everyone sleep on it. Once Tierney left, Mom's eyes lit up like a kid in a candy store. I could tell she liked him a lot.

"He's perfect."

"He's young," I argued.

"He has energy," she countered. "And he would work well with Amaya. Did you talk to her?"

"A little." I stretched my neck from side to side. "I told her the job was hers if she wanted it, but I'm not sure she does."

"Of course she does. She would love to work more with you." Mom stood, the bracelets on her tiny wrist jangling as she moved.

"Did she tell you that?" Try as I might, concealing my smile was impossible.

"No, silly. I can tell these things. After forty years in the wedding business, I know when I'm looking at soul mates." She winked and walked off, just as graceful as ever. And as scheming as ever.

By the time the sun began to drop, I could hardly stand it. I picked up the phone and dialed Amaya's number.

I fought off a curse when her voicemail picked up. What was I going to say? I hadn't thought it through at all. When the beep sounded I cleared my throat. "Amaya, hi. I just wanted to follow up with you." I thought for a moment. "I wanted to follow up with you about the chef that you met today and if you feel like he would be a good fit for The Promenade. Let me know, bye."

I hung up quickly and groaned while I buried my head in my hands. What was I thinking? I grabbed my things, pocketed my phone, and headed out. My whole life revolved around the office these days, so I thought I would go for a jog to clear my head.

As I ran through the streets of Savannah, watching people stroll through the public squares, I thought back to my ex, Tori, and the life I thought we would have had. It struck me in that moment that I didn't miss her and I guess I hadn't loved her the way I should have. Was love something I was capable of? As it was, I was trying to sell my mother's pride and joy outside of myself. That wasn't being very loving.

My phone began to buzz in my pocket so I came to a corner, stopped, and fished it out. Seeing Amaya's name pop up on the screen, I gave a breathless answer. "Hello?"

"Hey, I was just calling you back. You sound breathless. Everything okay?" Amaya's concern for me made my heart swell, but I attempted to tamp it back. She was merely returning my call, right?

"Oh, thanks for calling me back. Yeah, I'm just out for a jog in this beautiful weather we're having." *Beautiful weather? I sound like an idiot.* "I, um, wanted to get your opinion on the chef that you met earlier today."

A light chuckle came through the phone. "Well we did talk about him earlier but as I said, yes, I think he would be a good fit. I think he would be able to meet and maybe even exceed the expectations that you set for him. will you be interviewing anybody else?"

In truth, I had not thought to interview anybody else. I had lined him up last minute as an excuse for bringing her in. She didn't need to know that, though. "Well I do think he's the best that we've seen, and with your endorsement, I feel like we could offer him a position at The Promenade."

Her voice went from friendly to professional and I could tell I was now dealing with bridesmaid Amaya and not the girl who had brought me to meet her sister's new boyfriend. "Mr.

Daniels I don't even work for you at this point, so I don't feel comfortable giving an endorsement for anyone or anything. Please don't let this rest on my shoulders."

"Of course, of course. I don't mean to put that sort of pressure on you," I told her. "I'm just happy to get your insight."

"Well, I'm happy to give you my opinion."

"How is your sister?"

"What?"

"Your sister—what happened with the guy you brought me to meet?"

"Oh, that," Amaya said, sounding annoyed. "They have since parted ways as I suspected. Apparently, my sister thinks her biological clock is ticking which makes no sense because she's only twenty-one. I told her at twenty-six my biological clock is not exactly ticking yet so there's no way hers should be."

I hadn't known her exact age. She was only a few years younger than me and I felt relieved that she wasn't younger. "I'm glad to hear that she broke up with him since you didn't approve." At this point I was grasping for straws on what I might be able to say to keep her on the phone.

"It's not so much that I didn't approve of him as a person, just not for her at this point in her life. I feel like she'd be more suited to this Chef Tierney than to a professor almost fifteen years her senior."

An idea came to me in a flash. "Why don't we set up a meeting between them? How about I set up a second interview with Chef Tierney and you and your sister can be the taste testers."

"Mr. Daniels that is quite an idea," she chuckled. "And I think I like the way you're thinking. Let me know when and we will be there and," she added, "I hope you will be there too."

"Guaranteed." *Wild horses couldn't keep me away.* I finished my jog with renewed energy.

The next morning, I set up a second interview for Aaron Tierney a few days later. By then I hoped to know the future of the venue as well. I sent a text to Amaya with the details. I wasn't much on matchmaking, but helping her set her sister up with someone was turning out to be fun. And setting myself up with Amaya was becoming even more fun.

There was one last person interested in purchasing The Promenade. The more I thought about it, though, the more uneasy I was with the whole thing. I was growing more comfortable with the idea of staying in Savannah. The old city had a way of getting under your skin and settling its salty air in. Staying close to my mother was something else I realized was important. She wasn't getting younger and while she wasn't frail, I knew it would be coming someday.

My thoughts turned to Amaya. They were turning to her more and more with each passing day. Her desire to see me at this mock second interview with the chef bolstered my confidence in our mutual attraction. Could we run The Promenade together one day? The idea both warmed and terrified me.

Amaya

"Linny, this chef is not only amazing, but he's hot, too." I hoped this would convince her to hurry up so we could leave already. We were supposed to be seated for this special dinner in thirty minutes.

With a curling iron in one hand and hairspray in the other, Linaya was a flurry of activity. She wore a sapphire blue tiered sundress that showed off her sun kissed shoulders perfectly. It made me feel a little frumpy in the tailored red shirtdress I wore. It was a staple on my more casual work days.

I eyed my closet, knowing I didn't really have time to change clothes, but the tight pencil skirt called my name.

"I'm ready, let's go." Linaya smiled, her full fuchsia lips on display.

The red shirtdress stayed, then. We headed over to The Promenade and sailed past Orlando's office for the dining room. When we entered, I was met by a beautifully set table complete with candles and champagne flutes.

"Are you sure I was invited for this soiree? It's so romantic," Linaya whispered in my ear.

Three place settings of fine bone china graced the table. "Of course. But honestly, if you want to skip out so I can have an amazing dinner with a hot guy, I do not mind."

"You're here!" Orlando's voice came from across the room. "Please come in and have a seat. Chef is just about ready for you."

Ever the gentleman, Orlando kissed Linaya's hand before helping her into her chair and pushing her in. He did the same for me and I was thankful for the low light hiding my blush. He disappeared into the kitchen for a moment before coming back out with a bottle of sparkling wine.

"Tierney selected the pairing himself, so please let me know if you think it works," Orlando said. Before he served Linaya, he raised his brow to me. When I nodded, he poured her glass, though he kept it lower than our own.

I appreciated a man who looked out for people. Linaya wasn't his responsibility, but he still made the effort to be sure it was okay to serve her alcohol and he definitely underserved her as well. His attempt to match her up with the chef, even if it was a ploy to see me, was also appreciated.

Before serving the food, Aaron came out to greet us. His reddish hair was pulled back under a baseball cap, but his blue eyes shone like diamonds when he saw my sister before him.

"Mr. Daniels, Ms. Journet, a pleasure to see you again." He looked to Linaya. "It's a pleasure to meet you, miss. I'm Aaron Tierney and I'm hoping to be the chef at this fine establishment in the near future. Delicious, local, healthy food is my passion and I truly believe it's a form of art. I understand, Miss Journet, that you're a fashion major, so I'm sure you will understand."

It was as if my sister was star struck and seated before Liam Hemsworth as opposed to a young chef. Her eyes were huge and she seemed to soak in every word Aaron said. She could only nod in reply to him. Linaya was never at a loss for words. This was a first.

As he had before, Orlando asked Aaron to join us for the meal, and this time he accepted with a little hesitance. I wasn't sure if they had set this up beforehand, but a polo-clad waiter appeared with a fourth chair and then he retrieved an additional place setting. He seemed to know what he was doing without any direction. I shot a side-eye at Orlando and when he winked at me, I figured out his ruse.

As a foursome, we feasted on an entirely vegan dish that, Aaron proudly told me, was also nut and soy free. Chickpea noodles were served with a medley of roasted vegetables that anybody would swoon over. It was accompanied with a portabella steak that was seasoned to perfection. The conversation circled around the food, what farm it had come from, and just how artistic Aaron was. The last comment being from Linaya, of course.

"Aaron, truly, this was amazing. Could you serve this to two dozen people? Two hundred?" It was hard for me to turn my wedding coordinator switch off at times.

Aaron focused his baby blues from my sister to me. "With plenty of notice, which I understand I will have, it's absolutely possible. With wanting to use locally sourced items to be as farm-to-table as possible, I would need a good bit of notice if you wanted two hundred portabella steaks, but as an alternate vegan meal or for a smaller party, it wouldn't be problem at all."

"I love that it's all local," Linaya gushed. "It really inspires me to create fashion looks from the Savannah skyline. Mixed textures, colors you see locally every day." She spoke with her hands the same way I did.

Linaya and Aaron began an animated conversation about mixing colors and textures in food and fabric and I could tell that something was blossoming between them—be it friendship or something more, only time would tell.

I leaned over to Orlando. "This was brilliant. And I really like Aaron. I think you could turn this into a perfect luncheon spot if you wanted to."

Orlando's eyebrows shot up. "That's a brilliant idea. I've wondered what we could do with this space during the week. I've thought of conferences, of course, but having a small dining room for luncheon during the week would be genius."

Shrugging, I took a drink from my sparkling wine. "Just an idea. I'm full of good ideas."

"Clearly. I know we haven't made an official offer to you quite yet, Amaya, but I want you working with me." He got closer and I could see the golden ring around his dark brown eyes.

With him? He wanted me to work with him and not merely at The Promenade?

He caught his words just as I had. "I want you working here. With me. I think you might be just what this place needs. A fresh set of eyes, a beautiful face for the company."

"Really?"

There was so much more that he wasn't saying. I could feel it as easily as I could see it on his face. His eyes were bright, excited and his mouth was upturned in a was I had not seen before. I knew I mimicked his smile. He not only wanted me working there, but he wanted me close to him. Closer. And I was ready for it.

Thoughts of Kyle tried to push their way into my mind, but I pushed them right back out. This was no place for his narcissism. And Orlando, from what I was learning, was nothing like Kyle had been.

"What do you say?" The question lingered in his eyes.

"I would love to work more closely with you," I murmured, my lips very close to his ear.

When his eyes closed and his lips parted, I knew he was looking for more than just a working relationship. I didn't know what would happen or if it would work, but I knew that underneath all the hidden desire were two professionals.

Back in my car to head home, Linaya acted as if she had been proposed to. "Amaya, he's just fabulous. And he can cook. You know I can't cook, so this is perfect. And the way he sees color and art is so refreshing. He doesn't see it through a microscope like Josiah did. He sees art for the beauty it holds."

I laughed as I turned onto my street. "I noticed. You two had a lot in common."

"And did you see his eyes? Oh, those blue eyes were like oceans," she squealed. Taking a deep breath, she finally looked at me. "You and Orlando were quite cozy on the other side of the table."

"He wants me to work with him." I glanced in the rearview mirror and saw my eyes crinkle and my cheeks glow.

"Oh, work with him or for him?" She play punched me as I parked.

"He said with him. He said, and I quote, 'I want you working here. With me. I think you might be just what this place needs.' And he called me beautiful," I told her with a sigh.

Inside the house, we flopped on the couch. "You like him," she told me.

As if I needed to be told. "I know. I do." My smile fell then, and a scowl replaced it.

"Stop."

"Stop what?"

"Stop thinking about Kyle. He is not Kyle. He is not going to run you over then back up and do it again just to make sure he got all of you." Linaya reached her hand out to mine and pulled me close to her.

"I can't help the fear." And I couldn't. Enough bad things had happened with Kyle that I immediately looked for them. From being told I was wrong about every single thing, to him controlling what I wore, being in a healthy relationship was a foreign concept for me.

"He's not Kyle. You can recognize the fear and tell it to take a hike."

I looked up to my baby sister. "How did you get so wise?"

"My big sister taught me." She kissed my forehead. "Now, Aaron asked to take me to go to Telfair with him this weekend and I need something artsy to wear."

"A date already? Look at you! I'm so happy for you, Linny." I hugged her close. "This calls for ice cream."

Orlando

A MONTH AFTER SHE started working at The Promenade, Amaya had made herself indispensable as a hostess and event coordinator. New clients no longer came to
my office, but to hers, which was, admittedly, quite a bit
smaller than my own. At my mother's suggestion, Amaya
was given the larger office that was more accessible for clients
and I was moved down the hall to my mother's old office.

I hauled a stack of books and magazines to Amaya's new
office. "What is all this?"

She looked up from arranging the mahogany desk. "Trade
secrets," she whispered. When I raised my eyebrows, she
laughed. "The magazines are bridal, they help me stay current.
And the books are all trade books on event planning, wed-

dings, and organization. Being organized is really all anyone needs to be successful."

"Is that so?" I leaned on my, I mean her, desk.

"Absolutely. Organization with space, with time management, with everything keeps things running smoothly. It's the only way to do it. But I think you know that, Mr. Daniels." She had taken to calling me Mr. Daniels at work.

Calling me by my first name was reserved for outside of The Promenade. When she accepted my job offer, she said she would only accept it if she could take me out on a date. Who was I to argue? There went my rule to not date people I work with.

Besides, rules were meant to be broken, right?

The phone rang and she picked it up as she slid into the rolling chair. "The Promenade, Savannah's most sought-after event space, this is Amaya."

That had also been her idea, calling it Savannah's most sought-after event space. She was about to launch an entirely new marketing campaign that was as brilliant as she was beautiful. According to her, appealing to a high-level clientele would bring in more bookings at higher rates. She had asked a high profile client by the name of Ashley Harris if we could use some of her wedding photos in the ads and they were stunning. They made me want to get married. Almost. One day. Maybe.

I listened to her spirited conversation. "Absolutely. We can do that. Yes, we offer vegan options." She smiled at me and winked. "Let me look. How does Thursday at four sound?

And your name? Perfect, thank you Marissa, we'll see you then."

"The ads aren't even out but they're already creating buzz. Ashley is spreading the word amongst the elite of Savannah." Amaya shimmied her shoulders as she typed the appointment in the computer.

"The same one with the pictures?"

"The very one. She was raised a Savannah socialite and married the love of her life here not too long ago. It was a big to-do because her parents thought she was marrying down. But let me tell you, I have never seen two people more in love than her and Tyrell." She stared off in the distance for a moment.

"You remind me of someone I know," I said with a chuckle. I would never tell her that person was my mother. I'd let her ponder that.

"I'll take that as a compliment. I think," she said with a quizzical look.

"It is. It's a very good thing. Like Martha Stewart. Only not a criminal." I stood up straight and crossed my arms.

"It means you have excellent taste."

"I certainly do." I looked around the office. "I think that was the last of your things. Enjoy my office."

She beamed up at me from the chair. "Enjoy your hovel, Mr. Daniels."

I nodded. "Ms. Journet."

At five o'clock on the dot, Amaya appeared in my doorway and leaned on the jamb. "This room is so dark. You're like a recluse back here."

"Somebody forced me out of my office." I said, loosening my tie. "Are you ready?"

Wednesday nights were our standing date night. Friday and Saturdays were usually booked, so we had taken to mid-week dates. It kept things more casual and the wait times for a restaurant were usually much shorter.

"I am. And I'm excited about the theater. Linaya and Aaron are joining us," she said.

Tierney was working out to be a wonderful addition for us. Several of the weddings we had booked already had caterers, but he was starting off with our conferences and we were giving the luncheon thing a trial run. So far it was successful. And Amaya's sister's relationship with him was also successful. According to Amaya, Linaya was practically in love.

She hopped into my car with me, still in the pencil skirt she had worn at one of our first meetings. I loved her in that figure-hugging skirt, it gave her the perfect silhouette. It was paired with a coral colored sleeveless blouse that showed her decolletage without being too revealing. She looked perfect for a night at SCAD's theater.

Sure enough, standing outside were Linaya and Tierney. Amaya greeted the pair and I shook Tierney's hand. Linaya took me by the shoulders and gave me air kisses. She was definitely an eclectic soul and a wonderful compliment to Amaya.

Inside we found our seats and settled in to watch The Phantom of the Opera, one of Amaya's favorites. I had never been much of one for musical theater or operas, but I was learning the merits of them through her. For a previous date night she had ordered Thai food and we watched a musical on her television. For me, the way her face lit up during the climax of the show was worth the price of admission to the theater. It was the look of pure elation with no stress, no regrets. It was nothing but joy. One day I wanted to give her a reason to give that look to me.

She didn't know I was staring at her in that moment, of course. The stage took up all her attention, so she wasn't looking at me. But I was looking at her, all of her, in the soft glow of the theater.

When the lights went out entirely, she looked at me, the expression still on her face. The audience was clapping and whistling, so I couldn't hear what she said, but she took my hand and pulled me to standing. Then she turned back to the stage and began clapping and cheering herself. I clapped along, but my attention wasn't on the stage.

As we left, Linaya looped her arm through mine and pulled me to a stop. "I saw you watching her."

I felt like I had been caught with my hand in the cookie jar and I gulped. "You did?"

Her eyebrows rose. "Oh, yeah. And if I can ever get anyone to look at me the way you were looking at her..." She paused and sighed. "Tread carefully. She's been broken before. But I approve."

I nodded, understanding her slight warning. "Thank you. And you never know. Maybe this one will look at you like that." I gestured to Tierney. Linaya released my arm and grabbed his.

"We're off. That was fun." Linaya pulled her date closer to her. "Y'all have fun. Not too much fun, though." She winked at me. Or maybe at her sister. I wasn't sure.

Amaya's mouth formed an O. "That goes doubly for you two." She stepped after her sister, but I took her arm. "Linny, I mean it," she called after her sister.

When I held firm to her hand, she quieted. "She'll be okay. She's a big girl."

"When did that happen?" Amaya squeezed my hand. "Just last week she was five and heading to kindergarten."

"You two are close."

She looked at me with a pout. "We are. Growing up as the only Thai kids in town, eating strange Thai food when everyone else had sandwiches, we learned to stick together." It was then that she looked down at our still entwined fingers. "Do you think it's strange that I'm a quarter Asian?"

I pulled her close to me and we settled just outside the theater's lamplight. "Why would I think that's strange? You're the most gorgeous woman I've ever met, you're smart, you're close with your family. I see nothing amiss."

"I just, being Asian in the south is weird." She pulled her hand from mine and rubbed her arms.

"Says who?" My brow knit together in confusion. Who would say such a thing?

"It's just, Kyle always said..."

I put my finger to her lips. I had learned a little about her ex Kyle, and from what Linaya had just told me, I knew he was every bit as bad as he seemed. Probably worse. "Kyle wouldn't know a good thing if it bit him. You are not a perfect human being, because none of us are. But you are perfectly you. Never change. And I love that you come from a beautiful and rich culture."

I watched her throat constrict as she swallowed. "You do?"

"Only an idiot wouldn't, Amaya."

"Oh."

In that moment, she leaned in close to me, placing her hands on my chest. My hands instinctively went over hers and ran their way up her arms. Inches separated us and the distance was closing.

Taking the initiative, I placed my hands on the back of her head and closed the gap between us. My lips brushed hers lightly at first, then with more resolve. My mind raced, hoping she was going to kiss me back, and in a nanosecond she was. Her thin fingers pushed lightly on my collar as she dug her nails in. Her body followed, pressing into mine.

When we finally broke apart, Amaya took a deep breath. "That... That was..."

I finished for her. "That was amazing."

She giggled. "It was."

I furrowed my brow. "Wait. We might need to make sure that wasn't a fluke and try it again."

She laughed. "Oh, definitely. For science."

We spun around and I pushed her against the brick wall and kissed her again. This time deeper and longer. My hands skimmed down the length of her arms and wrapped around hers, pulling them up between us.

"Yeah, still amazing," I said between kisses.

"One more to make sure," she giggled. I was all too happy to oblige.

Amaya

ONCE AGAIN I FOUND myself donning a bridesmaid dress I would have never chosen in a million years. If I ever got married, I would have an incredibly hard time picking a bridesmaid's dress because I had seen and worn everything. This time it was a mint green ballgown with a dyed to match top hat. Even though I advised the bride, a mother of two named Riviera, against the hat, she had insisted, claiming the groom would find it hilarious.

The groomsmen began to cackle as the bridesmaids walked into the church narthex where they waited. I rolled my eyes at the four middle-aged men who were laughing so hard tears came to their eyes. I was, yet again, paired up with the worst of the bunch. Brides, I had come to realize, did this on purpose. I wasn't their friend, so I was paired with the most obnoxious of their groom's friends. That was so their own friends wouldn't have to deal with them. I understood, but that didn't make the awful guy any less awful for me.

This time it was a forty-year-old gym rat with huge muscles and bleached blonde hair. He was attractive, but he knew it and thought he was God's gift to women. Spoiler alert—he was not. He wiped his eyes as he approached me and slapped the top of the hat, causing it to shove into my ears. I winced from the pain and stepped back.

"Okay, everyone, let's get lined up." There was no pretense of being the bride's friend. I was a hired hand and everybody knew it. "Let's get our flower girl up front."

I ushered the bride's daughter, also donned in mint green but without the hat, to the front. Behind her went my gym rat, then the other three ladies and their groomsman. The bride and her son came in and brought up the end of the bridal party.

Checking Riviera's hair and dress one last time, I gave her a genuine smile. "Are you ready? You look spectacular."

She did not smile, but kept a perfectly neutral face. "I know. Let's go. I got a honeymoon in Hawaii to get to."

That genuine smile I gave her was because after this, I was done with her. I didn't often have bridezillas, but she had definitely become one. Perfection was never achievable, but I couldn't have told her that. Hopefully at The Promenade I would be able to turn down clients I thought might be a problem. Or at least not have to play bridesmaid for them.

We all marched down the aisle and took our places. This is when I usually went over my mental checklist for the reception. In this case, it would be next door at the local VFW. That was a new one for me, but the groom had been in the Army in his younger days. I had mastered the art of keeping a soft, happy expression on my face while mentally checking out and going over my list.

Something in the crowd caught my eye and a strange sensation came over me. I scanned the room as I felt my face begin to flush. There it was again, the sense that someone was watching me. Not the wedding, but me specifically. I began to scour the faces while trying to maintain composure of my own.

Sure enough, I spotted him. The auburn hair, the piercing blue eyes, and a wicked grin that I had fallen for two years before. Kyle. Our eyes met and his grin widened. I lifted my chin in defiance, but he copied my motion and I immediately lowered mine. *Stop, Amaya! Look away!* I casually moved my gaze, hoping I appeared casual even though my heart was racing and I could feel sweat roll down my neck.

Why wasn't Orlando here to save me? No, I could save myself. Why had I booked this bridezilla wedding? How did Kyle know this couple? I wanted to stomp my foot like a child and run away, but I couldn't. The clock at the back of the room told me I had three more hours. Could I do it? Of course I could. I could do anything. I could stand up to Kyle.

That didn't stop me from wishing Orlando was here, though. I turned back to the bridal couple just as they kissed.

With tongue. *Blech.* At a church, too. Pushing Kyle from my mind—okay, tucking him into a corner—I helped get the bridal party back around to the other side of the church and inside for pictures. The guests meandered over to the reception and I prayed with everything I had that Kyle had gone home or at least left the church.

The photographer wasn't familiar with me, so I couldn't count on him coming to my rescue. I set the family up for pictures and darted to my bag in the back of the church. Grabbing my phone, I texted my sister.

AMAYA: KYLE IS AT THIS WEDDING I'M WORKING. HELP!

LINAYA: NO! LEAVE. GET OUT OF THERE!

AMAYA: I CAN'T, I'M WORKING.

LINAYA: CALL ORLANDO.

AMAYA: NO.

LINAYA: WHY NOT?

The photographer called for bridesmaids, so I shoved my phone down the front of my dress and took my spot. I smiled, but I was sure I looked more panicked than happy. When the groomsmen joined us, the photographer had them wear our hats. Everyone laughed, but I felt like I was gong to get sick. Kyle was here.

Excused again for the bride and groom to take pictures with their children I fished my phone from my strapless bra.

ORLANDO: WHAT'S GOING ON? LINAYA JUST CALLED ME AND SAID YOU NEEDED ME.

UGH, MY SISTER!

AMAYA: I'M WORKING A WEDDING AND KYLE IS HERE.

I switched to my sister's text.

AMAYA: YOU CALLED ORLANDO?

LINAYA: YOU DIDN'T RESPOND! I PANICKED.

A new message from Orlando popped up.

ORLANDO: SEND ME A PIN OF WHERE YOU ARE. I'LL COME.

AMAYA: NO! I'M WORKING. I CAN'T HAVE A DATE.

ORLANDO: DON'T CARE. EVEN IF I DON'T COME IN, I'M COMING.

I quickly sent him a pin of my location and released a shaky breath. My phone went back into my dress as the bride called for me.

"My make-up is running," she yelled at me.

The make-up bag was right outside the door, so I grabbed it and touched her up to finish pictures. When those were done, we made our way over to the reception.

An uncle of the bride was acting as DJ and he introduced the bridal party. Muscles and I spun onto the floor and he dipped me low, catching me off guard. Once he had righted me, however, he pulled me close.

"If you're interested, I'm at the hotel across the street. Room 302. Meet me there at ten." Then he goosed me and sauntered off to where his buddies already had a table full of empty beer bottles.

No, thanks. Not even thanks. Just no. Hard pass.

I checked my phone to see if Orlando had arrived yet. Nothing. The newlyweds came in and immediately set up for their first dance. The bride's children were also supposed to dance next to them. I found the flower girl and brought her over to her brother, who was at least fifteen years older than her. He hoisted her up and carried her to the dance floor and began to twirl her around next to their mother and new stepfather.

My phone vibrated against my skin and I checked it.

ORLANDO: I'M RIGHT OUTSIDE. JUST IN CASE YOU NEED ME.

A sigh escaped my lips and I felt my shoulders relax. Even if I didn't need him, even if he didn't show his face, he was here for me. Any doubt about him in my mind slipped away in that moment. He showed up when called. If Kyle approached me, I would be ready.

And approach me he did. While everyone talked, laughed, and filled their plates from the buffet, Kyle sought me out.

"Amaya, look at you. That shade of green looks awful on you." He put his hands in his pockets and looked me up and down.

I stood to my full height, which wasn't much, but I would no longer back down from him. "This shade of green looks awful on everybody, Kyle. What do you want?"

"I thought I'd ask you for a dance." He held out his hand.

"No, thank you. I'm working." I turned my shoulder to him and took a sip of the tea in my hand.

He moved to be in my line of sight. "I heard. Zach said you're going up to his room for some extra work later. But I told him you're mine."

Now I did put my glass down. "You have absolutely zero ownership of me, Kyle. And for Zach, well, he's a pompous buffoon. I would never do that. Besides, my boyfriend is outside waiting for me."

With a scoff, he replied, "Sure he is. Let me guess, he's a hot model millionaire."

A sly smile came across my lips. "Hm. He is hot. And he is a millionaire. I think he could be a model." Orlando really could be a model.

Kyle grabbed my hand. "Come on, Amaya. Quit playing games with me. Show me this millionaire."

I pulled out my phone and texted Orlando a single word. "COME."

Kyle was pulling me harder toward the dance floor. "You're such a twit, Amaya. Nobody in their right mind would want you." He flung a racial slur towards me.

My feet dug into the floor and I yanked my arm, not caring if it dislocated. I was about to do something I had never done at a wedding—call attention to myself.

"Let go of me! STOP!"

Everything stopped. The laughter and chatter stopped. The sound of forks and cups stopped. Every eye turned toward us.

As if I was a medieval damsel in distress, Orlando appeared from the background. He charged ahead, took Kyle's hand off me, and turned with his eyes blazing. In one motion he clocked Kyle square across the jaw.

Sprawled on the floor, blood poured from Kyle's nose. He opened his mouth to speak, but the blood caused him to close it quickly.

Orlando stood over him, his chest heaving, his fist still balled. "When a woman tells you no, it means no. Go to—"

I put my hands on Orlando's arms before he could finish. He stopped and turned back to me. Strong arms enveloped me as he held me tight, his breath still ragged.

A panicked voice came from behind me. "Are you okay, Amaya?" Riviera and her groom stood there, wide-eyed.

I released Orlando and turned to her. "I'm so sorry. He wouldn't listen or let go."

The groom whispered to his bride and stepped away, pulling Kyle with him. Riviera came a little closer to me. "Kyle is George's nephew, but he is being escorted out. I'm so sorry this happened to you. I don't know what came over him, but I hope you're okay."

"You're not upset I ruined the reception?" My chin began to quake.

She stared at me, wide-eyed. "Honey, he was hurting you. You stand up for yourself, no matter what. Never let a man control you or handle you like that. My ex-husband was like that and I should have left long before I actually did."

Her attention turned to Orlando. "Would you like a drink? Ice for your hand?"

Flexing his right hand, he nodded. "That would be great."

"Now," Riviera said, turning back to me. "If you're okay, we'll cut the cake in five minutes."

The panic in my mind eased and bridesmaid Amaya came back into focus. "Five minutes, got it."

Perhaps I misjudged Riviera. She was a strong, independent woman and I had a newfound respect for her. She left to get Orlando ice and a drink and the crowd had resumed talking. I bit my lip and looked at Orlando.

"Thank you."

"He deserved it. But I think you could have handled yourself." He cupped my face with his hand.

"Just because I could have, doesn't mean I'm not glad you were here."

"You're okay?"

My wrist was a little sore, but it would recover. I nodded.

He winked at me and pulled me closer. "Looks like I'm invited to stay."

"Save me a dance after they cut the cake," I said as I leaned into him for a quick kiss before dashing off to get the cake knife.

Orlando

A T HOME THAT NIGHT, I replayed the events of the previous few hours in my head. When Linaya called me, I had thought something awful had happened to Amaya. While I felt a little silly pulling up to the dark VFW building, I figured I could catch up on my reading while I sat in the quiet. The text from Amaya simply saying to come launched me into action.

I knew she wouldn't have sent that without reason, but I was not ready for the sight before me when I came into the room. Dozens of people ignoring the girl trying desperately to get away from a man in a cheap suit. Then she had screamed and everything stopped. The people, the music, and my heart all stilled. Her words sliced through the air and right into my heart.

Before I knew what I was doing, I was in front of the sleazeball, decking him. I didn't care if I was hit back or arrested, nobody touched a woman—let alone Amaya—like that and got away with it. I think the bride's words to her afterward were just want she needed to hear. Sleazy men were sleazy men. And hopefully Kyle would take a hint from now on. I hoped I had broken his jaw. He deserved it.

My hand would recover, though it had been a while since I punched someone. Maybe I needed to take up boxing, it felt good. Maybe we needed to hold self-defense classes in the ballroom once a month for women in the community. I pulled out my phone and made a note to mention it to both Amaya and my mom. They would like the idea.

After the couple cut the cake, Amaya and I had danced to a slow song that came from speakers in the corners. There wasn't a proper DJ or anything, and Amaya said they had created a playlist that played on a three-hour loop. She had helped create the mix of songs.

When her time was up, I walked her outside, making sure no crazy exes were in sight. "You sure you're okay to get home?"

She nodded, leaning into me. "Yeah. He doesn't know where I live now and I doubt he'd bother to find out after that."

I kissed her forehead. "So you don't need a knight in shining armor to check your place over?"

I got a raised eyebrow in response. "I appreciate it, Orlando, but that's dangerous territory on its own. Besides, I think Linny will be at my place and will stay with me tonight to keep me safe. We princesses can handle ourselves."

"Duly noted. I have no doubt you can save yourself, but I do enjoy coming to the rescue every so often." I tucked a stray hair behind her ear. "Goodnight, Amaya."

Popping up on her tiptoes, she kissed me lightly. "Goodnight. And thank you. Truly."

So I came home, put on my joggers and a t-shirt, and wrapped my hand. I fell onto the couch and scrolled through social media, finally landing on Amaya's page. There were gorgeous photos of her in a variety of bridesmaid dresses. Most of the photos were not actually of her, but of brides and grooms—Amaya standing off to the side as a bridesmaid. An accessory to the event. In every photo, she was always a bridesmaid.

When my phone buzzed in my hand I startled and dropped it under the couch. "Hang on, hang on," I muttered as I reached for it. I yanked it up and answered in one motion. "Hello?"

"Orlando?"

It was Amaya. No. No, this was a feminine voice but was not Amaya. Why did I know this voice?

"Hello? Orlando?"

Tori. It was my ex-girlfriend. I gaped a moment before I stuttered her name. "T-Tori? Is that you?"

A sigh of relief came through the phone. "Yes, it's me. How are you?"

I could picture her sitting primly on a leather chair, her blonde hair perfectly tucked back, clothing immaculate. On paper, Tori was a perfect match for me. In reality, it was doomed from the start. We were similar, too similar. Both too goal-oriented to allow the other to shine. And those goals had led us to two different coasts.

"I'm good. Back in Savannah. How's Oregon?" I swallowed the lump in my throat. Why was she calling me?

"I miss the sunshine, but not the humidity, of Georgia," she replied with an awkward laugh.

My phone buzzed again. I looked at the screen, Amaya's face popped up. It would be too rude to hang up on Tori, I would have to call Amaya back. "What can I do for you?"

"Oh." It was as if she didn't have a reason for calling. "Right. I heard you're looking to sell The Promenade. I thought maybe you had reconsidered coming west."

Inwardly, I groaned. This was not happening. "I have entertained offers if anyone is interested, but I don't think I'm actively looking to sell anymore. And I have no intention of going west, Tori."

Never one to admit defeat, I could picture Tori squaring her shoulders and picking her chin up. "I suppose I misunderstood then. I did send a client of mine, Mr. James Worthy, the info on The Promenade and he was quite interested. But I can tell him I was misinformed."

"The James Worthy? That's a big name client." Color me impressed. Tori had moved up in the world.

"Well, I apologize for calling so late. I forgot it's three hours ahead there." An uneasy silence filled the air. "I hope you're well, Orlando."

"I am well. And happy. I hope you are, too." I meant it. We hadn't parted on bad terms, we just weren't right for each other.

"Yes, well. Goodbye then," she said, her voice soft and low. The phone clicked and she was gone.

I stared at nothing for a moment. "That was strange," I muttered into the air. Had she been calling solely about her client being interested? Maybe she was trying to brag about having one of the leading real estate tycoons as a client. But then I wondered if she missed me and truly wanted me to come out to Oregon.

The thought lingered in my mind for a moment. Would I be happy in Oregon? Likely not. I preferred the slower pace of Georgia, I had discovered. And, I realized, Tori was not the love of my life. There was no way I would pack up and move to be with her. I wasn't sure I would do that with Amaya, either, but we were new. I did, however, know I wanted to see where this thing with her was going. It felt like it could go the distance.

Remembering that she had called, I dialed her number and waited for her to pick up.

"Hey," she said. I hadn't noticed that she had an accent before, but after talking to Tori, I picked up a hint of a smooth southern lilt to her voice.

"Hey." The smile that came across my face could not be helped. "Sorry I missed you a minute ago, I had a business call."

"So late on a Saturday?" A yawn came through the phone.

"Sometimes business knows no hours." That was the truth.

And she agreed. "I know it. I'm glad this was an earlier wedding and not one I'd be at until midnight." She paused, but it held none of the ill ease the one with Tori had held. "Anyway, I wanted to call and thank you again."

I scratched the stubble on my chin. "Oh, I think you could have figured it out. But I'm glad to help. He was a…"

"Yeah, he is," she interrupted. "And I'm glad I didn't have to figure it out. I've never had that happen at a wedding before and I just froze. I didn't know what to do. If I had been at the beach or something I would have kicked him right where it counts. But I couldn't do that to my reputation as a business-woman."

"Maybe we need security at The Promenade."

She yawned again and I had the sudden urge to tuck her into bed and watch her sleep.

"No, I've done dozens, hundreds, of weddings and this was a first. Usually the worst thing is a handsy groomsman."

"I had a thought. What if we offered free self-defense classes once a month for women in the area?"

The sleepy tone she had perked up a little. "Really? That's a wonderful idea. I think Linny has taken classes, I can ask who did them."

"Let's talk about it on Monday," I suggested.

"Perfect. Write it down."

"Already did."

"Thanks again, Orlando. Truly. That meant the world to me."

I could hear her words getting slower as sleep began to claim her. "Anytime, hon."

She giggled. "Hon. That's cute. Goodnight."

We hung up and I grinned. I had felt exhausted, but after the call from Tori and talking to Amaya, my mind was racing. I looked up James Worthy, but low and behold, I had an email from him in waiting for me. It said he had spoken with Tori about acquiring a property on the east coast and she suggested mine. It would seem he already had the numbers in hand. It must be nice having more money than anybody else.

I wasn't too sure what to respond, so I closed the email for now. It could wait until Monday. The old me wouldn't have put off business because it was the weekend, but this new, slower-paced me certainly would.

Amaya

T HE FLOWERS ON MY desk Monday morning brought a smile to my face. A lovely spray of pinks and yellows brought color to my office and a blush to my cheeks. Orlando really was sweet, but this had been unnecessary. I checked the note. The flowers were not from Orlando, but from Riviera. *So sorry about everything Saturday. Enjoy the flowers and a dinner out on us! – George and Riviera Painter.*

"Whoa, who are those from?" Cordelia whistled as she came through the door. Her tiny frame took up no space, but the woman was a presence all her own.

"My bride and groom from this weekend. There was a little incident." I filled her in on what had happened and how Orlando came to my rescue.

"He likes you, you know," she said, wrinkling her nose.

She was just so cute. It made me miss my mom. "I know. I like him, too."

A manicured hand ran delicately over the blooms. "Make him think these are from another man. See if he gets jealous."

"Cordelia!" I was shocked she would suggest such a thing.

She winked and sauntered off, leaving me shaking my head behind her.

A text from my sister put me into slight panic mode.

LINAYA: MOMMY AND DADDY ARE COMING.

I missed my parents terribly, and while they didn't live more than three hours away in southern Georgia, it might as well be thirty hours away for all that we saw them. There were weekly phone calls where my very southern mother asked why we weren't married yet and my father told terrible dad jokes, but the visits were, regrettably, few and far between.

AMAYA: WHEN? WHY?

LINAYA: I TOLD THEM ABOUT AARON. THEY'RE COMING TO MEET HIM. AND I MIGHT HAVE TOLD THEM ABOUT OR-LANDO. AND WE HAVE TO PLAN MY GRADUATION PARTY! I GRADUATE IN A MONTH!

I almost forgot my baby sister would be part of the August commencement at SCAD. She had always planned to go to New York, but would she do that now with Aaron here in Savannah? They hadn't been dating long, but my sister was head over heels for the guy.

LINAYA: THEY'RE COMING UP FRIDAY. IS THIS A WED-DING WEEKEND?

My calendar showed there was a small event at The Promenade Saturday and I was not going to be wearing a hideous gown. I bet Cordelia would be willing to head that up, especially if it meant she got to meet my parents.

A text from my mom confirmed their travel plans.

MOM: CHANGE THOSE SPARE SHEETS. WE'RE COMING FRIDAY.

With arrangements made for Cordelia to handle the weekend event, Linaya and I spruced up my place for our parents' arrival. I had the spare bedroom for them since Linny was in a shared studio apartment, so they always stayed with me. We washed everything, picked up loads of fresh fruit from the market, and chewed our fingernails until they arrived.

"Sawadee!" Dad hollered at us from the other side of the door instead of knocking. The traditional Thai greeting was his way of announcing himself. When I opened the door, he repeated himself. "Sawadee, y'all!"

Mom pushed him aside and came through the door. "There's my girls." She kissed both our foreheads. "Linny, Amaya, let me see you."

Mom was tiny but mighty, much like Cordelia, but in a totally different way. Mom was loud and proud with red hair piled on top of her head, cheetah-print everything, and earrings that could take out a prize fighter. She was as ostentatious as Cordelia was demure. I had missed her.

Dad followed her in and dropped their luggage to give us hugs. Though he was half Asian, he had taken after his American father and towered over the three ladies in the room. At fifty-five, he was thin as a rail with the metabolism of a hummingbird.

"Let's go eat and you can tell us all about these men you've caught," he said as he clapped his hands together. "I want some shrimp and oysters."

"Just you wait, Emil," Mom said, smacking him on the arm. "I need the ladies' room, and let's visit for a minute."

Nope, nothing had changed at all. They were still our parents. Linaya looked at me and rolled her eyes at their antics.

The next day, Mom took Linaya shopping for graduation supplies while I took Dad with me to The Promenade to show him around. There was about an hour before the event happening in one of the smaller ballrooms, so I told him we needed to be quick. Our first stop was my office, which he was properly impressed by.

As we walked down the hall, Cordelia came our way and greeted us. "Who is this, Amaya? You bear a striking resemblance to him."

My entire life I was told I looked just like my father, while Linaya looked more like Mom. Thankfully, Dad was an attractive man.

"Cordelia, this is my father, Emil Journet. Dad, Cordelia Daniels. She's the owner of The Promenade." They shook hands.

"Actually, I'm the former owner. Orlando, my son, has taken over for me. But I still like to be here, and help your daughter out, when I can." She turned and walked with us down the hall.

"So Orlando is your son? We've heard a good bit about him from Amaya. Is he here today?" Dad made a show of looking around.

"He was here a bit ago," she replied. "I'm not sure where he might have gotten off to, though." She looked at me with a raised eyebrow.

"I'm not sure," I admitted. "I didn't warn him, I mean, tell him, we were coming by."

Cordelia laughed. "Smart move."

Around the corner we did find Orlando, speaking with Aaron.

"Well, Dad, I guess we can kill two birds with one stone. You get to meet them both at once." I stopped in front of Orlando and took his hand. "Dad, this is Orlando Daniels. And this is Aaron Tierney. Guys, my dad, Emil Journet."

Never had I seen two men stand straighter so quickly. They both were quick to shake Dad's hand and tell him how nice it was to meet him. For his part, Dad played right into it, puffing his chest and squeezing their hands. I could only shake my head at their displays.

"I'll leave you to it," Cordelia said. "It was a pleasure, Mr. Journet."

"Emil, please. And it was lovely to meet you. My wife will be sad she missed out." He bowed to her.

"I have a feeling I will meet her soon enough." Cordelia gave a slight wave and walked off, her steps silent.

"I'm sure these two have work to do today, Dad, so let's get out of their hair." I released Orlando and took my dad by the elbow.

He resisted my pulling. "Wait, wait. Why don't you two join us for dinner tonight?"

"Dad!"

Orlando flashed a mega-watt smile. "Sure."

Aaron nodded. "Sounds good."

"The girls will send you the details once we know them. Does seven sound good? We'll have to pick somewhere impressive since we have a real chef with us."

With called out goodbyes, I pulled my dad away to show him the garden area. "Dad you're a pain sometimes."

"Don't you want Mom and me to meet them?"

"Yes, but you put them on the spot."

"Nah." He put his hands in his pocket. "Hey, Amaya, do you know why Cinderella was so bad at soccer?"

I grumbled, but I loved his awful dad jokes. "No, Dad, I don't."

"Because she kept running away from the ball!"

My laughter echoed through the garden and a wren took off from its hiding spot. It was good to have my dad around, I had missed his corny jokes.

The jokes were plentiful that night at dinner. Dad fed us one after another and I'm pretty sure he endeared himself to both

Orlando and Aaron. Orlando's dad had been mostly absent after his parents split, and Aaron said his father took life way too seriously. Linaya and I couldn't imagine life without our dad. He was an accountant by day, but he actually worked comedy clubs at night.

Orlando fussed over my mother and she loved every moment of it. He complimented her hair, her style, how she had raised me, everything under the sun. "Truly, Anya, your daughter is a light in this world, and she must get it from you."

"Oh, darlin'," she cooed at him. "Flattery will get you everywhere."

"Worked for me," Dad chimed in with a wink. Linaya and I could only laugh.

"Emil, while I love the accountant I have set up, I'm open to having you take a look at our books," Orlando said. "You know as a businessman the bottom line is what it's really about. I would love to go over my five- and ten-year projections."

An elbow caught me in the ribs. "I like this one, Amy May," Dad said. "He's thinking ahead."

Orlando tilted his head to the side. "Amy May?"

I shrugged. "It's a nickname. Linny is Linny and Daddy calls me Amy May."

"It's her redneck name," Mom exclaimed.

Fire crept up my cheeks. I loved my parents, but they were certainly letting their south Georgia roots show. "Mom," I hissed.

But Orlando only laughed.

After we ate, Orlando pulled me to him. "Your parents are amazing."

"Amazingly embarrassing?"

"No, they're authentic and perfect as they are. I can see how they shaped you, the authentic and perfect person you are." He kissed my nose.

"We are all definitely authentic." My hand ran up his arm. "Thank you for meeting them and humoring them. I'm sorry I didn't ask if we were at the 'meet the parents' stage yet."

"You've met my mom."

"I knew your mom before I knew you," I reminded him.

"And that's worked out beautifully. My mom loves you." He winked.

My breath hitched, waiting to hear if he would follow that up with another love statement, but I knew it was too soon. It was too soon for me, so it had to be for him as well. Had I thought perhaps he would make a declaration? Had I hoped for it?

After dropping Linaya at her apartment and saying goodnight to my parents, I laid in bed and wondered why I thought he might say he loves me. We'd only been dating a short while. We'd both been burned before, so we had carefully danced around the fire instead of jumping right in.

You love him.

I do not.

Ha! Tell yourself that all you want, but you do.

Who made you the expert on me?

I am you. *So I am the expert. And you love him. It happened after he knocked Kyle out. You knew you loved him then.*

I closed my eyes and tried to fight the grin that spread across my face. It was a losing battle. A little squeal escaped my lips and I cozied down further in my blanket. My phone dinged, causing me to grab for it. Maybe it was Orlando. Instead, my sister's name was on the screen.

LINAYA: THAT WENT WELL.

AMAYA: IT DID.

LINAYA: DADDY REALLY LIKED THE GUYS.

AMAYA: LINNY, I THINK I LOVE ORLANDO.

LINAYA: I KNOW THAT, SILLY. IT'S OBVIOUS.

It was obvious? To who? Was it obvious to Orlando?

LINAYA: DON'T WORRY, HE'S JUST AS CLUELESS AS YOU.

AMAYA: HOW DO YOU ALWAYS KNOW WHAT I'M THINK-ING?

LINAYA: SISTER POWER.

AMAYA: SISTER POWER IS AWESOME. GOODNIGHT.

LINAYA: GOODNIGHT AMY MAY.

Orlando

I MIGHT BE IN love with Amaya. I wanted nothing more than to be with her. And meeting her parents was the icing on the cake. I knew I would end up tired of their over the top presentation eventually, but at the moment it was a breath of fresh air after growing up in a very structured home and maintaining that into adulthood.

The feelings I had also led to a firmer decision on my part. I wanted to stay in Savannah. I wanted to give up the stringent way I had been living up to this point and actually enjoy life. With Amaya, preferably. While The Promenade had never been officially on the market, I had certainly shown it off to potential buyers. Thankfully none had bitten so far. There was one last company I was waiting to hear from—Worthy.

What nobody else knew was that I had shown The Promenade to one of Worthy's people. Honestly, I tried to downplay the place to the woman who did the walk through. I pointed out every uneven stone, every tiny flaw. I hadn't meant to do that, but I had taken an instant dislike to the dour-faced woman and I didn't want her in my family's sanctuary.

I no longer wanted to sell. Sure I could have cancelled that appointment, but I wanted to see what was offered—if it was offered.

The second the phone rang I grabbed it up. This was the call I had been waiting for. The question was, what would be said? "Daniels."

"Mr. Daniels, James Worthy here." The voice was low and gruff.

"A pleasure, Mr. Worthy." I turned my chair backwards so I faced the wall.

"I've looked over the numbers several times," he said. "Your little venture there does quite well."

I nodded in agreement, though he couldn't see me. "It really does. It's been in my family for generations."

"Why do you want to sell?"

I scratched my head. "To be honest, I was looking to sell just to get out. I wanted to help my mother retire in style and get myself back to Atlanta as quickly as possible when I came here. This is a treasure and anybody would be lucky to own it." I was lucky to own it.

It might not pay what I made in Atlanta, but wasn't a high-stress corporate job either. I could relax, maybe even take a vacation now and then. Being near the ocean, my mother, and Amaya were all icing on the cake. I felt like I was punched in the gut.

"It's not what we're looking for at the moment. While it performs well, it's not big enough to entice me, I'm afraid."

Thankful for his answer, I sighed. "I appreciate your time, Mr. Worthy." He hung up and I swung back around to face my computer.

And I swung directly into the gaze of Amaya who stood stock still with her hands balled at her sides. Her face was tight and her color was more red than usual. I opened my mouth, unsure what I would say, but I closed it again. I had to do something. She was staring.

"You're selling The Promenade?" She blinked, but otherwise remained unmoved.

"Um..."

"You are selling The Promenade?" Her hands squeezed tighter. "After you bring me on, telling me how amazing it is here. After you told your sweet, caring mother that you would carry on your family's legacy." She closed her eyes for a moment and when she opened them, I felt sure fire would shoot forth from them. "You're selling?"

A string of expletives ran through my head, but those wouldn't get me out of this predicament. "Amaya," I started. "That was someone who was interested, but he's not buying. So nothing to worry about." I made a show of smiling and relaxing my shoulders.

I did not think the expression on my face conveyed that everything was fine. I think it conveyed absolute terror at her reaction. I had seen her with her game face on. I had seen her a little agitated. That paled in comparison to how she was looking at me. A look that would send any man to his knees, begging for mercy.

In a step, she was up against my desk. She put both her hands flat on the cool veneered surface and leaned down. "You hired me to work here. We started dating. You met my family. And nowhere in there did you mention any inkling for selling The Promenade. Were you just hoping nobody would notice?"

I knew people would notice, of course. Wait, that wasn't what she was asking. Was it? Her dark eyes were entrancing and the way she was leaning over made me want to kiss her. I shook my head to clear it. "No, no. I didn't want to say anything if nothing was going to come of it. And nothing has come of it, so no worries."

"You kept this from me, Orlando." Her doe eyes began to fill with tears. "Did you keep this from your mother, too? I bet she's clueless." Amaya pushed off the desk and turned on her stilettos, striding from my office and down the hall.

"Amaya, wait. Wait! Hear me out!" I jumped up and ran after her, but she barreled through the door and out to the parking lot in the pouring rain.

Not bothering with an umbrella, she climbed into her car and tore out of the parking lot while I stood next to one of the grand columns. I patted my pockets looking for my phone, but it wasn't there. It was still at my desk.

Back inside, I dialed her number, but it went right to voice-mail. "Amaya, please let me explain everything. Call me back."

I sat down and raked my hands through my hair. How had she ingrained herself into me so quickly? The idea of her walking out of my life forever made me nearly hyperventilate. I couldn't do this without her. Why had I been so stupid?

I tried her number again and again no answer. For a moment I considered calling Linaya, but I figured she would just as likely give me directions off a pier before telling me where Amaya had gone. I squeezed my eyes closed and slammed my fists on my desk.

"You love her." My mother's voice startled me. She stood in the doorway to my office, her hands clasped in front of her.

"Mom, she didn't let me explain," I started.

"That you were going to sell a piece of property that has been in my family for five generations?" The hurt in her eyes made me forget about Amaya for the moment. "I could hardly believe it, Orlando."

If I had felt at all broken before that moment, it was nothing compared to how it felt to hear my mother say those words.

"It was a foolish idea, Mom. I swear to you I will never sell The Promenade." Tears pricked my eyelids. Nobody wanted to disappoint their mother, especially when she was standing before you with tears on her cheeks.

She sat in the chair opposite me. "It's not even about the property, Orlando. It's that you didn't share your ideas or plans. I know that one day this land will no longer be in the family. I accept that. But for you do to this behind my back. It's shocking."

Never would I have described my mother as frail, but in that moment she was as frail as I had ever seen her. She looked weary and exhausted. Her entire life had been poured into this venue and I had been ready to pass it off without a word of her input or thought. I realized just how horrible I had been.

"Oh, Mom, I'm so sorry. I was only thinking about business and not about family. I realized my mistake, though, before this phone call. If he had made an offer, I would have refused it," I told her. "Over the last few months I've come to love it here. I think shifting my focus was exactly what I needed."

A slight smile warmed Mom's face. "I'm glad you feel that way now. Now, how about that girl?"

"Did she call you?"

"She texted me her resignation and told me what was going on. But I will just pretend the resignation didn't come through." She chuckled a little. "What are you waiting for, son?"

I tilted my head to the side and raised an eyebrow.

"Go after her!"

"Oh," I said, leaping up. "Where?"

"Do I have to do everything for you?"

I grinned. "I'll find her."

Amaya

I T USUALLY TAKES APPROXIMATELY three seconds for sand to cover me head to toe when I'm at the beach. It seemed that the time was cut in half if I'm wearing nice clothes. I had rolled my skirt up but it was still soaked. Sand and water droplets stuck to my eyelet blouse.

But I sat in the sand anyway, watching the tide roll in and out, thinking about what I had heard and how I had reacted. It was none of my business if Orlando sold The Promenade. I would have thought with us dating he would have told me he was even considering it, but he hadn't.

I was hurt more than anything. If he really wanted to sell it, that was his right. I didn't understand why he would have hired Aaron and me, but it was still his business. It was the fact that he hadn't trusted me enough to tell me. And here I had actually thought I was falling for him. Orlando Daniels was just as bad as the rest of them.

The sun was baking me as it bore down on my back. My phone was back in my car, so I wasn't entirely sure what time it was or how long I had been sitting and contemplating. In my haste, I fired a text to Cordelia and turned my phone off. Maybe I was overreacting just a touch.

Feeling a little more calm, I stood and picked up my heels. I should probably call him back. Turning toward the parking lot, I noticed someone watching me. Sunglasses covered his eyes, but his shoulders drooped and his hands were in his pockets. He almost looked like a puppy who had been scolded by his human.

It figures he would track me down. I'm not sure how he knew where I would be, but there he was, waiting. While my heart leapt upon seeing him, it also felt bitter that he hadn't trusted me or confided in me.

When he waved I trudged over to him, my heels hooked onto my fingers. Sand sloughed off me as I patted myself down. I stopped in front of Orlando and crossed my arms.

"Let me explain. Please." His voice was low and he did not meet my gaze. When I didn't answer, he took his own shoes and socks off. "Can we walk?"

I set my shoes next to his. "Sure. Let's walk."

We set off silently and I kept my eyes on the uneven terrain of the sand until we made it to the heavy, packed sand closer to the water. Orlando moved to be between me and the waves.

It took him a moment, but he finally opened up. "When I first came here, yes, I thought I would sell The Promenade. Potential new owners were set up to come look at it before I even got there, but I wanted a few weeks to give it a full assessment before they came. I intended to sell it, turn a profit, and set my mother up for a comfortable retirement before I went back to Atlanta."

I sucked in a breath. "You're going back to Atlanta?"

He stopped walking a moment. "I was going to. That had been my plan." He picked up a shell, then continued to walk. "I spent weeks running the numbers, checking the profits, making sure this was a viable business. But in that time I realized I loved the slower pace here, I enjoy not being so stressed out. And I enjoy seeing you every day. I didn't think I would, but I really like it here."

"You could have told me any of this," I said. "And you should have told your mother. I told her." I looked at him then, feeling guilty that I had ratted him out.

He shrugged slightly. "Yeah, she came to talk to me."

"What did she say?"

After a thought, Orlando grinned. "She told me to come after you. So I did."

"What about selling?" I drug my toes through the wet sand.

"She wasn't too happy. But she was more unhappy that I had let you get away." His hand reached out for mine. I considered pulling mine away, but I didn't. His fingers entwined with mine. "I'm truly sorry, Amaya. I shouldn't have kept it from you."

I stopped and looked up at him. "I'm hurt that you didn't trust me enough to tell me. If you want to sell your business, you can. Maybe you aren't in the same place with our relationship as I am, and that's okay, but I thought we had a mutual trust happening."

"We do, we do." He ran his hands over my bare arms. "I do trust you. I was stupid and clearly not thinking. My mom said the same things you said. And I told her I much preferred life here to life in Atlanta. I like running The Promenade and maintaining my other ventures from here. It's less pressure and I feel more relaxed now than I ever have."

He hesitated and we allowed the breeze to blow through our hair. "You have made me feel more relaxed than I ever have. I credit you with much of what has made me fall in love with Savannah."

Once again, I waited with bated breath, wondering if he would use the word love in conjunction with my name. Maybe I should say it first. Thoughts of Kyle tried to push to the forefront of my mind, but I squashed them back again.

"Orlando," I mused. I didn't know what else to say. There was both too much and not enough in my mind to form a coherent thought.

He pulled me close and kissed my hair. "Let's grab something to eat before we head back, huh?" When I nodded into his chest, he asked, "Do you forgive me?"

I nodded again and looked up at him. "If you can forgive me for reacting so poorly. I was so caught off guard I didn't know what to do."

"There's nothing to forgive. I would have done the same thing."

We made our way back to our cars and decided to ride together. Orlando could bring me back to mine later. We stopped by a little seafood shack that smelled like the sea and was coated in sand.

Before we left, we ventured out to the porch that was covered in crab traps and fishing gear but overlooked a beautiful inlet. The gear was from a hard day's work, not as décor, and we had to step over several fish scales that were clinging to my shoes. The view, however, far surpassed any obstacle we had to get through. The lighthouse stood tall in the distance, the sound of waves crashed in our ears, and the smell of salty air filled our noses. It both looked and smelled like home to me.

"This is where I would get married." I blurted it out before even realizing I was saying it.

I was left stunned when Orlando replied. "I agree. Let's do it."

My attention turned from the view to him. "Excuse me?" I almost choked but I managed to hold off while I stared him down.

He looked like a child playing his favorite game, face alight, body wound up tight. "Let's get married here."

I laughed because he sounded ridiculous, but my heart began to pound inside my chest. "Orlando, we're not engaged. We are not planning a wedding."

"That can be fixed." His eyebrows waggled as he put his arms around my waist.

The crash of waves must have messed with my hearing. "Don't joke about that, Mr. Daniels."

His expression changed from a kid in a candy store to one of quiet contemplation. "I'm not joking. Amaya, you have made my life worth waking up every day to see what new pleasures and treasures await me. You have brought me the ability to see beauty in the simple things again and to laugh again. I didn't realize all I was missing out on." He swallowed and I watched his Adam's apple dip. "I love you."

That was it. That was the declaration. My heart raced, my eyes filled with joyful tears, and I felt like I could take flight at any moment. "I love you, too."

"Really? That's such a relief." He put a hand to his chest.

I covered it with mine. "Really. And, also a relief."

"Should we get married?"

I wrinkled my nose and shook my head. "Not today."

"Not today, no," he said. "One day. Maybe one day soon."

"One day." I stood on my toes and kissed him lightly. "But you love me?"

Once he released my lips, he nodded. "I do. I realized it not too long ago."

"Same."

"My mother will be thrilled."

"So will mine. Linaya, too."

"Wait till they hear we're getting married on a porch covered with fish guts."

"One day."

"One day."

Orlando

WHILE WE HAD DECLARED our love and sort of agreed to get married, I thought it might be best to actually ask Amaya. First, though, I wanted to see her parents and ask her father for her hand. It was old-fashioned, but I think most southern families still appreciated the ceremony and gesture of formally asking for a daughter's hand in marriage.

It just so happened that Linaya's graduation meant a Journet family celebration and their parents coming to Savannah. The party was held at The Promenade, of course, and I thought that was a good time to pull her parents aside.

Knowing full well it wouldn't do to steal the limelight away from one sister to put it on the other, I focused my efforts at the party itself on proving what a good catch I was for Amaya. I made a toast, I brought Mrs. Journet coffee, and I danced with Amaya's grandmother. She was surprisingly good at the Macarena.

But before I had a chance to ask Mr. Journet if we could talk, he approached me. "Mr. Daniels, can we have a word?"

He was shorter than me by a few inches and had the kindest eyes I had ever seen, but I still found myself swallowing a lump in my throat upon hearing those words. I could only nod in agreement. We made our way out to the hallway as guests were leaving and laughing their way outside.

"Yes, sir?" I tried to look nonchalant, but was pretty sure I failed at that.

"Amy May tells me you've gotten pretty serious in the last few weeks." He crossed his arms at his chest.

"Yes. Yes, sir. We have. She's like nobody I've ever met before and I sincerely hope I make her as happy as she makes me." *Try to smile. Don't look like a creep. Relax, Daniels, relax!*

"Amaya has always been an odd mix of free spirit and business-like. Like she's not entirely sure of who she is. But we've noticed a change in her over the past month or so. She's more driven but also more relaxed. It's like she's finally comfortable in her own skin." He licked his lips before he continued. "I would guess I have you to credit for that?"

"I can't claim that, but I can say that she has helped me become more comfortable in my own skin. She's a wonderful woman." *It's now or never.* "I do love her, sir."

He smiled and clapped me on the back. "I can tell. You've bent over backwards today to show it not just to her, but to the entire family. Yai especially appreciates it."

"Mr. Journet—"

"Call me Emil."

I nodded. "Emil. I would like your permission to ask Amaya to marry me. If she'll have me. And you approve. And your wife approves. And Yai. I think Linaya would approve." Did that cover everyone? Why was I rambling?

Laughter filled the air and Emil put his hand out towards me. I took it eagerly. "Of course! Linny has already filled in with what Amaya hasn't told us. I'm happy to give my blessing to you, Orlando."

Relief washed over me. This was it. I could officially propose to Amaya now. "Thank you, sir. Of course, please not a word to Amaya until I can arrange a proposal."

He placed a finger to the side of his nose. "Mum's the word!"

The next morning I went to McFarland's jewelers to pick out a ring. They were the oldest jeweler in Savannah, nestled in a shop off Ellis Square, and were distantly related on my mother's side. If there was a ring unique enough for Amaya, it would be there.

I perused the displays while chatting with Nathan McFarland, the patriarch of the family. Each and every diamond ring looked like the one next to it. "Isn't there something else? Maybe not a diamond? Maybe an antique?"

"Show me a picture of this girl, son," came the weathered reply.

Several photos were on my phone and her social media and I scrolled until I found my favorite. Amaya in a fuchsia dress flowing out from behind her. Her eyes were crinkled almost shut and her mouth was open in a riotous laugh. She didn't hide her joy, but wore it for the whole world to see.

"This is her. Amaya." My heart swelled with pride upon showing her off.

I flicked the screen to show a better photo of her face. It was a lovely shot of her looking right at me over her shoulder, her tanned skin close to glowing in the fading sunlight. Brown doe eyes gazed right into the camera and the corners of her full lips were upturned. Maybe this was my favorite picture of her.

"Ah, yes, I know just the piece," Mr. McFarland said, tapping his temple. "Wait one moment."

He disappeared in the back for a few seconds and came out with an ornate navy blue box that looked like it was older than him. "This was made in 1844 by my grandfather Alexander. It's one of a kind."

The box was opened to reveal a gold ring shining bright with rubies. Small red jewels flanked the sides of the ring and in the center were gems arranged to look like a flower. It was stunning. He pulled it from the box and handed it to me. The blood-red rubies glinted in the light and I was mesmerized.

"If I were to turn Amaya into a ring, this would be it."

Old McFarland nodded. "Precisely."

The ring, however, was approaching two hundred years old and had been in the family all the while. "If it's been in the family this long, why sell it?"

"Grandfather had it made for his sweetheart, my grandmother. And you know, my grandmother and your great-grandmother were sisters. So truly, it's keeping it in the family." His eyes twinkled as he winked at me.

"It's perfect. But I have to ask how much it is." I winced, knowing I wouldn't like the price tag and hoping I could talk him down – for family.

Thankfully, he was willing to negotiate and with a little finesse, and a free event at The Promenade, I walked away with the perfect ring for the perfect girl. Now I needed to set my plan in motion.

On Monday, I popped my head into Amaya's office. "We had a last minute event come up for Friday."

Her face wrinkled up. "Friday? Really? What is it?" She averted her gaze to look at the calendar on her laptop.

"I think you'll like it. It's a proposal. Very sweet couple," I told her, inwardly high fiving myself.

Her head tilted to the side and she looked back up at me. "Someone booked for their proposal? That's interesting. Has anyone done that before?"

It was so hard keeping the huge grin from my face. "Not that I'm aware of." I shrugged in an effort to look calm while my insides were screaming that it was me.

Amaya went back to the laptop. "Well, they booked for six. Want to grab a late dinner afterward?" She beamed up at me as I came fully into the room.

I bent down and kissed her lightly. "Absolutely."

Before I could leave the room, though, she spoke again. "I don't see any files for this, babe. What are the names? What kind of set up? Will this be inside or in the garden?"

I swallowed and turned back to her. "Um, what would you do?"

A blank stare met me face on. "It's not about me. It's about this couple. What do they enjoy? Are they outdoorsy? More upmarket? Would she appreciate romance or not?" She pulled out a paper and passed it to me. "Didn't you get any information on them? How did I miss meeting this guy?"

Don't panic. Do not panic, she can smell fear. "He, uh, emailed me. I'll just forward that on to you and you can get what you need." I could feel the beads of sweat on my brow. I hadn't planned this through as well as I had thought.

"Perfect. Make sure he signs that contract, though." She blew me a kiss right as her phone rang. She winked as she answered and I turned from her doorway.

I made up a fake email address and emailed the 'details' to myself, which I then forwarded on to Amaya's email. Within minutes, she had emailed my fake account with a slew of questions, again with the reminder to sign the contract. Her mind for business was incredibly sexy.

By the end of the day I had hopefully told her everything she needed to know to set up for her own proposal in the garden of The Promenade – complete with candles, a petal-lined walk-way, and even a rented horse that would look like a unicorn. Because she deserved the most magical evening I could give her.

Amaya

T HE UNICORN WAS A bit much, but the handler assured me it would be fine and he would clean up after the animal if it created a mess in the garden. While it was a little outlandish, the horse had been covered with sparkles and the horn mounted on his head was beautiful. It did look magical. This young lady should be quite impressed with everything her guy had arranged.

I checked the petals on the walkway and set the hired photographer up behind a large topiary to be out of the way when he captured the magical moment. The guy, someone Orlando seemed to know named Oliver, had asked a lot of questions and gone with most of my suggestions. The unicorn, though, that was all him. And a nice touch, if I did say so myself.

Orlando met me in the hall. "If you will wait at the front for the guests of honor, I'll light the candles." He pulled a lighter from his pocket.

He was so cute, and I loved how involved he was becoming with the events. "Actually, you don't need to. They're all battery operated candles. That way they're not a fire hazard and they won't burn out."

The lighter was returned to his pocket. "Smart thinking." He licked his lips and shifted his eyes to the side. "Um, oh, I forgot something Oliver had wanted. I'll meet you out front." Quick as a fox, he took off down the hall and turned into his office.

I went to the front door to wait for the couple. He had said they would arrive together, with her thinking they were having a private dinner. If I had been told that, I would have been suspicious of a proposal. And then disappointed that there wasn't food. I had offered a private meal to him, but he had declined, saying their family would be waiting at a local bistro.

After nearly ten minutes, I checked my phone. It was after six and no sign of a car. I texted Orlando to see if he had heard anything.

Orlando: I haven't. They probably hit traffic.

Amaya: Right. Okay.

My senses were tingling. The air felt charged and I could tell something was about to happen. My heart sped up and I could feel little droplets of perspiration spring up on my neck. What was going on?

Footsteps behind me caused me to startle. Orlando came out from the shadow of the columns. "Nothing yet?"

"No," I said, craning my neck to see the road better.

"Why don't we wait inside? I think they can find the way."

There were so many rose petals scattered about, the path to the garden was clear. I took his hand and we moved inside. The air conditioning was a welcome relief to my thudding heart. I didn't know why I felt so wired.

Orlando kept hold of my hand and led me down the hall. Pink and red rose petals were crushed beneath our feet, releasing a heady, floral aroma. I heard the horse snort and I hoped it wouldn't do that during the proposal.

As I was led toward the garden, I stopped short. "We can't go out there and watch. That's inappropriate." I furrowed my brow as Orlando opened the door that led back outside.

"I promise it's not," he said, gently guiding me out.

He led me to the middle of the garden, surrounded by the candles and petals, the unicorn off to the side. It was then I realized there was no Oliver Dashing, but there was an Orlando Daniels. My eyes grew large and my mouth dropped open. He had done this for me!

My voice was barely a whisper as I questioned him. "Orlando?"

A finger was pressed to my lips. I kissed it gently. "Amaya, you swept into my life when I least expected it. I didn't understand what love looked like until you came into my world and opened me up to a whole new perspective. You are smart, kind, funny, and you put up with me. I can think of nothing I want more than to make you my wife."

Then he got down on one knee and opened a dark blue box, revealing a beautiful ruby red ring. "Marry me, Amaya. Please say you'll marry me."

I flung myself into his arms, almost knocking him over. "Yes! Of course, the answer is yes." I peppered him with kisses as he slipped the ring onto my finger.

Once we were back to standing, I studied the ring. It was stunning and exactly what I would have chosen for myself. "I love this ring, it's so unique."

"Just like you. I showed your picture to the jeweler and he brought this out to me. It's nearly two hundred years old." Orlando beamed with pride. "Now, I want you on the unicorn so we can take some pictures."

My eyes widened. "On the unicorn?"

Dark eyes sparkled back at me. "Absolutely. Because now is when the fairy tale begins."

I might have met Orlando Daniels as a bridesmaid, a perpetual one at that, but I would forever know him as his bride. And that was a role I was ready to step into with gusto.

Epilogue

Throwing out all my old bridesmaids dresses was much more emotional for me than I thought it would be. The lime green one that had looked horrid on everyone, the pink one with the black flowers all over it, the minidress I thought would show off everyone's goods – they all had to go. There was no need to keep them anymore and no room for them in our new place. Linaya would be transforming the old dresses into new creations for the upcoming prom season as she launched her own designs called "Savoir Savannah."

After the honeymoon, Orlando and I had moved into the small house adjacent to The Promenade. It had once been the gardener's home, but had long sat vacant. While we planned our wedding, we had also remodeled the gardener's house to our liking. It had two bedrooms and one bathroom, perfect for newlyweds. Once we were ready to move out, we could rent it for bridal parties or wedding nights. It had worked wonderfully for our own.

The honeymoon had been to St. Lucia where we basked in the tropical island sun and lazed the days away while Cordelia, aided by Linaya and Aaron, handled The Promenade back home. I suggested to Orlando that we open a second location for The Promenade in the Caribbean. He wasn't opposed to the idea.

I had decided that my days as a professional bridesmaid were behind me. I had a handful of contracts left to fulfill, but I wouldn't be taking on any more bridesmaid-for-hire jobs. Being the event coordinator for The Promenade was more than a full-time job. And since I had married into the family, it was now my business as well. Soon I hoped I would be able to hire an assistant.

Orlando popped his head into my office on a rainy, gloomy Wednesday evening. "Ready?"

We still maintained our weekly Wednesday dates. Cordelia had already told us she would be keeping her Wednesdays open in the future for babysitting jobs. Not just yet, I had told her.

"Where did you want to go tonight?" I asked as I shut my laptop for the night. There was nothing more pressing than my handsome husband with his deep chocolate eyes.

"Actually," he said, taking my hand as I stood, "I thought we'd order delivery to the house and watch a movie."

A crack of thunder and a flash of light made me jump. "I don't think I'll argue with that tonight. What movie?" I leaned into him and inhaled the scent of his cologne.

"Gladiator?" His mouth turned up as he crinkled his nose.

Of course he would want to watch an action-packed man movie. I sighed. "If that's what you want, sure."

"You know you like seeing Russell Crowe in that gladiator outfit," he teased.

True, but I would never tell him that. "I'd like to see you in that gladiator outfit." I kissed him softly as he pulled me close.

"Oh, I will get right on that. Gladiator cosplay." He winked. "We can both get in on that cosplay action."

We both laughed as we walked outside and into the rain. Thankfully it wasn't a torrential downpour, but it was still steady. The house was only about fifty yards from the main building and we didn't mind getting a little wet. We changed into comfortable clothes, ordered tandoori chicken and rice, and settled in to watch the movie.

My days of being a bridesmaid were now forever behind me, but I would revel in my role of forever being a bride to the dashing Mr. Daniels.

Afterword

Thank you so much for coming with me on this journey through Savannah with these fun-loving couples.

I wanted to share my deep admiration for the breathtaking beauty and undeniable wonder of Savannah, Georgia. The historic charm, cobblestone streets, and moss-draped oak trees create an enchanting atmosphere that has captured my heart.

It's no coincidence that I chose Savannah as the backdrop for my books; its unique blend of history, Southern hospitality, and picturesque landscapes have inspired the settings and stories within my writing. The city's rich cultural tapestry and vibrant character provide an endless source of inspiration, making it the perfect canvas for my stories.

As you explore the pages of my books, I hope you'll feel the same sense of awe and appreciation for Savannah that has fueled my passion for storytelling. The city's magic is not just a backdrop but an integral part of the narrative, adding an extra layer of depth and authenticity to the tales I weave.

Thank you for allowing me to share a glimpse of the profound connection I have with Savannah. May its beauty continue to captivate and inspire readers as much as it has inspired me.

Acknowledgements

As I sit down to express my gratitude at the end of this Savannah Sweethearts journey, I find I need to acknowledge the incredible support and inspiration that have paved the way for the creation of this book.

First, I extend my deepest thanks to you, dear readers. Your unwavering support and enthusiasm have fueled my passion for storytelling. It is your connection with the characters and the narrative that breathes life into these pages, and for that, I am truly grateful.

To my family, whose love and encouragement have been the bedrock of my endeavors, thank you. Your understanding, patience, and belief in my creative undertakings have been invaluable. Each word penned on these pages reflects the shared experiences, laughter, and love we have cherished together.

Lastly, but certainly not least, a heartfelt thank you to the city of Savannah. This enchanting place has not only served as a backdrop for my stories, but has become an integral part of my creative spirit. Its timeless beauty, rich history, and warm hospitality have woven themselves into these stories and into my heart.

About the Author

Allison Wells is a wife, mother, and sweet tea addict. Allison writes in two genres—Christian Women's Fiction and Sweet Romance. She writes what she calls "gritty Christian fiction," books that show the hard truths of life but ultimately are stories of redemption in the end. Her sweet romances are clean and fun with a dose of laughter (the best medicine). She loves to bring a word of hope to readers worldwide. Her motto is, "Life is short, eat the Oreos."

If you haven't already, find her online at whatallisonwrote.com.

Also By Allison

Hana Willis is too busy writing best-selling romance novels to worry about romance herself. But with her sister and her best friend walking down the aisle soon, Hana realizes it's time to start looking for her own Prince Charming instead of just writing about them.

Chas Rossi is the epitome of a successful businessman, but his parents' nagging that he start a family has him looking over every unattached woman he meets. When Hana walks through his door, he finds a woman who might be just what he's been looking for.

Pace McCoy never slows down between owning a bar and operating a dog rescue. With a failed engagement in his past, Pace has sworn off love. That is, until he gets to know Hana and her dog Lulu. Soon all his thoughts are about her and he's rethinking his take on love.

When both Chas and Pace take interest in Hana, she finds herself in a love triangle unlike anything in the books she writes. Chas is polished and driven, while Pace is rugged and kindhearted. How will she know which one is the one for her?

***

As the lackluster youngest daughter of a U.S. Senator, Roxie DePrive spends her life thirsting for one thing: to be loved unconditionally.

So, when her first boyfriend turns into her first marriage, Roxie's life undergoes a drastic change. And when that first marriage doesn't work out, she marries again. And again. Until Roxie marries five times.

The first marriage is puppy love, then dangerous love, convenient love, wishful love, and one that might possibly be the real deal. And yet, none of the men she marries can quench the thirst she feels in her heart. It's only when she meets a man who knows her entire life and all her mistakes that Roxie learns the power of something else—the deep and abiding peace of Living Water.

A modern retelling of the Woman at the Well in the New Testament, Living Water shows us that no matter our past, it's God's love that truly quenches the thirst of our souls.

9 798985 680027